CLOSER TO THE CHURCH

A Novel

LOUIS LEE SING

First published in 2022 by Hansib Publications
76 High Street, Hertford, SG14 3TA, UK

info@hansibpublications.com
www.hansibpublications.com

Copyright © Louis Lee Sing, 2022

Front cover design concept by Joash Alexander

ISBN 978-1-912662-79-1
ISBN 978-1-912662-80-7 (Kindle)
ISBN 978-1-912662-81-4 (ePub)

All rights reserved. No part of this publication may be reproduced, stored in a retrieval system, or transmitted, in any form or by any means, electronic, mechanical, photocopying, recording or otherwise, without the prior permission of the author.

Produced by Hansib Publications
Printed in Great Britain

To the many little people who blindly serve the Clerics – may you be justly rewarded!

BY THE SAME AUTHOR

*Conspiracy Against the
People: Local Government
in Trinidad (2014)*

*I Used To Live In
Heaven: Letters to My
Granddaughters (2016)*

TO CONTACT THE AUTHOR

EMAIL:
lleesing@gmail.com

ADDRESS:
P.O. Box 849, Port-of-Spain, Trinidad and Tobago

PHONE:
+1 (868) 624-7286

ACKNOWLEDGEMENTS

The process of preparing the written word for publication is never an easy one, regardless of the nature of the publication.

I am eternally grateful to my niece, Monique Assam-Peters, who painstakingly interpreted my handwritten script and made it digital. I also acknowledge with appreciation the cover design that was conceptualised and created by Joash Alexander.

To my wife, Reah, who was always present as I wrote, and who remains my living dictionary.

My niece, Rianna, for her editing eyes and my daughter, Ayn, who both assisted with the organisation of the final manuscript, and my sisters, Gwyneth-Ann and Judith, who were never too busy to listen to the development of the book particularly with the introduction of new characters.

To my sons, Rion and Daren, who facilitated, in so many ways, this business of my writing. Many thanks to Kash Ali and the Hansib Publications team for their professionalism.

GLOSSARY

Babash: Illegally distilled and very potent overproof rum. It is produced within the forests of rural districts and usually sold 'under the counter'.

Cooyah mouth: A gesture using your lips to point in the direction of someone you think is speaking nonsense.

Dougla: A person of mixed African and East Indian heritage.

Irie: Adjective describing anything good, nice or positive (originally Jamaican English/patois)

Ming-pilling: A miserly person or a very small space.

P2: To travel by foot from one destination to another (slang).

Pee straight: Local dialect referring to a male adolescent becoming an adult.

Standpipe: A freestanding water pipe and tap, usually encased in a short concrete post, to supply drinking water in rural areas.

PROLOGUE

NATHAN JOHN, A SIMPLE COUNTRY BOY FROM A place called Los Bajos in the east of Trinidad, was, for all his early schooling and upbringing, a good Roman Catholic.

By the time he began to "pee straight," as the elders in his community would say, he began to have misgivings about the Church, and the Church he often read of in the newspapers which he read from cover to cover.

His troubles with the Church and about the Church were compounded by the daily reports he received and listened to via his small radio, which he kept in his bedroom on a special table he built for himself using crude carpentry tools. In his growing mind, the deeds – or, more factually, the misdeeds – and cruel acts of the clergy against the innocent were often too much to listen to on a daily basis.

Yet his mother would demand that both he and his younger sister accompany her on her daily vigils to the parish church, which seemed too far away for his young feet. Throughout his childhood he did like all good Catholics do, and took his sacraments of baptism, first communion and, just before he turned twelve, the Holy Ghost descended upon him at Confirmation.

His years went by rapidly, and so did his mistrust of the clergy develop, despite his having very cordial relationships with the various parish priests who came and left as their seniors demanded and commanded.

Inside Nathan John resided an unexplained, nascent belief that, despite the smooth talking priest, the perfect ritual and the holy gospel, which he enjoyed reading and listening to, he was suspicious of the "too good to be true," the Church asked of you even before you could make an informed decision on doctrine.

As Nathan grew he was more occupied with the activities of children. The sports of cricket and football, played on the streets of his neighbourhood, gave him the energy young children crave the world over. The evidence suggested that he fared better at sport than in his academic pursuits.

Despite this very normal life, Nathan grew to become the single, very vocal voice that encouraged anyone who would listen to focus on the wrongdoing of religion, with specific focus on the church in his twin island nation of Trinidad and Tobago. His alertness to the multitude of religious operations in his homeland was remarkable for a boy of just over fourteen.

He not only listened to overseas reports, but he was saddened for weeks having read a newspaper, which told of a Hindu priest being convicted for the rape of an eleven-year-old girl in a village not too far from his place of abode. Reports of such abuses were common table-top discussion at many a family dinner, and Nathan took it all in. By his fifteenth year, he decided that he would do something to fight on behalf of all those who were now on a very long list of victims of clergy of all brands of religion.

Then the period – which he described as the period of revelations – arrived, with daily exposés and charges being laid against clergy from all around the world. Nathan, buoyed by the now universal revelations, decided to call a conference of persons of like minds.

With determination to turn spot and searchlights on the subject of abuse within the church, he visits one of the daily newspapers to announce that he would convene a 'Conference of the Un-Godly,' and solicits assistance from anyone who wishes to be part of the solution.

He gets one call, from a single mother of six children of the Muslim faith.

The conference not only focuses on abusers, but puts religion under the microscope. Nathan, finally, after a lifetime, exhales. The conference is the story that has driven him all his life.

So too the conference sharpens the focus of the woman who became Nathan's first acolyte, to become the woman she never knew she would be.

1

'CLOSER TO THE CHURCH OR CLOSER TO GOD?' questioned Nathan as he adjusted his chair, pushing it closer to the table while sitting. As he did so there was a low screeching sound, which echoed throughout the sparsely furnished, single-level dwelling the John family called home.

To the members of the Johns' inner family, this comment, presented in the form of a question, was Nathan's way of seeking an engagement – or an argument, depending on your tolerance – for Nathan's never ending commentaries on the Roman Catholic Church, within their poor, depressed and, as the more candid of their community would boldly state, oppressed neighbourhood.

For Nathan this was not just about getting his sister angry. It had more to do with the debates taking place, not only within his immediate community, but now also the topic of conversation at meal tables within homes, at restaurants and at cafes miles away. Wherever you visited the discussions filled the air, as ordinary people for the first time at last were debating what so many felt but dared not to say, lest they be perceived to be un-Christian and, by extension, un-godly.

Nathan knew more about the discussions taking place than did any of his family members. He, based on his long articulated views on the church, became the go-to person, as others sought clarity on the issues of the conversations now gripping his community and communities much further afield. Ordinary people, some who could no longer keep "still tongues," vented their anger over the revelations that were coming out each day, of yet another priest who had assaulted or raped a child.

The reports suggested that many of the priests pulled out of the closets of shame were not choosey, as, they suggested the men of cloth attacked little girls as well as little boys. More alarmingly, there was growing evidence they were more attracted to little boys. Some wagging tongues proffered, such was the preference of the perverted, depraved and vicious men who preyed on the children of God-fearing parents – many of those parents being mothers who fathered their offspring.

Neither Judith, Nathan's sister, nor his mother responded to his comment, which to those at the breakfast table was a daily ritual that brother and son Nathan shared with the wider community. They were bombarded daily by news of the Church, though the John family were not given to entangling other villagers in discussions on less contentious matters or the issues now confronting their Church. The women had absolutely no intention of getting involved in this debate, which both mother and daughter had long ago debated quietly out of the earshot of all others. They had taken the mutually agreed position that whatever happened within the Church were matters for the hierarchy of the Church. Both women shared a strong faith which they believed could not be easily broken.

Nathan was a son and brother, but from an early age he was given to a spirit of recklessness and rebellion. Ruth often wondered if it was punishment for his father's sins, which were numerous, or indeed her own basketful of so much dirty laundry. In an attempt to atone for her sins, she became fiercely Roman Catholic and worshipped at both the parish church's several altars as well her own chapel, which she had built and consecrated at the birth of her daughter Judith.

What sins did Ruth commit that placed such a burden on her, that for so many years caused her to light so many candles and in similar measure offer just as many novenas, was something Judith, an all caring and loving daughter, wondered, not once but too many times to recall. Yet she never once enquired of her most loving mother the reasons for her unrequited devotion to the Church, the use of wax candles of various colours and her devotion to novenas. Often she accompanied her mother to churches to conduct her rituals of prayer. These visits to the church altars invariably meant Mother Ruth prayed, while Judith sat and observed in silence.

Over a long period of being a silent participant, Judith began to wonder what the heavenly Father had in store for her. Some days she felt as if he had abandoned her and, though she never once expressed her thoughts aloud, she wondered if she, like her mother, was being punished for the deeds of her parents. On such days, these thoughts of sad enquiry often came when she looked at herself in the full length mirror, which was mounted at the end of the corridor on the wall between her mother's bedroom and hers.

Of the three rooms within the home Nathan was assigned the first room at the head of the corridor, he being the only male resident within the family home. The house stood on the cul-de-sac of a short street, which housed thirteen family homes and carried the postal number 13 Second Street, Los Bajos. Second Street was one of the twenty-two streets which formed the community of Los Bajos. To suggest Los Bajos was a well-planned community would be to err on the side of the planners who, like so many government officials, took the easy way out. The streets were all laced on the left-hand side of the Eastern Main Road, as you headed east coming from the westerly direction. You entered each street and you departed each street from the Eastern Main Road, which became busier as the years went by and the well-being of some citizens improved.

With such improvement each bought a car, be it new, second, third, fourth or fifth hand. Everyone saw the need for owning a vehicle, with the uncertainty of public transportation, and the people of Trinidad bought such cars as their wallets could afford. No one at 13, Second Street, Los Bajos, had the means to afford even a fifth-hand car, and so they got by using their feet, or "P2" as the villagers referred to those members of the community who by force of circumstance had to walk to where they wished to go.

This thing of walking was another of Nathan's bug bears, and he would raise these issues with Ruth. The family's lack of their own means of transportation was often raised but never debated, almost as often as he sought to lure his mother and sister into discussion on the holy, or maybe not so holy, Church.

Living on Second Street meant Ruth and daughter Judith had to negotiate twenty streets, or blocks of 6,000 feet each or thereabouts, each time she visited her church, which stood on the outskirts of the unnamed housing community that formed part of Los Bajos.

The government housing company, the National Housing Agency, having used most of the available lands to erect 2,700 houses, on reaching street twenty-two left a plot of land big enough to accommodate another seven houses. But its Board of Directors agreed one rainy evening at the Head Office at South Quay, Port-of-Spain, that it had neither the time nor the funds to build the infrastructure required for the seven or so houses. As one member of the Board of Directors noted, "It would cost us more to construct the street than it would cost us to build the houses!" With that statement and that statement alone, the remaining seven homes, which would have provided shelter to seven families or forty-nine needy persons, the Board of Directors of the National Housing Agency closed the construction at Los Bajos. Without knowing it at the time, they had opened up the opportunity for the Roman Catholics to find yet another location to establish a church and with it a place of Christian worship.

When the deed for the seven lots of land was signed and passed onto the local Archbishop, it counted for the sixty-second church owned and operated by the Roman Catholics within a land mass of 1,864 square miles.

Catholics were in Trinidad from the moment the infamous Christopher Columbus – lost at sea, frightened, troubled and bewitched – stumbled accidentally onto its shores. So relieved was he, it is recorded, the first thing he did was to kneel and give thanks. He changed the name of the island from Cairi Iere, which was the name given to it by its first people (the Arawak), to the very Christian name Trinidad, named for the symbols of the three mountain ranges he saw in all their glory; hence the Trinity.

Los Bajos became an important church parish for the Catholics in the east of Trinidad, and welcomed all who would come from the newly established, unnamed twenty-two streets of residences and the many smaller surrounding communities which encircled it. Within this parish, the John family of Ruth, Judith and Nathan grew to become an established family presence over the decade or so since the church first opened its doors.

It was within the walls of the very modest structure that Nathan was initiated into the faith for which he now had so many misgivings. At six years old, Nathan, holding Judith's hand while Ruth held the other, walked with his family into the newly constructed Catholic church, largely in response to the paper flyer placed in their mailbox. The flyer was signed by Father Tobias, the first clergyman to be assigned to manage the affairs of the new parish and the leader of the church. It appealed to all who received and read the flyer to come celebrate the consecration of the small modest structure.

The flyer did not suggest that only Catholics were invited. It read all were invited, and Ruth, besieged with her domestic and other struggles, saw this as an invitation from God. She believed with all her heart that the piece of paper she held in her left hand was signed by Father Tobias, but written by God.

It mattered not that the church was not a cathedral, but was, as her immediate neighbour to the right of No. 13 described the church, "a box house," meaning it was exceptionally small.

From the day it became public knowledge that the vacant land had been given to the church, there were heated discussions on the issue of the use of the available land. Some villagers argued that the space ought to have been given for a playing field, while others strongly articulated that, given the number of children of primary school age, the government should have built a primary school. When the brouhaha of whether a school was more important than a church died a natural death, like all village issues, some consoled themselves with the belief that maybe the church would build both a church building and a school house, given the size of the lot of land made available to it.

Through all of this Ruth said nothing, and as always kept her own council.

It was four weeks before the opening of the church when the common leaflet of an invitation arrived. It was classier than the ordinary circulars regularly left in the mailbox by government officials and other establishments wanting to advertise their wide and varied assortment of goods and services. Many of these paper advertisements or notices invariably went unread and were often simply crumpled in her left hand and eventually found safe storage in Ruth's kitchen garbage can, which she called a dustbin and was located immediately outside her kitchen or side door. The garbage bin was so positioned that you could not miss it either entering or leaving the home. Painted in fire engine red with white letters which shouted, 'Johns'.

The Johns' kitchen door was also the main portal used to enter and egress their home. This was considered a security measure by Ruth's husband of a very short-lived marriage. Anthony was his name, but Ruth and the neighbours on the street all called him Tony. For a while, albeit a short while, Tony played a pivotal role in the life of his newly minted family.

Tony was, during this period, everything a young wife and mother wanted in a husband and father. It was Tony's belief that bad people would choose the front door to enter and so he installed a number of bolts and other locking devices on the inside of the door, thus making it mandatory that the John family exited their home using the side door. Or, as Judith insisted: "It is the kitchen door Mother," in reference to the only entrance and exit to their home.

Judith believed that she could wish into life the opening of the front door to their home. She often thought about the closed front door, as well as so many small but unnerving matters she came to confront as she grew into womanhood.

All these idiosyncrasies were throwbacks to the time when her father and her mother were a smiling, if not laughing, happy young couple. How she wished she could wave her hand as if it was a magical wand, and completely erase the garbage left behind after what appeared at times to have been a period of untold bliss within the John household. A household and a marriage, which promised Ruth so much heaven and only delivered hell.

Judith, in her silence, as she read to keep herself occupied lest she became a 'raving lunatic,' sought to find answers to the mysteries of the Johns' home – a home built around herself, her brother and her mother.

Notwithstanding having five aunts and four uncles, in addition to fourteen cousins, the John family at 13 Second Street, Los Bajos, never saw their cousins, aunts or uncles. They neither knew their grandmothers or grandfathers, although all four grandparents were alive and in good health or, as the older folks often said, "they were alive and kicking".

The Douglasses were her mother's side of the family who treated Ruth and her small family as if neither their daughter, sister, aunt nor cousin ever existed. The Douglasses did what they could to stop Ruth, the pride of their family, from marrying Tony! They all sung from the same hymn book in painting a grim future between Ruth and the "boy from the gutter" as they described Tony, who had won Ruth's heart and with whom she wished to spend the rest of her life.

The Douglasses were known within the Parish Church to be not just pious but fanatically zealous in their belief of the teachings of the Church and in the execution of its practice. They prayed morning, noon and night. They, however, demonstrated little love for Tony in whose face they collectively closed the door. And when Ruth, headstrong and in love, decided against all the advice and threats to marry penniless Tony, they cut her off from the Douglass family when she became Mrs John. Later, when Tony had the audacity to walk away from Ruth and her two children, they became further enraged and illustrated their

Christian best behaviour by further ostracising Ruth, Judith and Nathan. These peculiarities of the relationships between the Johns and Douglases were just as difficult to understand or contemplate.

One evening, while engrossed in her reading, Judith came across a chapter which sought to focus on the mysteries surrounding the holy Mother Mary and the birth of her son Jesus Christ. As she read the detailed interpretation proposed by a theologian of African descent, whose mission was now based in a rural community of a southern state in the US, she was moved almost to laughter. In these paragraphs before her, she, for the first time, grasped fully the true meaning of her mystery and what a mystery meant. She both embraced and accepted conclusively that she, possessed of all her naivety, had been experiencing a series of mysteries for most of her life for which she sought answers. She clasped her hands in both acceptance and understanding that the mysteries of the John household would in good time be fully explained, if not by God, then by her mother. At this moment Nathan crossed her mind, as he so often did.

2

NATHAN SHE ADORED. HE WAS HER ELDER AND only brother. In earlier days they were truly a team, despite the fact that they were separated by three years, he being older and very male, and she female. Wherever Nathan roamed, Judith would be in tow. He loved playing football and cricket, games which were invariably played on one of the twenty-two streets within the Los Bajos Housing Development.

Judith, for much of Nathan's activities, was a spectator. She would be allowed to participate when one of the teams was short of players, and her roles were always restricted to the least important position on the playing surface or asphalt street that served as the playground for the children of Los Bajos. Judith was unfailingly assigned to "save goal" or be goalkeeper, which she became fairly good at, so much so that there were times Nathan would tease his little sister by suggesting she was the best goalkeeper in all of Los Bajos.

The story was no different when she had to become the twelfth man during a game of cricket. As twelfth man she was always asked to field at long-on, a fielding position behind the wicket keeper that is positioned behind the batter's wicket. Her view of the oncoming ball was always obscured by the wicket keeper, which gave her little time to stop the ball even at a distance of forty yards, and often she would miss stopping the ball to the annoyance of Nathan and his teammates. Whenever this happened he would promise Judith that, for the next match, she would not be placed in the fielding position which was generally an unpopular fielding position among all members of the team.

So too, whenever she got the chance to bat, she would be sent into bat at position number ten, and in this position rarely got to bat against a full over of bowling. She prided herself as being good with the bat, but dare not speak of herself as being a batsman.

In her small provincial community there could be no such thing as a batsman being a woman, and therefore she was sent to the wicket with the unwritten and unspoken, but clear, understanding that she made up the numbers and could not be allowed to make runs. If she added runs to the overall score she would have overshadowed the boys of Los Bajos, who even at that tender age defined roles for themselves as males and classified Nathan's baby sister Judith as a female.

Nathan often fought verbal and physical fights with his teammates, and, in his quiet moments, truly questioned whether he belonged to the group of boys with whom he fraternised. He was no longer the little boy who wore the white rosette and dark blue serge pants, which were the requirements for first communion. All of this, he recalled, was a couple of years back, very much his past, and the feelings that that was precisely where he wished such thoughts to remain were beginning to grow stronger. The treatment meted out to his little sister by his playmates was not something he took lightly, and he reasoned to himself, as the years passed, that even if he took her along with him he would ensure that she did not play. Therefore none of his friends would be in a position to suggest anything negative about her playing ability, or whether her contribution to the team caused them to lose.

As with most sports, when you win even the worst is overlooked. But to lose meant that good people became bad and, equally, the sweet became sour. So too it was on the twenty-two streets of Los Bajos. Nathan, having decided he would pull Judith out of harm's way, became unpopular with his team, who could not accept that she be made to watch from beyond the boundary given that the team was a "man short." Nathan would respond, "Not a *man*; a player short," in unqualified reference to his baby sister.

Equally, Judith was angry with Nathan as she could not understand his decision, in spite of him having explained his reasoning to her on three occasions. She, having been advised that she could and would not be allowed to play at future street competitions, became angry and elected not to join Nathan in the future.

This worked well for Nathan, who, for some time, would not be forced to treat with Judith's acceptance by his friends and acquaintances.

It would be months before Judith changed her mind, relented and asked Nathan if she could accompany him to his game, which, based on her brother's inherent excitement for the ensuing game, she reasoned was an important fixture within Los Bajos.

Nathan, notwithstanding his limitations with his height and being of small build, was one of the natural leaders among the several hundred children within Los Bajos. He was also a standout given his light brown complexion, which contrasted with the vast numbers of children of the community who were of varying shades of blackness.

Often the children referred to him as "white man" or "whitey" with a clear reference to his very light brown complexion. His sister Judith, though, carried a complexion that would be easily recognised as one having Black roots.

"This was village life across Trinidad," noted Ruth, in reference to the complexion of her two children.

It is within this environment of race, colour, class and religion that Nathan and Judith grew from being brother and sister who held their mother's hand on the streets of Los Bajos to children of reason. Eventually both were no longer interested in playing on the streets of their village, which now seemed puerile to both teenagers.

Nathan, nearing his eighteenth year, was becoming a known voice among the people of Los Bajos, and it was with this voice that he echoed the many concerns of hundreds who wanted answers about the inner workings of the many and various religions. Trinidad, more so than Tobago, was waking up religiously. The little people with concern and anger were becoming less tolerant with their demands for a better deal with the clergy of the multiple religions, which found Trinidad and Tobago fertile for the messages of their particular brands of the staircase to heaven.

Nathan the man emerged, and with a stealth-like sense of purpose he spoke to his audience wherever he found it. He deliberately avoided bars and watering holes, as he believed that nothing good could come out of a place that earned 'stupid money.' He argued that people who made money from the sale of alcohol earned stupid money.

Since his early teens, Nathan steadfastly refused to consume any alcoholic product. Meanwhile, he watched his peers and teammates begin with beers, and soon graduate to local rums and several concoctions of illegal forest-distilled and -brewed rums and spirits. He would see one of his more talented teammates blocking the water in the street drains, one Carnival J'ouvert morning and, try as he could, could not rouse him from the nightmare of sleep he invited into his life with the consumption of several glasses of bush rum.

Unaided, he brought Vishnu to his feet and walked him some seven miles to his house as no taxi would stop for drunk revellers. Upon reaching Vishnu's home and his single parent, his father, who was also very familiar with the behaviour of men when highly intoxicated, took one look at his fourteen-year old son and said: "What you bring him here for? Take him back to whoever give he the babash to drink."

Nathan, without engaging with Vishnu's father, brushed aside his senior who, from his behaviour, was himself under the influence of an unknown substance and was more cantankerous than he would be at his dry moments. Nathan ignored senior, and took his friend into the small wooden two-bedroom house senior and junior shared. Nathan always remembered, with a ghastly connection, tending to his friend's needs post his wanton consumption of products he believed were manufactured by the devil and his servants. These memories of not too long ago, married with the never ending list of reports of abuse by clergy of one religion or another, contributed to the development of one of the better informed as well as anchored young thinkers, on the topic of abuse by clergy the world over.

This passion for ferreting out wrongdoing came naturally to Nathan; it neither found him nor did he go in search of the challenge, which became his life's mission. Nathan John was anxious to push back against the vast and growing numbers of clergy who had crossed the line that defined good and evil. He also knew that many 'talked big' yet few were driven to action. He would be counted in the small group of those who not only talked, but equally took action on matters which demanded you walked your talk.

He had wrongdoers in his crosshairs and saw it as his assignment to expose and unearth the "bad," hiding deep within religious institutions. These clergymen were committing acts so terrible – some were before the criminal courts where magistrates and judges were ruling against such men wearing beads and robes while committing dastardly and criminal acts against children. Nathan could not entertain nor encourage these cover ups and protection extended to senior members of the clergy.

Nathan John was convinced that there were many who would stand with him, and that with the perfect plan the earth would bellow forth and expunge all filth from within the bowels of all religions – where wrong was far too long seen as right, and right treated as wrong.

Nathan John's anxieties over good and bad gave him focus and centred the manner in which he carried himself. His crusade against evil encouraged in him a tone and manner of speaking and, above all, a strength to debate all comers. In finding his centre, he became known as the boy who spoke without fear. He also gained a reputation as being a no-nonsense man in matters of religion.

3

"IT IS ABOUT MOSQUE, IT IS ABOUT TEMPLE, IT IS about church – mosque, temple and church guide us to salvation?" shouted Miriam. He was not making a statement, but rather questioning the reality of the benefits these religious places of worship had on the lives of the growing brood of children who were becoming more demanding as the months and years passed, with less and less food being available to nourish their growth.

Miriam had seven years earlier, very much against the wishes of all who cared for her, married Thomas. There was no courtship nor engagement. Miriam met Thomas at the local pastry shop situated on the Western Main Road, which meandered through village after village on the western peninsula of the island nation.

She stood next to him waiting to receive her order of three currant rolls, three cheese puffs, three tuna puffs and three chicken puffs. She would consume two of each item, while presenting the third of each item to her doting mother.

Miriam was the lone child of a union between her father who was of Arab lineage, and her mother who was a mix of Chinese and Creole White. In Trinidad, Creole White is described as being French Creole.

Both mother, Sammoy, and father, Phillip, worshipped their daughter Miriam. She was the love child of two people who loved passionately and made the lives of the people with whom they interacted richer and often far better.

Miriam Suielman lived at the top of Goodwood Park, and equally at the top of the food chain in one of the posh communities in West Trinidad, with her parents, where she enjoyed a happy and fun-filled life.

Thomas, decked in his Muslim light cream jubba, smiled his winning smile and enquired of Miriam, "Would you share your currant rolls with me?"

She looked back at him with her own million dollar smile, and remarked: "Why would I do that?"

To which he replied, "Because I asked you to."

Thus began a relationship which, at the best of times, saw Miriam follow Thomas' every wish; he never demanded or commanded. His was always a request, and Miriam, who prior to meeting Thomas was known as "Madam Independent," now as if with a flash of lightning became the willing servant of Thomas, the religious Muslim zealot of Rose Hill, East Dry River, Port-of-Spain.

This rapid transformation saw Miriam gradually abandon the many designer dresses and skin-fitting trousers which formerly adorned her attractive body, while simultaneously replacing her expensive modern women's wardrobe with the dull colours of navy blue and black full-length gowns that covered her slim frame from her head to her toes.

She became Muslim in one fell swoop, and, in the process, broke her parents' hearts. They neither understood nor could accept that Miriam, who they prepared to take control of their flourishing merchandising business, would abandon all she had been taught and choose to marry a "boy of no means."

"Where did we go wrong?" Phillip cried, as he viciously held onto Sammoy as if he could find the answers Sammoy always provided. In the weeks and months ahead they saw less of their beloved Miriam, who, as quickly as she was married and spirited away to Thomas' Rose Hill home, became pregnant and was expecting her first child – Phillip's and Sammoy's first grandchild.

Initially she visited once per week, and this then became twice per month. By the sixth month after Miriam left home, Phillip and Sammoy had seen their daughter a total of six times. Six times, which they counted and recorded on a calendar they kept above the family's breakfast table, situated within a small but friendly and warm enclave in the vast kitchen.

In happier times, it was seated around this table designed to accommodate six people that the Suielman family planned and discussed the family's future, but more so the future of Miriam Suielman.

Phillip and Sammoy Suielman still sat at this table most mornings having a strong brew of Hong Wing coffee. Both of Miriam's parents had been introduced to coffee since childhood by her grandparents. As children Phillip and Sammoy both lived in the capital city of Port-of-Spain, and grew up in homes where the cultures in some ways were similar. There were differences though, for Phillip represented the second generation of Syrian origin, and was schooled in both the traditions of the motherland and the newfound home of Trinidad. Sammoy, also of second generation, was schooled in the Chinese ways of language, cooking and caring for family. In the Suielman clan the direction of the family members was decided by father and grandfather, and Phillip was from an early age pointed toward the need to begin his own "store." Sammoy's father, who remained working class all his life, saw to it that his two daughters and their lone brother applied themselves to their school work, with all three children becoming professionals. Over the many years of wedded bliss, and in quiet moments as he sat and spoke with Sammoy, he would deliberately address her as Dr Sammoy, for she was indeed a highly certified medical doctor who many still visited when in need of emergency medical assistance.

In marrying Phillip thirty years earlier, she, without being asked or prompted in any way, chose to close her medical practice to join her husband's floundering business.

She had never seen his books or accounts, but she instinctively knew his business required a firm pair of eyes, a still firmer pair of ears and, just as critical, the firmest pair of hands. These she brought to Suielman and Sons and, within the first year of her presence, Phillip would be heard saying to the Suielman family, whenever they met that: "Marrying Sammoy was the best decision I have ever made." On each occasion his brothers would reply: "Have you ever made a decision?" meaning that the decision to get married was really made by his wife, who the family adored.

This love by the Suielmans for their in-law was both professional and family driven, as Sammoy was blessed with a personality of almost magical warmth and, like a spider in its web, ensnared anyone with whom she interacted.

Phillip had gone to see her professionally on the advice of his secretary, who 'swore on the Bible,' that Dr Sammoy was the best doctor in Trinidad and Tobago.

His secretary, Josephine, had listened to days of complaints by her boss that he was not well and could not explain the stomach pain he was having. Her boss also lamented that he had been to see his family doctor on two previous occasions, but still he could not get rid of the pain in his stomach.

Josephine, as she often did, said nothing, but called Dr Sammoy explained what she knew of her boss' illness and made an appointment for him to see Dr Sammoy. This having been done on leaving the office that Monday evening, she said to her boss without any emotion: "Mr Suielman, you have an appointment tomorrow morning at Dr Sammoy's office at 449 Dundonald Street at 10:15am. Please be on time, because Dr Sammoy is a very busy doctor," she added.

It seemed that Phillip did not hear his secretary until she was about to close the door on her way out. It was at this moment that he shouted: "Josephine, what the 'father' you mean by appointment with Dr Sammoy? Who asked you to make appointment for me to go and see a woman doctor?"

Josephine did not wait to hear the remainder of her boss' tirade as she hastily left Suielman and Sons Limited, on a bright, breezy Monday afternoon in the city of Port-of-Spain. Phillip was apprehensive about being attended to by a 'woman doctor,' yet he kept the appointment made for him and was on time, having ignored visiting his office before keeping his appointment with Dr Sammoy.

For Phillip, not going to his office before the doctor visit was out of character, as he by his rule or habit began and ended his days at his modest office situated above his store, on a wooden mezzanine he had built when he took possession of the rented property.

From his office window he could see all that was happening across his store, and many a morning he would be at his store by 6:30am, when he would sip his coffee and plan his day. None of this he did today; instead he elected to go directly to Dr Sammoy.

4

UPON HIS ARRIVAL, DR SAMMOY'S RECEPTIONIST greeted him and took the necessary personal details, advising in an officious tone that Dr Sammoy would see him shortly, given that she was somewhat delayed with an earlier patient. Phillip took this in stride as he had gotten used to waiting at his own family doctor's office. He was never happy waiting, and therefore made it a habit to never keep anyone waiting himself. He took up one of the old *TIME* magazines, which were neatly stacked on the left hand corner of the oblong teak table, which he calculated was approximately forty inches long by eighteen inches wide.

    Phillip was always counting, and as he settled into a chair near the reception table, for no apparent reason he attempted to count the number of magazines positioned on the table from which he took the outdated one he was now firmly clasping.

    He thumbed through the magazine as if looking for nothing in particular. He flipped page after page, but saw nothing in the yellowing pages of the magazine to capture his attention. He was about to get up to return the magazine to the stack on the table, when the receptionist in a soft voice said: "Mr Suielman, Dr Sammoy will see you now." As she beckoned him to follow her, an elderly man of Chinese descent came walking gingerly towards him, having already seen the doctor that he was about to meet for the first time.

    As their paths crossed, the receptionist said, "Mr Lee, kindly have a seat, I will be with you in a moment." She opened a door at the top of the short corridor and invited Phillip to have a seat at a very neat desk. The desk, made of aged teak, was spotless, and shone giving a glass-like image.

On the desk there laid only a legal size manila folder, upon which Phillip could discern his name neatly written, no doubt by the receptionist who operated almost robot like – yet she was both pleasant and professional.

Dr Sammoy entered her conference chamber and said in a firm, though endearing voice: "Mr Suielman, what can I do to assist you?" As she introduced herself she smiled, a smile the likes of which would haunt Phillip in the days, weeks and months to follow.

Phillip explained his troubles, or, more pointedly, his pains, to doctor Sammoy. She listened, and in response asked of Phillip whether he would subject himself to a physical examination, to which he readily consented.

Following a thorough physical examination, Dr Sammoy chatted with Phillip for another fifteen minutes. During this consultation she determined that Phillip loved to eat all the kinds of food that caused constipation, and in an almost maternal tone requested that he change his diet and begin a programme of exercise. She also gave him a prescription, which turned out to be a scheduled program of laxatives!

Phillip sat staring at Dr Sammoy, almost glued to the chair in her office. He was eventually dislodged from this chair when the receptionist knocked on the door and, just as professionally as she had ushered him into Dr Sammoy's office, invited him to leave. He turned to Dr Sammoy and said a curt good morning and followed the receptionist out to the reception area. He politely enquired about the cost of the visit, paid and left. He briskly made his way to his office, which was a stone's throw away given that he drove himself to keep his appointment. On his way to his office six blocks way, he thought of nothing other than the smile – Dr Sammoy's smile! What began for him as a doctor's visit would become by the end of the day an obsession.

That evening, Phillip sat in his office surrounded by all the worldly items that mattered much to him. He looked around his twelve feet by fourteen feet space, not understanding why he did not feel as buoyant as he normally did, particularly after a day of strong trading. On such days he would leave Suielman and Sons Limited a happy man, and the happiness would naturally begin in the very office after he had counted his day's take and secured the cash and cheques in the company's safe, well hidden behind several bolts of cloth, to be deposited early the following morning. Not even the magic of the feelings of personal achievement, which came naturally to him, were present on the day of his first visit to Dr Sammoy.

He looked around his office as if searching for something in particular, and his eyes stumbled on the corner where he kept the mementos of his sporting triumphs. Phillip was a keen swimmer, excellent at water polo and his favourite, breast stroke. Yet he did far better as a cyclist, dominating the longer races at club level during the years he remained in high school. His attendance there, however, was not made possible by passing the school exhibition exams, by which children at the primary school level were evaluated and allocated one of the limited places within the secondary school system.

Phillip could not matriculate even with his best efforts and though it was not advertised, the Suielman clan closed ranks and prevailed on all who mattered to open a bench space in one of the second-tier high schools' first form classrooms.

At college he did his school work well. As his mother told members of their closed, but growing Arab community who visited with the Suielmans, "Phillip is no fool, but he like his sports more than he likes his books."

His trophy corner underscored so much of what his dear mother so often spoke, and he kept this corner of his office flawless. He fixed, cleaned and placed each medal, trophy and sporting certificate in a specific pattern. All items placed told the story of the exploits and achievements of Phillip Suielman. He was extremely proud of his achievements, and would spend too many minutes explaining to people visiting his office the magic he felt for his sporting achievements.

How then was it at all possible, as he focused on his special corner, that he felt in his heart a spirit of emptiness? His thoughts, and his not knowing nor understanding what had befallen him, weighed heavily on a normal chirpy Woodbrook resident – who had not a care in the world.

Caught in his world of in-between too many thoughts he attempted to focus, and with each new thought, Dr Sammoy's smile and presence danced like streaks of yellow sunlight dazzling its way to a perfect sunset.

He did as he had always done – worked out what he interpreted to be good, and let it command him. At that moment his brain changed gears. He knew then what he had dismissed ten hours earlier; he had been struck by a baton of love, and the baton had hit not only his heart but also his head. Phillip, who before this day that began so normally had never felt such stirrings for anyone. He now knew he was hooked, if not smitten with love, for someone he had met briefly during a medical examination and consultation.

What did this mean for his future? He got up from his desk, which was positioned under the glass window overlooking the store beneath. He looked down, scanning each aisle of cloth and each counter, which carried specific goods and merchandise. Phillip learned to care for his store from working at uncle Ellie's store, and later when his father, Benjamin Suielman, allowed him into Suielman and Sons Limited. Suielman Senior managed his business no differently than had his father. Each child was first sent to the business of a close relative to be apprenticed. Though the word apprentice was never used, the boys were told they were to report to Uncles "to learn the business." Only when the assigned uncle was convinced the young lad was sufficiently proficient in the administration of the store would he, with a simple ceremony, call the nephew on the last Friday of the month and request the "boy" to sit with him. "Nephew," he would begin, "you have been here with me for almost two years. Isn't that so?" he would question – though he was making a statement.

Invariably, Phillip's uncle took him through the same ritual other young Arab boys experienced in similar situations. Phillip never forgot his meeting with uncle Ellie, who was always as fond of Phillip as Phillip was fond of him. Uncle Ellie explained to Phillip that, from next month, meaning the following day, he would begin working at Suielman and Sons Limited – he being one of the sons. He impressed upon Phillip the importance of he, Phillip, doing a good job immediately. "When you go to work tomorrow, I expect you to be better than all your father's employees, your brothers and your father. The last two years here with me have been better than any university could offer you," he said to Phillip, with a firmness Phillip had never before seen in his uncle Ellie. "You are not going to Suielman and Sons as if you have any special role, because you don't. You go there to do what everyone who is already there does on a daily basis – you go there to build the business," he added.

Phillip knew his uncle Ellie, and therefore knew he was not finished with his exit interview. Uncle Ellie paused as if catching a second wind and then said in the most caring voice: "Nephew, you were given to me in the hope that I would take all the sports out of your head and get you to focus on your business. I was asked by your father to begin preparing you to control and manage Suielman and Sons Limited. I don't know what is in your father's heart or mind, given that you have two brothers, both older than you and who are in the business. But I do know when he sent you to me, his exact words were, 'Do what you must to prepare the boy to take over the running of Suielman and Sons.' I have done my best, not for you, but for my eldest brother," he concluded. All of this flooded Phillip's mind. It wasn't that these moments had not returned to him over the years, but he found it strange that such thoughts, which he never shared with anyone, would suddenly surface from deep inside his consciousness.

He agonised that it must have been his illness, though as he reflected, he no longer felt the degree of pain in his stomach he had previously endured prior to his visit with Dr Sammoy.

His thoughts suggested to him a life changing moment. He understood fully the change, and he knew the moment was present. He now reckoned his life's assignment would be to do what he must to encourage Dr Sammoy to see in him what he saw in her – a person to whom Phillip would give his life unconditionally.

5

PHILLIP GOT HOME TO THE SUIELMAN'S BUNGALOW at Ana Street, Woodbrook. He bade everyone good evening, sat with his mother and had a strong black Arabic coffee. As he poured his serving into the small demitasse cup he could smell the cardamom, which though distinct in taste could not overpower the aroma of the blend of coffee.

He consumed his coffee almost with one huge slurp, closed his eyes for one brief moment as he savoured the quality of the served coffee and as he opened his eyes he saw a vision of Dr Sammoy. At this instant, he smiled at his mother and excused himself from the family's conversation and repaired to his bedroom situated in a little annex to the rear of the Suielmans' well-appointed residence.

Now within the confines of his comfortable bedroom, he found his reclining chair and dropped into it. He sat and stared at his sixty inch smart television, not bothering to power it on, in the silence of his room. It was lit only by flashes of light that penetrated his thin, almost see-through drapes. This light he shared with anyone now using Ana Street, and the world beyond it.

As darkness finally came he resolved to visit Dr Sammoy unannounced. His daring plan also involved taking with him a box of the finest chocolates and one dozen red roses. He knew red roses suggested that there was intimacy, which did not exist, but he reasoned if he had to illustrate his inner feelings he ought to do so with a strong and equally positive gesture. Phillip knew in this battle for Dr Sammoy's attention, if not heart, he had only his heart to loose, and so pressed forward with his foot fully on the accelerator of life.

He knocked on Dr Sammoy's office door and entered. As he entered the reception, he discerned it must be a busy day for the woman he hoped he could convince to be his wife. All chairs were taken.

He planned to leave both chocolates and flowers with her receptionist with a request to pass the items to Dr Sammoy. Phillip earlier that morning had written a most warm and endearing letter to Dr Sammoy, asking her to give consideration to the frailty of his heart, and pleaded with her to allow him to demonstrate his worthiness.

All of his plans went well, except that he did not anticipate that when he entered the reception office Dr Sammoy would be standing next to her receptionist. In that moment he froze. The fast talking Phillip just could not move. Years later he explained to his wife, when asked about that moment, he would advise he wanted to retreat out the door backwards, but his feet could not move.

It was a moment of untold awkwardness for Dr Sammoy, her receptionist and Phillip, as the office full of patients looked on curiously, most with eyes wide open and others with smirks on their faces.

Eventually the receptionist, realising the ridiculousness of the moment, broke the ice. She said: "Dr Sammoy, would you wish to discuss this long outstanding matter within your office?"

Dr Sammoy took the prompt and invited Mr Suielman into her office, where she asked that he be seated, and she regaining some composure and took her seat behind her desk.

Phillip, long used to having his way with women, was for the first time very slow to act. Almost robot like, he immediately got back to his feet and apologised. "Madam, Dr Sammoy, forgive me for arriving at your office unannounced, without an appointment and uninvited. But madam Doctor, I had to find a way to meet with you, and it was my intention to leave these most beautiful flowers and high quality chocolates with your receptionist for delivery to you. Madam Doctor, I have included with the chocolates a letter, which explains everything. Will you treat a poor soul such as I with the kindness to read the note, when you have time? Now madam Doctor I know you are busy, and I ask you to forgive me for being so foolish to believe I could impishly impose myself as I have done. I must leave promptly, hoping I have not upset you in any way," he ended, and rose from sitting to leave.

Before he could move, Dr Sammoy, who by this time had regained her command of her office, asked if he would remain seated. She said to Phillip: "Mr Suielman, where is the letter you have spoken of?" In response Phillip got up, took hold of the chocolates, removed the letter he earlier affixed to the box and meekly passed both letter and chocolates to Dr Sammoy.

She slowly opened the envelope and took out the letter, and began to read:

Dear Dr Sammoy,
I hope this letter and chocolates get to you, as I plan on delivering both to your office receptionist, who I hope will not throw both into the kitchen garbage.

Doc, I am not one given to impulse, nor am I one to go around writing letters of one's feelings (of the heart) to a total stranger.

I have had the extremely good fortune of meeting you two days ago, and since that moment I have not experienced a waking moment during which you and your magical smile have not, in ways unimagined, bewitched my consciousness. For me to have not done something to bring to life the spirit of my innermost feelings, which I now happily embrace, would have been to say to the universe I am foolish – a meek and stupidly cowardly soul, truly unworthy of your time.

I have therefore thrown all caution to the wind in the hope that the greatest of all architects will see the truth and worthiness of my feelings, and would bless me with the opportunity to be able to meet with you at a personal level. There you may find the space to determine if I am worthy of you as a life-long partner.

I cannot ask just yet, but with time I will ask you to determine if I am worthy to be your life partner. Please

forgive me for being as forward as I am, but I do believe in God and the scriptures do state: 'ask and you shall receive.'
   I am asking, Dr Sammoy, will you agree to have coffee with me?
   I remain madly moved by your spirit.
   Always,
   Phillip Suielman

As she finished reading the letter tears came to her eyes. She did not know Phillip Suielman except as a very recent first time patient, nor did she know of him.
   Her dear father always reminded his children "that it is important to know of persons with who you do business." This was not about business though, it was about life. She did not know this man sitting before her, who not only brought her red roses with all their implications, but also chocolates and a letter of the heart – his heart. She was too overcome by the moment to think this through, and so as she was always reminded by her father, she elected to allow night to be her counsel.
   Having read the letter, she said to Phillip jokingly: "This is quite a letter, are you an author?" Phillip was about to respond, but she waved her left hand as if saying no need to respond.
   Finally Dr Sammoy spoke with feelings she kept suppressed for a long time. "Mr Suielman, I truly don't know you, and I am not sure I may want to get to know you, but I am moved that you think so much of me, given that you only met me for half an hour before today. That being said, it would be poor manners if I were to reject your flowers and chocolates, the latter I am fond of. But may I request of you if in future that when you bring flowers to one with whom you do not enjoy an intimate relationship, you bring that person yellow coloured flowers?"
   With that she smiled and got up to suggest the audience was over. As she stood she added: "About your invitation for coffee, I accept. Will you allow me the luxury of visiting with you unannounced, uninvited and without an

appointment? Will you be so kind as to leave your business address with Marisa, my receptionist?"

She stretched out her hands and shock hands with Phillip. The interaction had as much impact on Dr Sammoy as it did on Phillip Suielman. Dr Sammoy had no time to ponder as she had kept her patients waiting based on the unplanned interruption caused by Mr Suielman, the Arab who came bearing gifts.

Dr Sammoy completed a full schedule and more, as she looked after the needs of six additional patients who were not on the schedule. There were always days at her office like the one she was about to complete, but none of the days focused her so sharply on the subject of the opposite sex, if that person was not a patient.

Today for the first time she became aware that she was not only a well-respected, in demand, medical practitioner, she had now come to grips with the fact that she was a woman.

That evening, as she prepared to leave the office for her yoga class, she looked at herself from head to toes. She was forced to whisper to herself, "Sammoy, you are not only brilliant, you are a damn beautiful woman, with spirit and charm."

6

IN THE ENSUING EIGHT MONTHS, SHE WAS FORCED to use both her wits and brilliance to ensure her heart never out-manoeuvred her head.

She first initiated contact with Phillip Suielman approximately twenty-eight days following his memorable visit to her practice. During this period she enjoyed moments of smiles, laughter and above all concern for precisely what action she ought to take, to address this matter of the heart. Phillip Suielman was not the first man to have been attracted to her, there were many.

She had two reasonably serious relationships while abroad at university in Ireland, which lasted just a couple months short of a year. Each ended when her partners found out that she, though a loving, caring and passionate woman who would do most things for you, remained firm and never wavered on the matter of the big one – sex. Both men, although she advised them of her position on the subject early in their relationship, were so smitten by her beauty, charm and her "way with words," elected to pursue her in a relationship. They convinced themselves that in the course of time she would let her guard down, thus allowing her quiet passions to erupt. The reality, that such a possibility was impossible, would eventually, like seeds of corn planted, pop forth with proper nurturing, and with set time frames become a reality.

On each occasion neither saw themselves as suitors, and stayed around beyond nine months only to recognise what Sammoy the brilliant and beautiful had made clear, near a year earlier – their fate.

Since these episodes, she spared little time in working on relationships. Yes she dated, but never went beyond the odd dinner or lunch date. Her work and studies occupied her time as she excelled in keeping good her commitment to make her father proud.

At twenty-eight years old, Sammoy was already qualified and practising for nearly four years. Her achievements at a leading college of surgeons at Dublin, Ireland, amazed her professors and student body, both in her year group and in groups years ahead of her. She had developed a reputation of being not only very bright, but the go to student if the medicine being taught confused and required 'lay woman' interpretations.

In this regard, groups of students studying at the lower levels would come to her for assistance, and she, despite her own work load, found time and space to conduct tutorials. "It was always fascinating to see Sammoy surrounded by eight juniors, with her teaching and her group listening with undivided attention," said Sammoy's roommate Elena Singh, in describing her colleague in an interview with a Campus Newspaper.

Sammoy dutifully did her day's work at her office, seeing her scheduled last patient just after two o' clock in the afternoon. Not on impulse, she had the evening before decided she would keep her promise to visit with Phillip Suielman unannounced and without appointment. Sammoy did not know whether she would meet Phillip, but she planned on leaving a note, which she had prepared later that evening just per chance he was not at his place of business.

She mused to herself this could well be the opportunity to close the chapter on Phillip Suielman – the Arab with the gifts. Sammoy also wondered whether it would be awkward to continue seeing the man as a patient even though she had seen him only once.

With her patients all cared for and all files returned to Marissa's safe hands she visited her powder room, whereupon she looked at herself and believed she never looked better, despite not wearing a drop of makeup. Noting that single detail, she turned, retrieved her handbag from her desk bottom drawer and quietly departed her side exit, which opened onto the garage.

She drove as she always did, at a cautiously moderate speed, arriving in the vicinity of Suielman and Sons Limited. The neighbourhood was covered with a range of stores carrying a variety of merchandise. Stores offering clothing for both male and female, fabric, jewellery, medicine, furniture, appliances, coffee shops and a lone American restaurant surrounded Suielman and Sons. Despite the density of the hoardings of these shops, Suielman and Sons commanded mindshare and radiated a strong presence on the block.

The go-to-doctor found a parking lot a block away, at one of the parking lots operated by the Roman Catholic Church. She parked, collected her parking sticker and gingerly walked to Suielman and Sons Limited, where she proposed to keep her promise to visit, "uninvited, unannounced and without an appointment."

Phillip Suielman, unknowingly, had at his first visit to Dr Sammoy put in train three words that would characterise her future actions in her relationship with him. She was about to cross the street to get to her destination, when something made her stop and look up at the building which housed Phillip Suielman's store.

As she did so, she pictured the possibility that one day Phillip Suielman would truly have a grand establishment. That is how Sammoy was; she always wanted the best for others, even strangers, and Phillip Suielman was a stranger.

She briskly made her way inside, and enquired of the first store clerk who approached her: "Where could I find Mr Phillip Suielman?" The clerk, a woman of medium build and of African origins, looked no older than eighteen years old and her demeanour suggested she was fresh out of secondary school. She looked at Sammoy with a smile, and turned her back to point to the mezzanine where Phillip's office was located.

Sammoy did not bother to enquire how to get to the office, as she saw the metal staircase situated outside the building. Approximately twenty-four steps, broken by a landing just after the fourteenth step, with another landing outside the entrance door to the office.

Dr Sammoy reached the entrance door having alighted the twenty-four steps in record time. Being something of a fitness buff, she had fashioned the habits of jogging, swimming when possible, and had become an ardent acolyte of yoga.

Dr Sammoy knocked gently, three firm knocks which kept a rhythm, each knock being evenly separated by time and space. The knocks bore almost instant results as Josephine, secretary and 'Girl Friday' to Phillip Suielman and patient of the doctor, opened the locked door and was met with Sammoy's warm, piercing eyes. In that moment both women instantly recognised each other, one as a medical practitioner and the other as a patient.

Dr Sammoy was the first to break the ice, she said in her oh-so-gentle voice: "I am here to see Mr Suielman."

Josephine with haste ushered her into the office and took her straight to Phillip Suielman's office door, which she opened and looked in. She said, "Dr Sammoy is here to see you."

There was a moment far longer than a moment before Phillip Suielman responded. It might have been surprise and a combination of relief and disbelief which caused the prolonged pause, but he finally, almost leopard-like, rose from his chair. With a smile a mile wide, he stretched out his hand to greet the woman he prayed would keep her promise to visit with him for coffee under her terms, which in a meaningful way had been fashioned by him, the pursuer.

Both shook hands as if they were long and well acquainted, and each allowed the other the moments to adjust to the truly unusualness of the moment. It was by no means awkward; if anything it was unique.

Josephine stood in awe as so many thoughts flashed through her mind. Top of her list of concerns: did Dr Sammoy visit with bad news about her boss's medial visit over his stomach? She closed the door and quietly retired to her desk, fully conscious that her boss and Dr Sammoy required privacy.

Phillip invited Dr Sammoy to sit at one of the two chairs which were placed at the front of his desk, and politely enquired if he could occupy the other. In response Sammoy answered: "Mr Suielman, this is your office. I have come to have coffee with you, under terms and conditions of which you are and must be familiar."

"Madam, your wish is my command," Phillip responded.

He had begun to relax for the first time since he met Sammoy weeks ago. Now he entertained that he could dream beyond his delivery of chocolates and flowers.

Following near one hour of polite but healthy exchange of conversation, about everything from politics to business, Sammoy asked Phillip: "Mr Suielman, where is the coffee you promised the Madam Doctor?" With that said she offered her magical smile, and would in the not too distant future gift the gem of her smile to her one and only child – Miriam Suielman.

Phillip on a normal day consumed several cups of strong Arabic coffee, which his mother dutifully prepared for him each morning and which she would store in a Thermos. Notwithstanding how many times he would say to his mother, "Mom the name is Thermos," she would continue to say to him: "Here is your Icey-hot of coffee."

Phillip looked at Dr Sammoy and said to her: "Madam Doctor, I wonder if I could encourage you to share with me my own coffee, which has been prepared by my mother's own two hands." Not taking any chances to convince her, he added, "She makes the best coffee you could find anywhere in Port-of-Spain."

Sammoy would learn over the years just how much of a salesman Phillip Suielman was, and whenever he wished to close the deal he would invoke the superlative of best to illustrate the highest quality. On this occasion, she was about to test his theory of the best coffee.

Mrs Suielman, who she did not know, made her coffee strong, thick and black. She prepared it the Arab way. Whereas the Spanish drank a deep black coffee, the coffee which Phillip Suielman poured out of his Thermos was mildly mud-like and very robust.

Sammoy had three very small cups during the hour and a half she visited. The coffee would come to mean much more to both Phillip and Sammoy, and in the months ahead as they began to truly express their feelings for each other, it would not be unusual for Phillip to arrive at her practice carrying with him his Thermos of coffee. She would interrupt her schedule of attending to the needs of her patients to have coffee with a man she was fond of, and with whom she was certain her feelings went beyond a stick of fire.

Phillip Suielman and Dr Sammoy built their love first, then built their business together, and later as a man and wife they built a family, with the lone child the creator allowed to them.

The sweetness of their union was, with every new day, passed unto their offspring Miriam.

Miriam from the cradle was given an abundance of blessings, harvested from the work of her parents in so many areas of their lives, and they graciously passed to their offspring untold possibilities. She gave no indication that she would deviate from the path that had been cut for her. Whenever the grass was high and challenging, Phillip and Sammoy Suielman, like a good lion and lioness, were always there to clear the path so that their darling daughter Miriam would have a life of easy passage.

She was schooled at the best schools, firstly at private school for her primary school education followed by one of the leading convents at Port-of-Spain. Phillip often boasted: "One of the elite girls' schools on the island."

No sooner had Miriam completed her O-Level examinations, she was tutored to specifically undertake the American SAT Examinations. With her own high aptitude and professional tutorage she aced the exams, and was enrolled at a leading women's college on the outskirts of Boston, USA.

"Maybe it was the education institution that she attended, which made her vulnerable to this boy," Phillip noted to Sammoy, as they spoke about Miriam for the millionth time. They would begin speaking about the prices of food and the beautiful fruits on the trees in the huge backyard, but invariably their conversations would return to Miriam and her new world, and what all of it meant to the Phillip and Sammoy Suielman clan.

7

SIX MILES AS THE CROW FLIES, MIRIAM WAS SERVING lunch to her two younger children. Despite the burden of having six within a six year period, she had no regrets about her children. She largely home schooled them, though she crossed swords with Thomas who wanted them to attend the Islamic school on the compound with the mosque.

Blessed with four boys and two girls she gave special attention to her girl children, knowing they could never experience the world that she did.

Miriam was always pragmatic as a girl, and became much more so as a woman. Her world was one, where her needs and wants were equally satisfied. Her meeting Thomas and her marriage to him ushered her into a life of poverty at the beginning, and with each additional child she came to accept abject poverty as the lowest form of human existence.

Thomas was firm that she should not ask her parents for anything material, as he would provide for his family. She knew that if she wanted she could withdraw funds from her personal savings account, but this he also forbade. He was the husband and leader of the household and he alone would provide, even as the evidence suggested he was less than capable of providing anything to keep his family of six children properly fed, clothed and sheltered.

When she first moved into Rose Hill the very cramped two-bedroom was not what she was used to, but Thomas at that time smiled and promised that soon they would be moving to more spacious quarters.

"That was too long ago," Miriam pondered when the third child arrived. Then there was the fourth – another boy, which Miriam mused seemed to give Thomas a new verve, a reason to go on with life. It was as if his Rose Hill household was the best kept, well fed and happiest household in all of La La Land.

She on the other hand had begun, since the birth of child number two, to recognise the life she had chosen, and gave consideration to returning to her Goodwood Park happiness. Miriam, despite all her pains, feared that such a move could become violent. She had not seen this side of Thomas, but too many of his Muslim sisters in speaking with her at times would let slip that Thomas was one of the regulators, or put another way, one of the enforcers, within his mosque.

Now she was the mother of a brood of six children, and had a husband who, despite his apparent inability to effectively father any of the six, was quite happy to seek a seventh child.

Miriam's mind finally awoke from all manner of slumber, and so on a quiet Tuesday afternoon she said to her closest neighbour: "Jesse, could you keep an eye on the children for an hour? I will be back shortly." Before leaving, she disconnected the twenty-pound cylinder of propane gas which fuelled the stove. Miriam wanted no mishaps in her absence.

8

UPON LEAVING HER HOME SHE CALLED SUZIE, HER lifelong friend, having shared a desk with her throughout primary school and into convent, which now seemed so far away. She had previously made contact with Suzie two weeks earlier to say to her, "I now need your professional services." Having made arrangements for the date and time, she hung up her phone and contemplated her next move.

Miriam arrived at Suzie's and was met by an empty office, as was her request. There were no patients, nor receptionists – only Dr Suzie Stefano.

Both women loved each other as only close sisters could, having in earlier years as girls shared so much. As young women they were, as some elders are wont to say, "like ring on finger." During their formative years Miriam would sleep over at the Stefanos', and Suzie would do the same at the Suielmans'. When the girls were finally able to go clubbing, neither would not be allowed to go if the other was not available. Thus it was not surprising to Miriam that she met a vacant office, as she had not spoken to Suzie after that never to be forgotten day when Thomas eased his way into her life and she opened hers to him.

She now surmised that her bestie instinctively understood her needs, and Suzie in turn understood that Miriam would not have contacted her unless she had pressing challenges.

When the two women saw each other, they each paused and smiled long-lost smiles, neither wanting the other to feel less than the other, nor indeed more than the other. They embraced each other for the best part of a minute, during which Suzie whispered in Miriam's right ear: "What can I do to assist?"

Suzie held Miriam's hand very much as they had done as girls so long ago, and led her into her examination and operating room. When Miriam left to 'catch' her taxi forty minutes later she felt sad, but she knew her good friend Suzie had seen to it that some of her troubles were over. Suzie, who was often referred to by a cross section of society as the best gynaecologist within the city, was equally fulfilled that she had begun what both women would come to accept as the beginning of the repair job on her dearest friend Miriam.

It was left to Miriam to ensure that Thomas did not become suspicious of the act, which ensured that despite Thomas the zealot's desire for a far bigger family, his with Miriam would not grow beyond six children.

The days grew into weeks, and Miriam felt stronger mentally and physically. She spent more time reading the Quran and becoming familiar with Islamic materials. She also gave extra lessons to children in need. Word circulated far and wide within the communities of East Dry River about the perceived brightness of Miriam's children, which caused the neighbourhood parents to come knocking at her door seeking unpaid assistance with their children's education.

Miriam observed that many who came to her were under thirty five years old, and were in many instances functionally illiterate. She now contended with home schooling her six children during the day, and assisting approximately one dozen children in the evenings sitting on the floor of her humble living and dining room. She also noted that many who came to her were Muslims, and this reinforced in her mind the need to seriously begin understanding this thing called Islam in the context of poor communities.

As a scholar Miriam took her genius from her mother Sammoy, while her cunning and her street sense undoubtedly sprung from her father Phillip. She would never be rash about her plans, nor would she respond to Thomas, when she knew he would be unbending. Her world, she concluded following her meeting with Suzie, would be in support of her six children. Nothing would henceforth stand in her way of ensuring her children climbed out of Rose Hill and into a far better space.

Her reading of the Quran gave her an understanding of a better tomorrow, and steered her in her belief that the interpretation of the special book by many of its followers, like the interpretations of the Bible by Christians close at home and further afield, was perhaps the challenge to be surmounted.

Despite her understanding of the books of two religions – over which wars have been fought, with millions of lives lost throughout the ages – she was in no position to give focus to her views on these fundamental issues of Islam nor, indeed, Christianity.

It was the restrictions which troubled Miriam, of not being able to discuss nor debate the issue of the impact Islam was having on the lives of the women and children of Islam. It frustrated her more than the physical hardship she endured, each hour of each day of each month and each of the six years she lived at Rose Hill as the wife of an Islamic zealot named Thomas. Who could she speak with? There was no one she could trust to illustrate the contradictions of the men who wore their 'topes' and 'jalaps' as signs of their strength and belief in the creator, but who if measured by the lives they led demonstrated anything but good examples of the Prophet.

Miriam largely kept her own counsel, not knowing how the strongly articulated views of a woman convert would impact the culture of the mosque which her fanatic of a husband attended.

Miriam was always thinking, especially as she washed cleaned and cooked. It was during these long hours she fashioned her arguments about Islam, or perhaps Islamic men. These talking points were rarely used, as she long saw herself as an outsider within Rose Hill, East-Dry-River, and the mosque where Thomas held rank and status but for which he received little rewards for his long hours of efforts.

Behind her back, the very neighbours who would knock on her door to ask that she give lessons to their children, and to write letters both private and official, were the very neighbours who called her 'whitee,' noted Avalon, one of the Christian ladies at Rose Hill.

Avalon lived four houses up the Hill from Miriam, being a resident of long standing within the community. She too kept to herself, but had a reputation of having a nose that smelled upwind, ears that heard long distance and eyes that could see around corners. With these attributes Avalon enjoyed a level of distance from her neighbours, which she both welcomed and used for her own interest and comforts. She however took to Miriam, as evidenced by the warm welcome she extended to her, shortly after it was established that she was not only new but also the married Mrs of Thomas' home.

Avalon listened to the "users," as she referred to a group of her neighbours, of whom she often said: "They can't help themselves, they must talk people business." She knew that the life of the woman four houses lower down the hill was, in her mind, the business of too many in the small, stifling community. To her Miriam was special, and did not deserve to be the topic of any standpipe gossip.

Avalon, sitting on her six feet by ten feet veranda, kept surveillance on "all who came and all who went." What she did not see her ears heard, as she listened to the conversations of all who passed her home on their way to their various destinations.

Avalon was given to recalling to herself incidents and events which, at the time, touched her soul. These were the facts of Rose Hill which she knew first-hand and, as if in a trance, she would recount such moments as if speaking to her now deceased sister.

She looked into the narrow, paved main artery into and out of Rose Hill and as she did so, her memory bank kicked in and she began speaking as if reporting to her deceased sister. She spoke softly, not wishing anyone beyond her thin plywood wall to hear what she said.

Avalon said to herself: "I remember late one evening as I lay in bed in the darkness of my small but comfortable room. I heard and recognised the voices of two hill people, meaning Rose Hill residents. They were not speaking loudly, but they were having a good go at bad mouthing the dear lady named Miriam, whom they called 'Whitey'. In their wickedness, they spoke of Whitey being rich, but choosing to keep Thomas and his children living in that 'ming-pilling' shack. 'She real terrible, she could easily take she family to live in the west where she come from,' one of them concluded."

"This kind of gossip from two people who can't write dey name and often visit with Mrs Miriam for help of one kind or another," thought Avalon.

Miriam knew much of this. Not that Avalon had said anything to her, but she knew. Her father taught her to always treat the postman or post lady well, as they not only delivered letters, but equally brought you the neighbourhood news – both good and bad.

Operating with the cards stacked against her, Miriam smiled. She had learned to smile a long time ago – "when you could close the door on the person in front of, you smile." These skills she mastered during her summer vacations spent at Suielman and Sons Limited, doing what both her parents insisted was her apprenticeship. Miriam in the process became adept at the smile, but managed it never wishing to deceive anyone. As she grew into womanhood, her smiles more often than not had meaning.

It was this "Miriam smile" which made life so much easier for the light skinned woman, who though she cared for all her neighbours knew that their business was their business and not matters for which she need detain her thoughts.

Miriam not only taught herself the "use of English," that is, the match of words and the application of dictionary, she had always been attracted to the calypso and the richness of the double entendre of its poetry. She was the young woman who, in the world she once knew, found time to join her parents during the carnival season. Keeping step with her parents, she also attended many calypso and calypso related events. It was at these events that Miriam's interest in calypso peaked, and allowed her to sharpen her skills at double meanings of many a calypso presented by the artists.

In so many ways she learned well, and often spoke with double meanings in her conversation with Thomas, who responded to what he assumed he heard. So too in communicating with her neighbours, who she accepted were people of poor manners, and who never having been "taught any better" could not improve the lot of their miserable lives.

She never saw anyone as being a loser, though in her quiet moments she was driven to conclude she was surrounded by neighbours who could and would not rise beyond who they were. Therefore if bad mouthing a neighbour provided a booster, then she resigned herself to both humour and to entertain each of them whenever their paths crossed.

In this way she used double entendre to its fullest. However there were matters for which she chose simple, straightforward, clearly articulated language. In such circumstances she had no desire to be misunderstood.

9

IT WAS LATE ONE EVENING, AND SHE SAT READING the Quran. Thomas arrived home as he usually did, nearing ten pm. She raised her head from the holy book, looked out the window near where she sat in an old squeaky rocking chair and welcomed her husband as she had done for all of six years.

It was not a greeting she had planned, but it might have been an inspiration from the holy book. She looked up and said softly, almost whispering: "It is about mosque, it is about temple, it is about church. All three are intended to guide us to salvation."

She continued, as if driven by the backing of a full orchestra, with she being the lone performer. "We may not have food on our plates, we may not have milk to put before our children as they sit at our meal tables, but for church, temple and mosque we find resources to dress them up in preparation for the best costumed character. And once dressed to dazzle, whether by foot, mule cart or motorcar we get ourselves and our babies to one kind of service or another – for that is what matters," she concluded.

As Miriam said these words Thomas was taken aback, given that over the six years and six children his wife had never once spoken about his faith, nor the faith of others. On this night she not only spoke of and to Christians and Hindus, but she dared to lump his beloved Islam with the other two devil religions.

Miriam finished her statement, and her husband glared at her with a look of disdain. A thousand memories of neglect and sadness flowed through her memory of two thousand, five hundred and fifty five days of a most difficult marriage.

During the past seventy two months, there were few days she remembered as being great days – though there were good days. Yet, try as she might, she could never erase from her consciousness who she was, and what the future held for the four boys and two girls who carried her blood within their veins. Nor could she detach herself from her past, nor from the person she accepted her true self.

There was not a day when Miriam, the daughter of Phillip and Sammoy Suielman, who never, ever needed for anything, and who from her cradle was cared for by an extended family and who grew to embrace and accept peace of mind as a mighty blessing, didn't yearn for at least a small bit of what she deemed to be heaven.

She had met and fallen in love with a man who once offered her a sense of nobleness, and who existed in the dreamy world of love. Then she met the real him – Thomas.

Thomas this night revealed who he was, and what feelings he felt for the woman he so quickly married and then impregnated for six years consistently. He knew after that day that his relationship with Miriam would have changed irrevocably.

His instincts told him his wife was no longer smitten by him. Over the last four months she would remain reading or correcting the examinations she had given to her students, and only retired to bed when he was deep down in slumber land.

He stood with the sudden turmoil confounding his sanctuary. He looked at Miriam, wanting to lash out at her, but he knew other senior brothers at the mosque who made the error of hitting their wives and/or women were demoted in rank, and in some instances given strokes by the imam. Though shaking with rage and with his fist clenched, he looked away from Miriam and retired to their cubby-hole kitchen, to find out what his now inscrutable wife may have prepared and left for him.

He sat and ate his bowl of soup cold, as he was too angry to heat up his meal. That would have meant putting it in a small pot on the stove top and stirring the thick rich soup. There was no microwave nor toaster oven in the house. The last time Miriam used a toaster oven was the day she met Thomas, and at her mother's request she warmed a currant roll for her.

Tonight she listened from the adjoining space as her husband set his meal on the table for himself. This was a first in six years, as she would not allow him to do so before tonight's revelation.

Having gobbled his cold soup he moved silently to their night sleeping quarters, not bothering to look in on the six children who shared the larger of the two spaces utilised as bedrooms at Rose Hill. He performed his nightly absolutions, climbed into bed and attempted to fall off to sleep. But that single statement by Miriam caused Thomas to come to grips with the reality, that while his kettle was boiling, the water within his kettle was not getting any hotter. He wondered as he had never done before. Would his wife suddenly come to terms with just who he was? Would she return home to her parents, as he had long suggested to her not to do?

Thomas lived in discomfort knowing of Miriam's background and previous lifestyle. The society which she once shared, and which fashioned her as a younger woman, was structured where the rich and wealthy stayed together and partied happily together. At times like these, when he allowed himself to stray from earlier pledges he made to himself and his imam that he would not allow the "high and mighty" to rule either his heart or his head, he felt in himself a tremendous spirit of weakness. Over much of his life he rumbled with the rough and difficult from his very urban environment. He had physically fought many a battle as part of a gang of young Turks from Rose Hill and the surrounding communities of East Dry River, Port-of-Spain.

Late one evening, when he was just fourteen years old, he held a gun to the head of one of his rivals and squeezed the trigger. There was no explosion, though – the Beretta pistol jammed. Having failed once he squeezed again, and still there was no loud explosion of sound which comes from the firing of a gun. Meanwhile the young rival, who stood and stared death not once but twice within seconds, bolted.

He left Thomas holding an unfired pistol, which jammed and changed his short life forever.

The incident, though not ending in physical tragedy, created a psychological challenge for Thomas, his fellow gang members and their rivals. They all knew now that Thomas was not just talk; he was made of the metal that would shoot to kill, and they gave him due respect, ensuring they were on good terms with the skinny, young Rasta from Rose Hill.

From that day onwards, Thomas reformed himself. He never carried a gun thereafter, conscious that he would kill someone if he had to use a gun – he would with one shot ensure one kill.

All these unpleasant memories of so long ago returned to him, as if he saw himself once again running through the tracks which linked Rose Hill to the neighbouring East-Dry-River districts, chasing after Manto and Bootu, members of a rival gang. Such memories did not come often, but came always when he felt threatened in any way. Miriam's "verse and scripture" had pierced his well-constructed and concealed armour and left him vulnerable. He felt naked and exposed, and felt equal disdain for himself, having allowed his wife over whom he exerted so much control to, with a simple statement, ruffle his feathers and in the process weaken a relationship which made him more of a man than he really was.

His biggest fear was not going back to wielding a gun and chasing Manto and Bootu, within the dimly lit track above Clifton Street, East-Dry-River. No, his fear was being in competition with the class of people from which Miriam originated. So too were his fears of the middle class and the classes between them and the poor.

Growing up within the East-Dry-River, he knew that the poor, like poor people wherever they resided or inhabited on the planet Earth, are firmly tied to the bottom of the ladder. The other classes occupy the rungs between the bottom and the top, guaranteeing that the social structure remained in place. Having pulled his trigger more than once, he resolved to move up the ladder even if it meant displacing some of the classes on the rungs between him and those who stood at the top.

The intensity of his bitter feelings towards Miriam, over what she said of his religion, convinced him he would never ever be allowed to climb the ladder. He hated the ladder before him. He knew only too well that Miriam loved him, and this he clung to as he finally allowed sleep to overtake his tired body and his beaten, restless and troubled spirit.

Miriam, seated in her chair and having closed her window to the world of Rose Hill, focused on her reading, knowing the day would come when she would have to stand up to be counted not as a brainless, unthinking Islamic woman, but as a widely read and studied Muslim, mother and wife.

Her subconscious mandated that the stories of the poor, especially the poor women, be they Hindu, Christian and above all Islamic women, be told, to facilitate review, debate and discussion. Yet more importantly it must lead to corrective action coming to all women, especially the many trapped in situations which began as relationships in which men promised the moon, if not the stars, and instead delivered abuse, fear and in too many instances an unspoken form of imprisonment.

10

MIRIAM'S DESIRE TO FIX WHAT PSYCHOLOGISTS, medical doctors, social workers and senior police officers argued could not be changed, encouraged in her a self-imposed mission – Miriam resolved to put wrongs right. How she would initiate the process would come in the form of an almost 'unwritten' article, in the third most popular daily newspaper of the three daily newspapers on the island.

The article, with the by-line Staff Reporter, began: "Community activist from east Trinidad says he will convene an international conference, to debate abuses within all religious organisations. The activist, Nathan John of Los Bajos, said his international conference will put the spotlight on all the underhand dealings within the three dominant religions within the twin island Republic of Trinidad and Tobago. Mr John underscored that he hoped citizens who had something to say on all the issues confronting the churches would be welcomed.

"When asked how he would be funding his conference, Nathan John replied: "God will provide." The conference will be held during the last week of April, and persons interested are encouraged to contact the organiser, Nathan John, at phone number..."

Marian made a note of Nathan John's phone number and resolved to call, if only to enquire. This she did some days later, in between her list of maternal and household chores.

When Nathan answered his phone Miriam paused before continuing, almost as if she was having second thoughts about the call. Eventually she enquired: "Is this Nathan John, and are you the man planning the conference on abuses within churches?"

Nathan was equally astonished to have had such an early response and enquiry, not having even assembled a team yet. He planned on discussing it with his colleagues within the Los Bajos Community Council, of which he was secretary.

Nathan eventually replied: "Yes I am Nathan John, and in answer to your question I am the person hoping to host the conference."

With his response came a raucous laugh from Miriam and a sharp quip. "What do you mean by hoping?" She added to her sustained laughter. Miriam had not laughed with so much passion for a long time – certainly not in the last six years of seeking to please and to conform within Thomas' Muslim environment.

Eventually Nathan asked, almost as if he was speaking with his sister Judith: "Do you smell a joke somewhere?"

Miriam replied: "You just said you are hoping to have a conference, yet the newspaper published that you are having a conference – isn't that worth laughing over?"

Nathan immediately grasped Miriam's frustration. He apologised, and further explained that while he had skills in getting information published, he was at his wits end in getting 'the idea' of his conference organised.

Miriam listened, and enquired if he would agree to meet her at the city's market the following morning at nine am. When Nathan enquired why the market, she was blunt and to the point. "I don't want my husband to know I am about to tell the world of the troubles Islamic women face within their faith."

Nathan did not enquire what she meant, but asked politely: "Where will I find you and what do you look like?"

"You must recognise me, as I will be the lone Muslim-dressed woman, standing near to the lady who sells swizzle sticks, mortars and pestles, at the north-western corner of the second block at the market from the entrance, on the western side gate" she outlined to an attentive Nathan. Anyone listening in on the telephone exchange between Miriam and Nathan that memorable morning would forever be convinced that sometimes all it takes is one phone call to change lives, sometimes families and sometimes communities and countries.

Miriam's single telephone call to Nathan John initiated a chain of actions and reactions, which once set in motion began a change process that would, in the weeks and months ahead, not only move Nathan much closer to his long desired ambitions of taking on the Church, but expose it for what he felt was, it being too secretive about its secrets.

Nathan's actions when he started his crusade may have been to tease his overzealously Christian mother and sister, but his critiques over time began to take on a level of seriousness.

Judith recalls, in discussing the planned conference with her mother and other parishioners of the Los Bajos Community, that being very close to Nathan she could discern the morphing of Nathan the village boy into Nathan the activist.

With Nathan the change came quickly, said Judith. She explained to her group of women who all wanted to know more about her brother, to know exactly what happened to the sweet little boy from No. 13, Second Street, Los Bajos, who sang so sweetly at church choir and who was the life of the annual church harvest and Christmas bazaar. They could not reconcile what they perceived to be dramatic changes in the demeanour of a good Catholic member of the Christian community, into someone aggressively in opposition to the church that not only educated him, but provided a platform for his overall social development.

"Nathan is and had been upset for quite some time with the issues of the church," noted Judith. "He became angry each time a report of abuse by a priest against children surfaced. His concerns are that the church is complicit, both in its treatment of the abuse and in its methodology in keeping these matters secret." Judith underscored with a wave of her hand, as if to illustrate her support for her rebellious brother. "The die has been cast, and Nathan will do what he must to host a successful conference – how successful is anyone's guess," she concluded.

Truly the "die was cast," for as Judith spoke to her little group, Nathan was meeting with Miriam. Working together, she would change his life and he would change hers in ways neither could imagine or wished to imagine at the time of their first meeting at the Port-of-Spain Central Market.

Nathan saw her form, from a distance of five hundred yards or so as he walked from block one of the market to get to block two. He could make out the figure of a woman dressed in Muslim clothing from the crown of her head to the soles of her feet. She wore light brown clothing, and he estimated she was approximately five feet, six inches in height. Nathan still calculated using imperial measurements, choosing to ignore the metric system, which he found confusing, but which was established to be the official system of measurements within his island home.

He was still calculating her height as he walked up to her and asked: "Are you Miriam?"

To which she replied with a huge smile, "Miriam in the flesh, though you won't know that with my hijab and abaya." Miriam, from the moment she laid eyes on Nathan, knew she would genuinely wish to assist him.

She confided in Judith months later: "In Nathan I found someone who spoke his truths despite the pain his truths carried."

Nathan and Miriam settled for their meeting sitting on two wooden boxes, which belonged to the swizzle stick vendor. She knew Miriam from visiting and purchasing from her stall, and did not find it odd that a total stranger would meet with her customer and settle to sitting on two wooden boxes to conduct a meeting. She distracted herself a couple of times during the meeting between Miriam and Nathan to look over her shoulder to see what her known customer and her stranger of a visitor were doing. The vendor was a worldly woman well into her sixties, and knew when men met married women in the market that mischief could be afoot. Following three twists of her neck and her well perfected glances, she was convinced this meeting was genuine and above board. She reckoned that if they were up to no-good, they would not sit out in the open behind her market stall to get on with 'slackness.' All the while Nathan was explaining to Miriam why he was driven to host the 'Conference of the Un-Godly,' which was the name he had chosen.

Miriam did not say to Nathan that she did not like the name, as this could be dealt with at a later stage. She was more interested in understanding his concept, his format, the resources available to him, and she pressed him for answers. "Are you certain you want this to be an international conference?" she enquired in her most compelling voice.

Next she asked: "Where do you plan to host the conference?" Without giving Nathan time to respond, she added: "Do you have a conference hotel in mind, and more importantly do you have a conference secretariat?" She paused to give Nathan a moment to both reflect and to respond.

Nathan now understood that despite his wanting to host a conference it seemed in so many ways to be beyond him and the resources he commanded, which when detailed on a 'dinner mint' wrapper, amounted to zero.

His response, when it finally came, was fashioned with nine words, which he softly shared: "It looks like I have bigger plans than possibilities."

Miriam saw the dejection in Nathan, and for the first time since she made that instinctive call which brought them together for this meeting, she felt she had met a person of utmost sincerity. "To admit defeat when confronted with the facts is a good thing," she said, "but to give up so easily is not the sign of a man who wishes to right the wrongs of his church."

This was the wake-up call Nathan needed, and it came from someone who had only in recent times begun to awake from six years of her own slumber. "Well when, where and how do we begin?" questioned Nathan, fully conscious that Miriam was the leader in this matter of hosting his conference as he reviewed what had just happened. Miriam Suielman, the woman somewhat older than he was, may have also become his leader.

Miriam glanced at her watch, which was hidden under the left sleeve of her brown, loosely fitted top, and her face took on a look of concern. He observed and said nothing. He knew zilch about this mystery woman who had suddenly entered his life, his conference and who on the evidence before him, could turn out to be his saviour and the one upon whose shoulders the hosting of the conference of the "ungodly" would be convened and hopefully celebrated.

Having checked the time Miriam said, as she looked Nathan squarely in the face and forced him to lock eyes with her: "We have made progress, and we have much work to do. I will prepare a checklist for our next meeting, can you do the same? Could you also jot down all your thoughts – just about everything on this conference," she added with a broad smile returning to her face, where moments earlier she carried an intense, almost woe-be-gone look having learnt the time.

Miriam was about to bid Nathan farewell, when he was moved to enquire of her: "When will we next meet, and more importantly, where will we be meeting?" Miriam's thoughts were locked in so many places; she was here with Nathan at the Port-of-Spain market, while her mind was running in a number of domestic compartments.

She had already given thought to the questions posed by the conference convenor and co-ordinator, but chose not to decide on the meeting time and place until she sketched out a plan and initiated some of its details. She surmised, and rightfully so, that it was neither good for her nor for Nathan to be meeting, not having progressed beyond the discussion of their meeting just concluded. Both needed to see and feel some measure of progress if this conference that they both highly anticipated were to remain a project with purpose and passion.

Miriam, from where she stood and what she had experienced since leaving her parents' home and chose to live at Rose Hill, East-Dry-River, knew the world was changing. Not for the better, but some would argue for the worst – she knew on the evidence before her the world was quietly but quickly changing for the worst.

She reasoned Nathan's conference could be one of the moments of recall, when people of all faiths and persuasions could come together in an atmosphere of civility and pleasantries, and truly put the brakes on a world that was slipping into untold darkness. She embraced the idea that she would be one of the instruments through which meaningful change would be initiated, and she committed to being such an instrument regardless of the difficulties her actions would initiate between her and her fiercely Muslim husband.

She finally said to Nathan: "I will contact you with the date, time and place of our next meeting. Please do your homework – our conference will be held, and it will be a success."

Nathan was quick to respond: "I will do my homework and I hope you do yours." He laughed as he added: "I like the words we have shared today, but I am especially moved by two words – our conference." With that they turned away from each other, but did not move on before each thanked Mrs Jocelyn, the swizzle stick vendor, for allowing them the meeting space and the two boxes upon which they sat to host the first planning meeting of their conference.

11

AS MIRIAM WALKED AWAY, SHE DID NOT LOOK BACK. Had she done so, she would have seen Nathan stop, turn and look in her direction for as long as he could see her. As he looked his mind was blank, and overwhelmed by the blessing that came his way in the presence of Miriam, he uttered not a word as there was nothing to be said.

Miriam made her way out of the market using the exit which brought market goers to the Eastern Main Road, having crossed the Priority Bus Route. She turned over each tiny detail of the meeting, and as she learned so long ago working with her father, each component of a plan ought to and could be looped to create an even more defining component. Each was a block in the wall, and when finally assembled, presented the complete wall, which allowed ordinary people an opportunity to see the work of the master mason.

She felt the nascent spirit of the conference deep within her, which she rightfully sensed was overpowering her. All the feelings were innocent and holy, yet embodied a sense of rebelliousness.

She wondered whether the youth and boldness of Nathan was impacting her beyond the work they had both chosen. As quickly as this thought entered her brainwaves she dismissed it out-of-hand. Nathan might have been brave enough to want to host this land breaking conference, but to her he was just a good boy.

She visualised her checklist, and at the top of the list was written that she must go home and speak with Mom and Dad. Her list also carried an item next to which she pencilled three asterisks. Finding a name for the conference would not be the easiest of assignments, and at this point Miriam decided she would walk the three miles to Rose Hill as it gave her time to think.

On this day of the inaugural planning meeting there was no sun in the sky – or if it was there she did not feel its rays. She observed that the sky carried all the tell-tale signs of an impending wet season, during which showers would pour down on the city as if in defiance and in competition with the sun. These showers came without warning. She hoped today to be spared such a shower as she made her way to the space she shared with her six children and her husband, which she reluctantly described as home.

Always observant, Miriam could tell when the rains were likely to pour forth from the sky. Her desire to know also encouraged her to ask questions of others, and there were instances when she simply listened and learned.

She must have been just nine years old when her father Phillip Suielman decided that she should play golf, and he took her to learn the rudiments of a game that she wished in her silent moments she could still play. She enjoyed the openness and nature, which most golf courses offered, but she particularly loved the public golf course at Chaguaramas on the north western peninsula of Trinidad.

Here she not only became proficient at golf, developing a quality swing under the watchful eyes of coach Yearwood, a former national professional, but learned as much of the abundance of flora and wildlife of the majestic acreage that embraces the course. Miriam told everyone when she spoke of the golf course: "The tranquillity which encircles you is interrupted only by the chattering of howling monkeys, and when mating the sounds turn to loud aggressive roars."

It is at Chaguaramas that Miriam learned from coach Yearwood: "Whenever you hear the monkeys making lots of noises, know it will rain within half an hour."

During the years that she perfected her golf craft, before she journeyed from Trinidad to university at Boston, she would witness the phenomenon of the sounds of the monkeys. As told by coach Yearwood, it was followed by huge showers of rain approximately twenty to thirty minutes after they filled the air with their loud chatter, which sounded more like lions roaring. Such experiences assisted in sharpening her keenness about weather patterns, which to her represented and remained a constant wherever her travels took her.

On this overcast, breezy morning leaving the market, where the air always seemed still, she embraced the breezy blowing at her back, and the sensation she felt that even the wind was pushing her on to a successful staging of Nathan's conference.

For some months now, Miriam did not know when she prayed if she prayed to Allah, the God of her husband, or to Christ, the God she believed she knew intimately.

Miriam was not an over-zealous anything; she lived her life throughout her childhood years always wanting to please her mother and father. Both represented her world, and though she never to the best of her memory could remember verbally expressing her love for Sammoy and Phillip Suielman, she made known her love in doing the things she knew they both wished for from their offspring. She set her standard to become an exceptional person.

She demonstrated at an early age a willingness, which bordered on passion, to be part of the Suielman world of business. As a toddler she cried behind her parents as they went off to work and left her in the care of Suzanna, the Suielman lifelong helper.

Suzanna was not a maid, as some believed she was – she was part of the family. She joined Phillip and Sammoy shortly after they got married, taking care of the small, well-appointed home they owned at Fitt Street, Woodbrook. Later she would move into her own studio apartment, which Phillip had added to the Suielmans' newly acquired Goodwood Park home.

Suzanna organised the household with the flair and professionalism one associates with a student of protocol and hospitality. She was neither seen nor heard, but was always a "wink" away if needed by Sammoy or Phillip. With the birth of Miriam, Suzanna assured both parents that they need not worry about the new-born, as she would always be there for both parents and their girl child. This promise she kept, and she was as shattered as Sammoy and Phillip were when Miriam, without so much as batting her eyes, announced she was getting married, and with the speed of lightening moved away leaving most everything she owned behind at Goodwood Park.

Suzanna, though she constantly cleaned Miriam's bedroom, never cleared or moved anything from where her "special one," as she called her, left it. She never said it, but for many a night she prayed herself to sleep, appealing to her God to return Miriam, her "special one," to her parents' home.

She believed and remained convinced that there was something 'un-godly' about the sudden and gut-rending separation of Miriam from the household. All these feelings of hurt, sometimes bordering on despair, caused her to leave Miriam's space exactly as she left it. She reasoned that God would intervene and return her to her only true family.

Suzanna was in many ways Miriam's sounding board. Miriam came to her at all hours either day or night, to seek solutions on matters that troubled her; she sought answers on just about everything. She was always asking questions of Sammoy and Phillip, and in their absence she found Suzanna wherever she was and whatever she was engaged in, to ask her questions for which she needed answers.

What counsel Suzanna, a girl with four Caribbean Examination Council passes, offered to her parents, she gave in equal measure to Miriam throughout her life. On weekday mornings, Miriam cried behind her parents as they left to administer over their areas of responsibilities at Suielman and Sons Ltd. Suzanna would swoop toddler Miriam up off the floor and place her on her shoulders as she went about her own responsibilities at the Suielmans' home.

As Miriam grew, so too did the family business, which Phillip nurtured followed by Sammoy, who, with an eye for detail and a diligence for not spending a bad cent, gave Frederick Street in Port-of-Spain one of the fanciest department stores. This was the world Miriam loved to go to, as she not only grasped the rudiments of business but like a strong sponge she absorbed the don'ts of her parents business. To Miriam the dos were always easy – it was the don'ts to which she gave focus and spent much time avoiding.

She turned onto Piccadilly Street, East-Dry-River, with the late morning breeze still strong on her back. In her mind she added to her check list, "Do plan to raise $300K USD". She thought in US dollars even though she operated in Trinidad and Tobago. Miriam was conscious the conference would cost much more than $300,000 dollars, but reasoned if the conference attracted participants from both near and far then it would not only pay for itself, it could generate a surplus. Miriam turned onto Rose Hill and began to ascend the short but steep incline.

As Miriam drew near to her door, Nathan was well on his way home. He was seated on the near left seat of the maxi-taxi that would bring him to the Arima Borough, and at the Borough he would find another taxi to bring him to Los Bajos.

During the slow but steady journey he mulled over the discussions of the morning, and pondered the possible success of his much hoped for conference. In Miriam he found a pleasant, slightly older and wiser person than himself, who he accepted could open doors – she was not only pretty, but wise and white.

In this moment he allowed himself the space, if not the luxury, to dream, and to begin to believe the 'Conference of the Un-Godly' would move from just being an idea to a reality. He smiled and uttered aloud: "a big reality, a huge reality."

Nathan did not hear himself, but the seven passengers within the maxi-taxi heard and in unison looked in his direction. He never noticed the curious looks which jabbed at him, for he was in his own world, beginning to live his reality. Nathan was having flashes of the possibilities of seeing speaker after speaker, as well as presenter after presenter, tell their various and many stories of life behind the high walls of religious institutions.

He, for as long as he could recall, read everything he could find on religion, with all its goodness and its darkness. He always told his sister Judith that he could embrace the good of her church, but he slammed the damned for all the evil committed in the name of the Lord.

He was as curious about other religions as he was about Christians. For him the assignment would never be restricted to Christianity, who had closets to be emptied. The assignment was wider and deeper, and he reasoned if there were closets within Christianity, then there were wardrobes elsewhere. He hoped the 'Conference of the Un-Godly' would be a world spring-cleaning of those who hid behind their rituals and robes.

12

NATHAN AND MIRIAM DID NOT SPEAK ONE WEEK later as planned. No calls came from her to him, nor did they speak for two weeks as still not a call came.

During the week after the meeting he expected to hear from Miriam, who he accepted would be the senior partner in the hosting of this historic conference. Not having heard from her, he counselled himself that she would contact him the following week. As week two passed with silence he, despite losing hope, elected to give her the benefit of all doubts. He concluded there must be a good, if not a very good, reason for 'Miriam the wise' abandoning him so quickly.

Nathan was growing up quickly; he accepted that not all persons kept their promises, inclusive of a number of persons he knew for most of his life who often broke their promises. With Miriam, he was so overwhelmed that he could not busy himself in believing that she too was not a promise keeper.

Week three following the meeting began without incident as per the pattern of the two previous weeks, and continued with Nathan finally accepting that he would neither hear from Miriam, nor would there be a conference.

Sunday turned to Monday, and Tuesday into Wednesday. At precisely 8:00am, Nathan's phone rang, and the voice at the other end instructed: "Don't say anything, just listen." Nathan did as he was told, and Miriam speaking said: "Can we meet tomorrow at 9:30am, same place?"

Nathan's reply, when he finally adjusted his mind, was curt: "Sure thing, I will be there."

Before he could add another word Miriam added: "And be on time." And she hung up.

Nathan kept the phone to his ear almost as if he expected to hear Miriam giving further instructions. When he finally lowered the phone, he smiled a broad smile, clenched his fist and cuffed the air downwards as he shouted: "Yes!"

He had almost lost faith, but the wise and white and veiled Muslim woman was still on his side. The renewed possibilities of his conference once again shone like the bright sun, which he witnessed as he sat in his bedroom, looking through his glass louvered window in his community of Los Bajos.

It took Miriam all of near three weeks to detail her plan. She knew for her plan to succeed she would have to enrol the support and services of the Suielman clan, namely her mother and father, who she had not seen in five years and six months.

This worried her immensely, as she knew she had broken the most important rule of the Suielmans – she had abandoned her family.

Phillip had drilled into her very being the significance of always putting the family first. Often to illustrate his point, he would with his right bent index finger gently knock her forehead as he said in a whisper: "Miriam, nothing is more important than family; always put the family first."

Sometimes, as he taught her the values of family, he would add: "Your family is not only your mother and I; it is also your grandmother, your aunts and uncles. It is your cousins and their in laws, but in this link of the Suielmans our family must include Suzanna and all our employees at Suielman and Sons Limited." On the rare occasion he would add, as if to reinforce the point: "Miriam, never forget you met Suzanna here. She was occupying space here before you were born and you must always see her as family."

During and following these classes of family indoctrination, she could not help but deeply reflect on the true meaning of the word family and its implications for her future as a wife. Miriam witnessed that employees at Suielman and Sons Limited, time and again, would knock and enter her parents' offices unannounced. Upon an invitation in, they would sit at the desk of her father and, more often than not, request financial assistance to attend to some matter within their family. Upon listening he seldom asked questions, but responded: "When do you need it for?"

Early in her marriage to Phillip, Dr Sammoy curiously observed the procession of employees who came to see her husband, invariably to request financial assistance. She once told her daughter as they spoke about this unusual Suielman corporate culture: "I could not, try as I might, work out the mechanics of your dad's logic in dispensing cash to his employees without so much as a signed voucher. From day one I observed, but I never said anything to him. He knew I had concerns. One evening as we were having coffee at the office he said to me: 'Sammoy, I have observed that each time one of our people come to me for help you look on without saying anything. I know you are troubled.'

"I still did not respond – though I kept an even keener facial expression. Your dad proceeded to assure me: 'Sammoy, if I don't help these people where will they go for help? Do you want them to steal our goods and do their own retailing?' He ended our conversation that evening almost as if dismissing the money he "gave away" to our employees, with the words: 'Anyhow it is small money.'"

Sammoy understood her husband, and though she changed many systems and added many-a-procedure, she never commented nor interfered with Phillip's own welfare programmes within Suielman and Sons. He saw every employee as being part of his family, and it was the responsibility of the leader of the family to put its people first.

These memories of her years of schooling on the importance of the family, at the feet of the man she loved deeply, returned with the intensity of a tidal wave, gushing over her entire being, pushing her in too many directions. All she wished was that the power of the wave would send her hurling to the waiting arms of Phillip Suielman. She had abandoned him for her husband Thomas, who she believed at that unfortunate moment that she loved, and who, though he never said it, forced her to forsake her family.

She planned in her head the head the best strategy. This she changed a thousand times, and eventually said she would just go home.

13

MIRIAM, DRESSED IN HER MUSLIM CLOTHING, WITH a cloth shoulder bag swinging across her shoulder, got out of the maxi-taxi and began her trek into Goodwood Park on the west of Port-of-Spain. Her first hundred metres was the hardest walking she had ever done, and Miriam walked almost everywhere she visited within Port-of-Spain, and so walking to her parents' home was by any yardstick not a difficult task. Yet she felt cramps in her legs and pains in her stomach.

These pains she knew were pains of expectation; she wondered what awaited her at her family's home.

She deliberately did not call to say she was coming home. It was not her intention to surprise nor alarm her mother, father or Suzanna, but all her intuition pushed her to arrive unannounced.

Three days earlier she had called her father's office, and deliberately did not say to Josephine who was calling. She merely enquired: "Could I speak with Mr Phillip Suielman?" It was her intention to say to her father, had he answered: "Dad, I am coming to see you at home next Thursday." She had already made up her mind that her father would have been so taken unawares he would be lost for words, and she planned to add: "See you soon dad, I love you."

Josephine's response changed her plan. In a most officious voice she said: "Mr Suielman is not in office and will not be here for the week."

Miriam, always on her feet, countered: "Do you know where I might find him? I have a proposal for him. Can I find him at home?"

Josephine's professionalism kicked in, and she said: "I can't say if Mr Suielman is at home, but I do believe I could get a message to him."

Miriam replied very curtly: "I do not believe that will be necessary. I will get back to you when your boss is back at his desk."

Miriam deduced that her father was away from the office, and for whatever reason he was at home. She took the decision to visit her parents unannounced, and as her father always said, uninvited. She also reasoned that it would be the least stressful, for all members of the Suielman family.

Having turned the main bend at Goodwood Park she paused and looked around her old neighbourhood, of which she had so many fond memories. Miriam could walk the Goodwood Park Hills blindly, as prior to her unplanned departure from the community she spent many hours jogging and exercising on the very road she now travelled to, to an unknown reception at the Suielman residence.

Miriam would later relate to Suzie Steffano: "As I walked, I was reminded of the Stations of the Cross of Christ. Each step I took I could feel neighbours' eyes peeping from behind drapes. This was unusual, as none of my former neighbours had the character to come out and say hello. Those piercing eyes, staring at me as I alighted the slopes of Goodwood Park, were like lashes on my back. I dare say at the lower levels of the hill there were fewer eyes, but as I got further up the road each house had its sentry with eyes that were neither welcoming nor inviting."

Miriam also shared with Suzie: "My biggest fear was that someone who might have recognised me may have called my parents' home to alert them: 'Your daughter is within the neighbourhood.' Thankfully no one did that, and I made quick steps of the last mile to the home of Sammoy and Phillip Suielman," she added.

When Miriam arrived at the gate she retrieved her sixteen year-old key and placed it in the lock. Before turning the key, too many memories flowed through her person. There were also doubts at the very moment she was about to turn her key, about whether her parents may have changed the lock during her absence. Miriam slowly turned her key and heard a recognisable click, and she entered her home so long after she was last here.

She did not go to the front door, but made a beeline for the rear or the kitchen entrance, which adjoined the carport built to accommodate four cars.

When Phillip Suielman bought the house to create a home for himself and Sammoy he met a modest garage, which accommodated two cars, but soon had his cousin Anton (who was by no means an architect by profession) design and develop new plans to create a space for four cars.

Anton was Phillip's cousin on his mother's side of the family, and fitted the description of being a jack of all trades. "Just where did Anton learn to draw up plans, and perform the long list of services required for the legal approval of construction?" Sammoy questioned her husband one evening, as they discussed the extension of what she, always conscious of her pennies, described as an 'oversized, not needed' space.

Both Phillip and Sammoy had vehicles, he a Toyota Hi-Lux and she a Toyota Prado. Both believed the Toyota brand was the best available, and most durable, vehicle in Trinidad. Phillip, for as long as he owned a vehicle, chose a truck to provide for his personal needs, but more importantly to be able to transport goods in an emergency. You might say Sammoy's approach was similar, given that she too often turned down her seats to accommodate the movement of goods of one kind or another.

Knowing they were a two-car family, Sammoy enquired of Phillip, "Why are we expanding the garage to accommodate four cars?"

In response, Phillip, always with a strong rebuttal, said, "Dr Sammoy, don't you have a hobby which involves wood working? Well, Dr Sammoy, the extra space is to facilitate you doing your hobby," he added with a smirk on his face.

It was revealed that Anton, before settling down within his parents' establishment, served as an apprentice draftsman at an establishment owned and operated by a firm of French Creole architects.

There as a teenager he looked on, listened and learned the rudiments of architecture. He was thinking of becoming an architect, but his father had other plans and one day he visited the company where his son worked. Between his conversations with the senior architect with whom Anton worked and his coming to sit at Anton's desk, and almost as if speaking to no one in particular, he said so that all within the office could hear: "I have tried to tell the boy that he will amount to nothing sitting at these funny tables, scribbling lines and numbers.

"He is too smart to know the difference of working for yourself, doing what you must to earn your way legally. He is too smart to grasp that what now attracts him will only bring him grief and, to be certain, little money. If you see this boy, say to him his father wishes him well." As he concluded he left, with all nine employees and seven senior architects and principals of the firm with open mouths.

Anton was stunned by his father's appearance and unwelcome remarks. He was between tears and anger, but deep within he knew his father wanted the best for him, to come to Charlotte Street and apply his clearly recognisable discipline to their family business, which was in need of guidance, innovation, and a sense of newness.

At that moment, however, he wished the earth would open up and consume him. He felt pained and embarrassed, and mulled over the statement of his father. He recognised how much hurt he had created. He had hurt his father with whom he enjoyed an excellent relationship, to cause him to come to the establishment where he worked and to not only meet with his superior, but to create 'a scene', which no doubt would be talked about for a lifetime at a space not used to such interventions.

He wanted to grab his short list of belongings and bolt, and these thoughts squeezed at him. He heard first one clap, then two, then a chorus of applause from his colleagues. This was his co-workers' way of suggesting to him the matter was closed.

A week later Anton reported for work at his family's business, which sat at the middle of the block, between Prince and Queen Streets on Charlotte Street.

That morning, as he entered the cluttered space, he said to his father: "Good morning Pop. That was quite a speech at the other place."

His father looked at him and smiled, got up from his desk, reached out to his son and hugged him – never wanting to let go of him. When he finally released him, he pulled out his chair and said to Anton: "Please son, please take your seat. I have been keeping it warm for you."

With the increased garage space Sammoy Suielman did indeed find time to make use of the newfound covered space, which allowed her to explore a skill her father possessed and which he executed with passion.

As she built new creations of furniture she often would stand back from a just-completed piece, to examine it to determine imperfections. On these occasions her work brought smiles to her face, and in that instance she would remember her father and the joy his limited woodworking skills gave to him. And to her too, who was always available to hold down a piece of "board," as he called it, to allow him to cut it with his well sharpened hand saw.

He never worked with the precision tools she now possessed, and yet his work was neat and something to marvel at. He always insisted: "Sammoy, you measure twice and you cut once." His reasoning, he insisted, was learned the hard way. "When I first became interested in woodwork I was busy, busy, always ready to cut, and I made mistakes as I did not take time to measure accurately. Now I am no longer busy I take my time to measure, and so I make less mistakes," he added.

Sammoy had improved vastly on all she learned from her father, and added her own wisdom of quality machinery, keeping up to date with the latest equipment coming out of her father's mother land – China.

When she needed to unwind she would be found in her workshop, putting finishing touches to something she may have begun and now sought to complete.

Going to the door at the back of the home meant having to walk between the cars, which were parked to the entrance of the garage, and then through Sammoy's woodworking shop. Phillip, in defining Sammoy's space, placed several twelve-by-four-by-four inches posts along the floor, to ensure no one driving in would move beyond the fourteen feet of space he allocated within the garage for his Dr Sammoy's woodworking space.

It was inside this zone that Miriam got to when she realised her mother was busy at work, sanding an object before her. She froze, not talking or wanting to take another step for fear of having to confront her mother, for whom she carried an unending love which could not be measured or weighed.

The subject of one's love for their mother, she had often raised over the years as a subject for discussion with her childhood friends. She invariably told her friends that while she had extreme love for her father, it is to her mother she could not describe the depths of her love. She once said to Suzie Stefano: "I love my mother Sammoy Suielman to the infinite degree."

On that occasion, Suzie, who knew when not to press Miriam, added: "That surely sums up the 'mostest' of all loves," and ended the discussion.

This teenage discussion came to her as she stood in one spot, unable to move and as if controlled by an unknown force.

Her mother was also having one of her not too rare moments of intuition, and she, in sync, switched off her electric sander and placed it on her work table. She looked at the work before her, but could not see it. Instinctively she sensed Miriam's presence, and without looking around in Miriam's direction she said: "Miriam, is that you?"

Miriam in that moment lost control of her physical being. She could not recall for weeks and months following this magical moment what transpired with her mother. She came to her senses clinging to her mother, with her mother's short but sharp fingernails clawing into her sides as she, lost to the moment, clawed her own nails into her mother. So passionate was the embrace by mother for daughter and daughter for mother.

When they did finally release each other from the chain of love, Sammoy looked at her daughter from head to toes as only a mother knows. She, in a whisper, said: "Welcome home. How are you and how have you been?

She said nothing further, but held Miriam by her right thumb as she always did and led her inside the office den, where Phillip lay snoozing on the couch with the television watching him as he slept.

Sammoy gently nudged her husband and whispered: "Phillip, there is someone here to see you."

As he opened his eyes he could vaguely recognise Miriam, but the thought that his daughter was in the room in Suielman space roused him. He awoke and instantly sprung to his feet and stood in front of his daughter, not knowing whether he was having a dream, or the reality that his daughter was finally at home visiting. Daughter and father embraced, and all the challenges of the past six years vanished.

He held onto Miriam and would not let go. His embrace communicated both fear and relief. Fear that if he let go of his embrace she would once again disappear from his reach, and relief that he could finally hug his daughter as fathers are supposed to embrace their children.

This long overdue and haunting embrace after some minutes came to an end, as Sammoy tapped both her husband and daughter gently on their shoulders and said; "Enough is enough. There are others waiting to hug and to be hugged," and she turned to Suzanna.

Suzanna was standing inside the kitchen cooking a cow heel soup, one of Miriam's favourite meals, when she got a glimpse of Dr Sammoy leading a veiled woman who looked like Miriam into the family's home office.

At moments like these, she never entered the den unless summoned. At this point she too felt the Miriam magic, and threw caution to the wind and boldly stood behind Miriam as she embraced her father. Now it was her turn to hug the girl who left home six years ago, and now returned as a mother and a woman to the family.

Each had questions to ask of Miriam, and Miriam had questions to ask of her mother and father. The one question only Sammoy could ask, and raised only after Miriam and

Suzanna released each other, was: "Miriam, how long will you be with us on this occasion?"

Miriam turned to her mother and father who stood side by side holding hands, which Miriam had come to recognise as being a trait of her parents whenever either one needed support.

As they stood facing their daughter, they knew that all three members of the Suielman family, as they stood in the den, each needed support from each other.

Miriam, never one to look away or to postpone answering difficult questions, said: "I am going through some challenges. However, today I am only here for a couple of hours."

14

"THERE ARE MATTERS I AM INVOLVED IN, AND I require the advice of my two best advisers, even though you may now believe I do not heed your advice," she exclaimed.

Sammoy broke into her famous smile, which as she grew older helped to highlight her Chinese ancestry. This smile of Sammoy's had a way of breaking the ice, relieving the weight of burdens and above all bringing the trinity of Suielmans together.

Suzanna knew when to excuse herself, which she did, but not before asking Miriam, who she told everyone was her daughter, "Sweetheart, will you be staying for lunch? I knew you were coming home; I have cooked your favourite meal – cow heel soup."

The news of this particular dish warmed both Miriam's heart and stomach. She reflected that she had not eaten it since she left home. She also reflected on the strains the mere mention of cow heel soup brought between her and Thomas, who referred to it as 'cow hell' soup. Today, she was going to sit with her parents and enjoy the best-cooked bowl of cow heel soup courtesy of Suzanna, the best adviser any young woman could find anywhere.

Sammoy, and Phillip did not move beyond the den, so anxious were they to learn about the events which finally caused their daughter to return to them unannounced and without appointment.

Phillip, even before they were seated, said: "Miriam, is everything ok?" Before she could answer he added: "How are the children?" Once Miriam assured her parents that all on the home front was as good as it could be, they allowed her to share with them what brought her home.

Phillip and Sammoy would sit spellbound for another three quarters of an hour, as their daughter told her story.

"Mom and Dad, this is a weird story, but one you must listen to very closely. I have been reading the Quran and the Bible daily, and I have been doing so for hours at end. Within the pages of both books I have found that there is only good, yet as you look around the world and examine and review the actions of many of the clergy within all religions, you are left to wonder whether these clerics and religious officials are serving the faith, themselves or the highest being. It is these sacred books that have caused me to want to further review and analyse the work and actions of those who claim to be servants of the most high. Such a review I now believe is necessary, both at a national and international level."

With this she paused, and Sammoy, as if searching for something beyond Miriam's statement, enquired: "Does any of this review have anything to do with your husband – Thomas?"

Miriam replied with a firmness to which only her mother Sammoy was familiar: "Yes, he must be analysed and reviewed."

Having said this, Sammoy opened her eyes widely and responded: "Whatever you are contemplating, we ask you to be very careful, for even though you have shared the same bed, you do not know what you are dealing with."

Neither Phillip nor Sammoy ever revealed to Miriam that they had, early in her marriage, investigated the background of her husband Thomas. Both mother and father, on the basis of the report compiled by a very senior and competent officer of the local Police Special Branch, suffered more nightmares than they wished.

They were now confronted with yet another challenge involving the boy from Rose Hill, East-Dry-River.

Miriam, not to be detained, continued her presentation to her parents: "Despite my reading, I earlier reasoned that, despite my wanting to do something, – there was nothing I could do. Then I saw an article in the newspaper, which outlined that someone was interested in hosting a conference here in Trinidad to address the very concerns I wish addressed," Miriam added.

The silence in the Suielmans' den was unparalleled, for even as the birds outside the sound-proofed, air conditioned room whistled, all within the room were aware but not distracted, as Miriam told her story.

"I responded to the contact given in the newspaper, and I am now in contact with the sole organiser of this conference. The person is a charismatic young man, five years my junior, but a highly committed and good person. Since meeting him I have concluded that I am now leading him, and he has become a most willing support act."

Having expressed her thoughts of Nathan, Sammoy blurted out: "Stop, stop. Are you certain this is not another love affair being started?"

Sammoy Suielman never forgave herself for not intervening forcefully when the three Suielmans sat in the very room to speak of the Muslim boy Miriam had met, and was determined to marry after two weeks of friendship. This was just about six years ago, and today Sammoy was being told about another boy, five years younger than her daughter.

Miriam gave her mother a look of disdain, yet she kept her composure and responded: "No mother. This is not about a man, but more about the behaviour of all men. At least this man who you have described as a boy is not only concerned about the affairs of a single man or religion, he is concerned about the behaviour of all men and all religions," she emphasised.

Continuing, she added: "At least he has the 'cojones' to want to fix the church that some of us visit and pray at, while turning a blind eye to the many sins of those elected and appointed to lead the very sinners of the Church," she added, looking at her mother straight in her eyes.

Given the mounting tension, her father intervened and said to his wife: "Let her finish tell her story."

Elaborating, Marian added: "The boy of which I speak is Nathan John, who lives a simple life in the village of Los Bajos. He and I share the common vision of hosting an international conference, which must be appropriately named. The title of the conference will be critical if we are to attract a high quality audience of international scholarship and participants," Miriam proffered.

Phillip, though concerned but not troubled, listened attentively to all his daughter had to say. Though never once being the organiser, he had attended many a conference and trade show and had always marvelled at the level of organisation which went into such conferences.

Each time he returned from a conference, he would share with anyone who cared to listen: "These people plan and direct you from registration to the bathroom." That was his take on the professional administration of the trade shows which he attended. All these experiences, like a sandstorm in the desert, flowed through his consciousness at an unnerving speed, and he wondered at the same speed whether his prodigal daughter could pull off the kind of conference she talked of and wished for.

Miriam, as if reading her father's mind, stopped speaking and fixed her focus on him. He in turn responded, speaking slowly: "Miriam, staging this conference won't be easy. If I hear you well, the only person involved is the 'ideas man' from Los Bajos? An event like this requires a lot of money, which has to be located."

Her father was already ahead of her as he was seeing and feeling her conference. She knew how her father conceived and gave life to his plans. His intervention now was like the sweet sound of her favourite steelband, Exodus Steel Orchestra, led by one of her neighbours. She almost said it, but remained silent, even as she smiled for the first time since she, her mother and father began their own conference on the work she had chosen – the staging of a conference all three of them knew would upset many and create equal 'confusion' within the island community.

Her father continued giving his vision of things he felt Miriam should do, as he said to her, "Pay attention to these things. You will need to charge participants a registration fee, and you should do so in US dollars," Phillip suggested.

Phillip spoke non-stop for near twenty minutes, offering his vision, giving guidance and bringing to Miriam an awareness of the immense undertaking she now wished to perform. To underscore his point on the magnitude of the proposal he opened his eyes, opened his hands as wide as his aging body would allow, and said: "Miriam, this is a mammoth assignment you have embarked on." These words were not Philip Suielman's everyday vocabulary. He never saw anything as being too big or too large. With Phillip, everything was 'doable,' as she knew her father believed he could climb every mountain. No summit was beyond his efforts, yet he had, not a moment earlier, suggested her undertaking was a mammoth one.

Whenever her father used the word 'mammoth,' he was uncertain of success.

Miriam chose not to question her father, nor engage him on anything negative, as she knew such actions on her part could negatively impact the assistance she sought from her mother and father.

Phillip's next comment brought the biggest smile to her face, as he said: "But nothing has ever beaten Phillip Suielman, and no church conference will defeat him. Miriam, count me in as an active member of your team." He turned to his beloved wife, who at that moment seemed to be in a state of shock, and asked: "Dr Sammoy, are you in or are you out? We have to support our daughter."

Sammoy Suielman sat back in her chair, and her actions suggested that she hoped the repositioning of her body on the chair would give her the counsel she sought and guidance she needed at this defining moment.

For Dr Sammoy there were too many considerations, which she needed resolved before she could respond. She thought of the likely responses to come from Thomas. She instinctively knew this conference would create enemies for the Suielmans in every pocket of the very petty community of communities, which made up the twin island republic. Dr Sammoy, the anchor of the Suielman family, was now the centre of the family discussion.

She knew she had moved from being mother and wife to Dr Sammoy, as her questions suggested concern. Equally

Sammoy Suielman, mother to Miriam, knew in her heart that on the matter before her she dared to think with her heart, but demanded that she be guided by her head. She knew, having sat and listened to Miriam's compelling presentation and her husband's response of support, that she had to be both balanced and pragmatic. Her own inner voices told her that both persons she loved and cared the most for would be upset, but she knew if she truly cared for them both, she would have to speak from her head. On the matter before them the heart had no place being present. This matter was not and could be no reverie. Now was not the moment to be benign.

She cleared her throat, raised her right hand almost as a judge at court is wont to do to gain the attention of those before him, and she began to speak slowly. She never once addressed her husband. It was as if he was not present, as if he were not sitting in the room. Her thoughts and comments were for her daughter.

"Miriam, I have listened to all you have said, and I am moved by your commitment to define a better space for our people and nation. I am deeply moved that you care so much for the well-being of our people, and I sense you are more driven by the challenges faced by women of all strata of our society. Make no noises only for the women of Rose Hill, as there are women on this very hill we share who suffer more demeaning and miserable lives at the hands of their wicked husbands, if you can call a man who beats his wife a husband. What is worse? It is these very violent men who are first out of the pew to line up for communion at mass, whether it be Fridays or Sundays.

"I have prefaced what I wish to say, as I believe what you have chosen to do in the hosting of this conference, is both good and noble. It will bring you no new friends, and may I add you are very likely to lose friends and family, as you will step on toes as you open the doors of the closets of many. There are people who will neither cheer nor jeer, but know that this is a land of both the brilliant and the dullard. What you will do will be a crushing culmination of centuries of abuse by mostly men abusing women, and in some instances women abusing men, and this too happens on the hill. What goes on within all these houses painted white is not the same colour as the colour of the houses, as more blood has been spilled through abuses. You see these women smiling at church on Sunday morning, but underneath their neat dresses, their bodies are blue-black from the previous night's abuse," she advised.

Through it all, neither Miriam nor her father interrupted her mother, who continued speaking to the very reasons of the importance of the proposed work of the conference.

Dr Sammoy continued speaking, underscoring her understanding of the subject from very personal, professional and first-hand knowledge of the topic, she having had to counsel and treat women from all areas of the very stratified society in which she lived and operated.

"Miriam, I am saying all of this to suggest to you that, as much as we need debate and discussion on religion, you are about to engage Trinidad and Tobago in a debate on the merits and demerits of religion. If there's one thing we have in abundance, or maybe too much of, it's religion. As you begin your quest to evaluate this 'convention of religions,' know there will be push back. Such push back will come in all colours. There will be rash as well as wilful responses, and these replies will be hurtful, wicked and personal. You will need to be particularly mindful," and as she said these words she closed her teeth, seeking to over-emphasise the need for Miriam to be weary of the unknown, "that Thomas will be one of those wanting to stop this conference from coming to life. Know that Thomas is not the smooth-talking man you believe he is, and don't forget this."

"For all that I have said, I want this project to be a success. But because I love you more than anything or anyone, including your father, I must ask you to forget this conference. It will become a living nightmare."

As she said this, a coldness covered her. Miriam noticed that her mother's clothes within seconds became drenched, and for an instant, neither her father, mother nor Miriam moved. All were prisoners of this defining moment.

Phillip, sitting next to his wife, embraced her. With a most supportive voice he enquired: "Sammoy, are you alright?"

In response she cupped both hands and placed them at her temples and said nothing, as she looked her husband in his eyes and nodded to confirm everything was indeed OK.

Phillip gently urged her to her feet and led her in the direction of their bedroom. As he did this he looked at Miriam and spoke to her with his eyes to say, "I am coming back – now."

15

MIRIAM HAD OVER THE YEARS LEARNED TO communicate with her parents without speaking. A skill that was very useful while operating at Suielman and Sons.

She first became intrigued by her parents' ability to speak to each other without uttering a word; instead they spoke using eyes, mouths and other movements of the face. This they used as they worked among their employees, and at such times when she was still very much a child and both her mother and father wanted to say no, when she wished to hear yes to some request she had made.

As her mother and father left the room, she became acutely aware of the road she had chosen, and above all, how much of a challenge the 'Conference of the Un-Godly' would be.

She marvelled at the wisdom of her mother, as she always did – Dr Sammoy was truly brilliant, not only in her chosen profession of medicine, but more so as a thinker and one from whom you could always solicit a meaningful opinion.

Miriam knew that from her mother she did not necessarily get the response she sought, and it is this objectivity she absorbed and shared with her brood of six, as well as the scores of adults and children who visited with her seeking support of one kind or another at her Rose Hill dwelling.

Today, she saw clearly the immediate road ahead, which she knew would be arduous and rough, but she convinced herself that with the assistance of Nathan John and the God she believed in, the conference would become a successful reality.

If she learned anything from meeting with her parents, it was that they supported the ideals which were driving her forward.

She also knew that her father would support her, and sadly while her mother knew and understood what she wanted, she would not support the hosting of the conference for so many sound reasons – chief of all would be the response from her husband Thomas, with whom she had over the past month enjoyed a less than cordial relationship.

She also believed she would any day be told by Thomas: "I divorce you, I divorce you, I divorce you."

If ever there would be grounds for her fundamentalist husband to take action against her, this role she embraced as co-host to the conference offered him an excuse. And she feared there could be other, much more deadly, responses. But she, having long contemplated both likely possibilities and implication, took the road of no return.

If her mother knew anything of her daughter, she fully accepted that she would need counsel, and she would offer such counsel on the matter through the channel of her husband.

During the ensuing moment after her parents' departure from the family den, Miriam mulled over all that transpired and so much more. What she could not contemplate was that, as she sat back in the huge brown leather single chair, another discussion was taking place inside her parents' bedroom.

"Phillip, I want you to know I truly want no part of it – it is too dangerous. What Miriam is doing is important, not only for us here in Trinidad, but this is really something for the world. All the issues she has raised afflict the world, and must be addressed, but why Miriam?

"Regardless of my position, I want you to keep your promise and assist her. She will need funding – lots of money. And you must convince some within your community to help. All of this must be done quietly, as you don't want to disturb a wasps' nest." Sammoy next asked Phillip: "How much money do you intend pledging to her?"

Phillip, at this time, had not given thought to any of the points raised by his wife, and he responded: "I have not given it any thought."

She in turn smiled and responded: "You're supporting the conference, and don't know your first responsibility to your daughter will be making available seed money. Between you and Miriam, it will be necessary to raise upwards of two million TT dollars to make this conference a success. And though I want to have nothing to do with it, I will pledge 300,000 TT dollars from my personal accounts. The money is hers anyway, it is just that, with that husband of hers, she has refused to accept anything from us," she emphasised.

Upon hearing Sammoy's pledge, Phillip said: "If you are giving 300,000 I will match that, so she is off to a good start. Now let me go and break the news to her." He cuddled his wife, giving her a bear hug and a kiss on her forehead. It was moments like this which kept Phillip and Sammoy in love with each other. To them the decades had taught one lesson, and that is, it is imperative to grow from all challenges.

Phillip entered the den and found his daughter sound asleep, and was reminded of a million memories of her falling asleep in her favourite chair. He did not wish to shake her from what in his thoughts must have been peaceful and needed rest, but he remembered her earlier comment that she had come for a short time. So as he had done countless times over the years he whispered her name, and as she had always responded, she opened her eyes and smiled.

Her waking words confirmed to Phillip that his daughter must have been weary, and so the short sleep in a familiar and comforting environment suggested she was now refreshed. Before she could speak, Phillip said: "Miriam, are you sure you are up to the task?"

In a slow and thoughtful way Miriam nodded her head, firstly upwards then downwards, to confirm to her father she was not only ready for the task, but was excited.

"Miriam, you will need lots of cash, and I will do what I can to raise money quietly within the community. For your own protection I will serve as your treasurer. Let me, as your treasurer, advise that the conference balance as of today stands at 600,000 dollars," Phillip added with a sheepish smile.

Miriam had been taught from the cradle not to illustrate her emotions outwardly. She quietly asked Phillip where had it come from, to which he replied: "Half from your mother and half from me."

"Did mother not say she did not wish to have any part in the conference?" Miriam asked.

"Yes she did, and so she wishes all to believe, but you are a Suielman and no Suielman can be involved in a project and not have the support of the clan," he underscored. "However, I want you to know she will not speak to you on this conference, but you will be counselled and you will be guided."

Miriam did not know how to interpret her father's words, and she decided to "leave well alone." As she began to thank her father there was a knock on the den's door, and the door opened as Suzanna pushed her head inside and announced: "Soup is ready Lady Miriam," to which they all laughed and briskly moved to the breakfast enclave where three places were set.

16

THE STARS ALIGN, AND WHEN THEY DO, PEOPLE from all walks of life come together as if driven by unseen forces.

"How else do I explain my meeting with Nathan John, a young man who on the surface is just another ordinary young person you meet on the streets? I bumped into Nathan while visiting the Birdsong Steelpan yard, weeks before the Carnival. He was there like the plus one hundred of us, who came to listen to the planned Panorama rendition of our favourite steelband. As the evening progressed we got to talking, and Nathan shared with me that he was co-ordinating an international conference on religion, called 'Conference of the Un-Godly.'

Anthony's wife looked at him from the kitchen sink where she was cleaning dishes, and in response to her husband enquired: "Where yuh going with this conversation about this boy Nathan?"

Anthony, sitting at the dining room table, looked at his wife Helen and responded: "I eh going a place, I merely sharing with you an interesting conversation I had with a young man who has a lot to say about you Catholics."

Anthony knew the mention of Catholics would invoke the ire of his partner. Yet Helen said nothing. She kept silent and continued soaping and washing the sink full of dishes.

Anthony was, as the game hunters of the community would say, "caught in his own trap." He continued speaking as if he was addressing his wife, even though she had by her actions ceased to engage her husband in conversation.

"Well this boy Nathan John shared with me his plans for his soon to be convened conference, right here in the capital city of Port-of-Spain. He is bringing into Trinidad and Tobago people from all over the world. And he is hoping to expose all the ills taking place within the Church – your Church," he added, hoping to spark a response from his now silent wife.

Even as he sought to draw her into his discussion, she kept her distance and did not even give him her normal pursed lips and simultaneously lifted chin. This action of the pursed lips and a quick lifting of the chin are known within the village as a 'cooyah mouth.'

Despite Helen pouring cold water on his efforts to engage her, Anthony kept on sharing his experience and discussion with Nathan John.

Anthony was very moved by Nathan's conviction, and though he largely listened to the young man from Los Bajos, he never sheared his personal story. He for some near fifty years held a negative view of the Roman Catholic Church. This disdain for the Church began within a parish church sacristy, decades earlier, and though it began with what he felt was a personal attack on him by a holy man, his feelings for the Church became more negative as the years and decades went by, with more revelations of abuses by officials of the church.

Anthony never saw his challenge as being of an extreme abuse, but he paid close attention to each new bit of information which told of the weaknesses of men who wore robes and used the authority these robes gave them to abuse the young, and not so young but vulnerable little people.

Anthony knew his story would upset his siblings, and so kept his own counsel on all matters of the Church. His story was not about sexual abuse, but as he saw it he wished to tell the 'Conference of the Un-Godly' his story.

He never told Helen of his time as an acolyte, or why he felt so strongly about the Church, but hearing Nathan speak he not only knew he wanted to be present at the conference, but he wanted to document his feelings on the matter of abuses within the Church. It might have been the cold shoulder he got from Helen, or it could have been the time had finally come for Anthony to put pen to paper and share the views he had kept pent up inside of him for almost fifty years.

He was like his newfound young friend, feeling the frenzy of the virus of thoughts, sweeping the world about abuses within religious bodies.

Anthony got up, went to his bedroom, retrieved a stack of writing paper and began to write as if driven by an unseen force. When he did pause, he did so to reflect on the chronology of the facts as he remembered. For him this moment represented the culmination of years of wanting finally to respond to the aging Irish priest, who dared to raise his hands to his younger brother for being a boy and doing the things boys do. He had come at Anthony with the same vicious intent that, were it not for his holding the church's crucifix and pushing it forth as protection, he would have endured the same hostile blows that were administered to Jerome and George.

Each time he thought of that morning of Palm Sunday so many years ago, the anxiety, the dread of the moments returned. He was time and time again confronted by the limits of what is correct in the context of the roles and responsibilities of clergy, both senior and junior, in the conduct of their functions as saviours of souls, if not saviours of people – little people.

Anthony could not get out of his mind the rage he saw in his parish priest that early morning. He conceptualised over the years the possible dire outcomes had he, being the eldest of the boys, reacted to the aggression of a white Irish man, 'priest or no priest,' who had the effrontery to strike his younger brother and friend, doing so with rage and anger, spewing a level of hate and meanness he had not since experienced.

At this moment, as he recalled the unforgettable moment, he recoiled as if the experience was alive – happening all over again.

Anthony sometimes would spontaneously clench his fist as if holding the crucifix, and raise both his hands simultaneously as if in defence of himself from his attacker – the Irish parish priest so long departed. He knew he suffered then, and he continued to suffer from the tell-tale Palm Sunday experience and all the events which followed.

Anthony lived through the immediate period following the experience of that memorable Palm Sunday doing what the young do so well – he moved on, and moved away from the Roman Catholic Church. It was easy to do, as it was a period when young people of colour were beginning to speak to the issues of their Blackness, and were for the first time in the modern history of the independent nation demanding a fair share of the nation's wealth.

Anthony, forever conscious of who he was, saw the assault by the parish priest as an attack on his colour by a white Irish man, and as he would later write, he could not dislodge this major premise from his fertile mind.

Anthony's story, as he documented, begins.

17

MOTHER, GOD BLESS HER SOUL, ALWAYS PREACHED to me, "Closer to church, further from God." She was a wise woman in so many ways. What crushed her was to discern that people who genuflected night and day before the church's altar, and made novenas as if investing in repentance for too many past sins, were in so many ways neither worthy nor true in their outward and visible demonstration of being servants of the higher-most-one.

She in her youth was very conscious of her responsibility to encourage her large brood, to be ever mindful of their responsibility to be a good Christian not only at baptism, but to be a genuine and wholesome Christian if not Catholic.

She by her actions encouraged in her children a love for each other, a love for friends, and demanded that each of her children recognise what it meant to be a Catholic – more importantly, what was required of "them" to be good and wholesome Christians.

I believe she saw being a good Christian as being superior to being a good Catholic. For her it was not a case of the end justifying the means, but very much the other way around. She explained her beliefs not with over-zealous visits and rituals at the church, but rather she expressed her beliefs in her God by her own forceful actions.

She lived a Christian life – greed was never a word in her vocabulary, nor her being. Whatever little she had did not belong to her, nor to her family.

Ownership of such small worldly possessions of food remained the possession of no one within the household until she deemed it so. Perhaps a more apt description of food within the confines of very occupied quarters has to do with a mother who always knew her responsibilities went beyond providing for her immediate and growing group – as evident by her consciousness that she had responsibility far beyond her eight children.

The Christian she was, she consistently provided meals for a number of individuals that she called boarders.

This phase of her being a good Christian must have been taken from the teaching of the life of the Christ.

My infant mind would record these Christian actions, and later in life would discern the tremendous outpouring of giving that were mother's natural characteristics. For her, giving was not only an everyday occurrence. For her, caring and sharing with others was as common as the fowl cocks who controlled our backyard and who always advised of the time of the day with their crowing.

She emulated the Christ who the scriptures underscored took five loaves and two little fishes and fed the multitudes. Such was her generosity, her giving and caring in every way. She qualified to be both a good Christian, but more so a good Catholic. Yet in later years she retained her Christian values and even her God, but she turned away from the Catholic Church.

It is this quantum leap which began within me a search to finding answers to my own feelings about the Catholic Church. I, long before my mother turned to the Unity religion, had good reason to want to seek another Christian platform other than the Roman Catholic Church.

For a good many years I was anchored in the ritual of Roman Catholicism, having been baptised and having subsequently performed the sacraments of First Communion and Confirmation. I surmised then that, having performed their three sacraments, I was good with my God. I did all the sacraments not because I wanted to do so, but because the Church demanded it of me. In all of this, the sacraments of Baptism, First Communion and Confirmation are imposed on you by the time you celebrated your twelfth birthday.

At twelve years, what do you know, or really understand and appreciate, of the sacrament of the Holy Ghost with all its mystery? And at birth, sometimes one day old or one month old or one week old, you are supposed to be brought from the darkness of your birth into a new a wondrous life, as the ritual of the holy oil combined with holy water touches you, while your godparents speak on your behalf as you promptly renounce Satan and all his wickedness. At Baptism I may not have known anything of the value of the ritual, but I inherited two beautiful people to be my godparents. Myrtle, the eldest cousin on my mother's side, became my godmother, while my father's youngest brother was chosen to be my godfather. Neither were ever called upon to play the roles assigned to them, but in adulthood I reasoned on the evidence that, had they been so called, they would have performed with credits. In essence – both were good Catholics.

At Confirmation, you are serenaded with the most powerful combination of words in the famous Catholic hymn: "Holy Ghost come down upon thy children, Give them grace and make them thine,

Tender powers in heart sublime"

This is the Catholic Church at its purest, with its rituals of bells, thurible and incense, with its ornate statues and brass candlesticks and high fashion garments worn by its priests, bishops and its officials.

Everything about the Roman Catholic Church holds it mysteries, and encourages questions from inside and outside its ranks. Like the officiates of the Church, the poor faithful are expected to be equally adorned at all ceremonies. And so at each of my taking of the sacrament, my dear mother had to find the resources to purchase a blue serge pair of trousers, a white shirt, a medallion and ribbon and a must-have rosette. These burdens never went unnoticed by me, even as a child.

The rosette, a rose made of white or red ribbon approximately an inch thick and weaved into a rose, cost quite a penny, and so by the time my first communion arrived my mother had become adept at creating her own rosettes. Each time I think of the Catholics I have visions of her sitting at her old wood-framed Singer sewing machine, fixing in place and stitching each row of satin ribbon which gave life to a cloth rose made of satin fabric. I watched her from the edge of our bed – I shared a bed with my brothers and sisters – as she, i.e. my darling mother, with the smallest of needles and a perpetual most natural smile, fashioned her rosette for her children in response to the demands of the Catholic Church. On the day of the ritual she would also attend the function in a garment she dressed up to reflect the moment, and she would duly do the same for my two brothers and four sisters. She saw it as being ultimately important that the family be part of the ritual, which my elder sisters would have experienced and were forced to revisit each time one of their siblings, way down the ranks, took their sacraments.

The silence of the sacristy was interrupted with what at first appeared as if Jerome and George were once again at each other, which was a common trait of these two, in their early teens and full of energy. Both boys attended a Roman Catholic secondary school out in a suburb to the north east of the capital city, Port-of-Spain.

Jerome lived up the hill, four streets from the church, while George lived some distance away in the well-ordered district of Barataria. This community was well laid out with twelve streets in an east to west direction, while there were ten avenues operating from north to south. The first street was situated in the north with the twelfth street being furthest south, while the avenue was to the east with 10th Avenue being furthest west. Barataria was one of the early, but better laid out communities within the East-West Corridor of Trinidad's northern communities. The church stood on the hill at the entrance to the majestic main road, which joined Sixth Avenue as you passed First Street and Sixth Avenue.

For many, Sixth Avenue is seen as the main artery of Barataria. Barataria is also a melting pot for the races and religions and classes of Trinidad. It is in this context that the children of Barataria are more aware of race and religion, and are more racially tolerant than children of other, more homogenously Indian or African communities.

George was more aware of life than Jerome, and though just a year apart, often led Jerome to mischief, so common to boys.

This Palm Sunday morning was the day after the stripping of palms in preparation for distribution. Anyone familiar with sacristies would know the silence was always overwhelming. You could hear a bug crawling or the wings of a butterfly flapping. Those unheard sounds that each human, in their own way, dreams of hearing. But how could I ever know how my butterflies sounded on this holy morning, having been shook awake from my deep slumber by a most caring mother, who from her cradle was always a child of the holy Roman Catholic Church? She was born a Catholic, not Anglican, from a very poor family, which by their in-house rules and regulations was not working class in thinking. In every other way my mother represented a long-lost and in some ways dying period, in the history of an equally long-lost British colony.

She was in many ways the typical woman of her time. She was a mother, wife, patriot, a devoted Catholic and ardent follower of the island's premier and later prime minister. She was all of these things in that order. She was a special kind of woman, and both her husband and brood of eight children knew what a gem of a person she was. To our family she was a special, very special, woman of her age.

This devotion caused her to wake earlier than usual this Palm Sunday, and to ensure her two sons Anthony and Jerome were "up and about" and dressed for church service. She had laundered the acolyte gowns, ensuring they were "lily white," properly starched and hung on two makeshift hangers. She could not afford to buy clothes hangers, so to ensure her family's clothing was kept without wrinkles she tied stripped pieces of cloth to pieces of wood eighteen inches long to create makeshift clothes hangers, which she hung on pieces of bent wire within our cupboards or to nails strategically placed outside of them.

It was from one of these nails that we removed our stiffly starched and lily white gowns, lifting them by their makeshift hangers, and headed for the church on the hill.

We entered the sacristy, and as customary pulled over our gowns on top of our Sunday clothing. Jerome, having robed, left the sacristy to join his friend George, while I remained within, assisting the Sexton to ensure all was in order for the morning's first scheduled Mass. This first Mass on Palm Sunday morning was very important, as it is during this first service that the Palms to be distributed are blessed with much fanfare and ceremony.

Over the years I became familiar with the ritual, and now found it to be routine and more of a chore than the magic I felt about a similar ceremony four years earlier. Yet I remained active, performing the responsibilities of a senior acolyte often present on the right side of the altar during services.

At fifteen years of age, I had come to appreciate that, though I received no remunerations for my services, I was flattered that the girls of the parish and students of the nearby convent over the years became more attracted to me and me to them.

While I was not talkative I went about my duties as an acolyte with quite professionalism, and you would not know I was within the sacristy unless I was asked a question or requested to perform a specific function.

I was not an aggressive person, but was known to be quite capable at holding my own in a street fight among the boys of the community, and equally was known to come to the defence of my younger brother, who took no prisoners.

As I recall, as if by telepathy I would be advised that he was in a fight, and before I knew it would find myself in the midst of battle in his defence. I would later learn he was responsible for issuing the first blow. This is who we were, young men with strong beliefs of the importance of letting others know that we would defend ourselves – together.

With this mind-set we saw attacks from anyone as actions to be addressed with equal force.

This Sunday, holy Palm Sunday, reflected nothing holy, as the raging Irishman sought to administer blows, I told my parents later that Sunday morning when the news of the incident reached home that if I did not have my crucifix in my hand, which thwarted the priest, anything could have happened within the sacristy of the church.

When I was certain there would be no further attacks on me, I put down the crucifix, took off my gown and encouraged my brother to disrobe. Together we left the sacristy, never to return.

In time I would begin to view the Roman Catholic Church through a microscope, and this ongoing process effectively ended my commitment to religion as I was schooled to understand and to accept. During the period that I began to question the virtues of being Catholic, my mother also slowly gravitated to another form of Christianity, and so any inducement to return to the religion of my family was rejected. I saw little meaning in a church that at one time had looked as shinning as the brass adornment on its marble altars.

Now Anthony suddenly put down his pen and looked at the pages before him, all numbered but not placed in numerical order, as during his writing he would pull a page from the pile to reference check what he had earlier written.

He penned a final two paragraphs:

I have shared all of this with you so that you may fully understand that I have come to this conference with no axe to grind, only a mill to turn.

It is my sincerest hope that you will discern who I am and what I am, and what are my perspectives and expected outcomes for the conference.

In his mind, he reasoned, if there was a 'Conference of the Un-Godly,' he would tell his story. He, as he sat at this dining table watching his completed conference paper, became anxious. Or as his doctors would say, he experienced an anxiety attack.

At these moments, such as the moment of having finally written his story, he felt as if he lost control of his body and often would cling to a table or wall, convinced he was about to fall to the floor.

18

ANTHONY, THROUGHOUT HIS ADULT LIFE, NEVER fell, but was convinced that if he did not cling to a sturdy structure, he surely would.

This illness, which not one, but three medical minds remained convinced was a clear-cut case of anxiety attacks, came to Anthony during periods of stress. He questioned why he was feeling stressed, having finally completed a secret task he had long undertaken, but until now had remained undone. Anthony surmised his anxiousness was driven by his achievement of having completed a secretly held desire to tell the world of his experiences as an altar boy.

With this burden no longer a burden, he felt conflicted. Why was he experiencing symptoms of anxiety and not relief? He wondered.

He remained seated, thinking aloud and oblivious of Helen's presence within the adjoining living room.

"When I get up on that conference floor and present my story, then the world will know the true meaning of Irishman and priest," he blurted out, as if convincing an unseen person that he was ready to spill the beans. He had kept his hurt a secret for over five decades.

Upon hearing her docile husband speak about an Irishman and a priest she turned in her chair and continued listening, but Anthony said not another word.

He slowly pulled together his thirty two pages, which carried his written report.

As he stacked and secured his writing he silently committed to make contact with Nathan John the following day, if only to confirm his support for the conference and to advise of his attendance if God willed it. He also wished to offer to Nathan any assistance he could offer.

Early the following morning, Anthony, very much out of both routine and character, placed a call to Nathan John.

Had Helen been up and about she would have been shocked to see her spouse making a phone call before having his favourite cup of tea. Anthony never did anything before painstakingly sipping his tea until his mug was empty. Nor would he engage in any kind of activity unless he had his breakfast, for which he waited until Helen awoke, prepared and served it.

Today was somehow different – Anthony was on the phone having made a third call, as Nathan John did not answer his first or second. He was about to give up, the phone having rung seven times, when a soft sounding voice answered: "You are calling Nathan's phone; can I assist you?"

Anthony was not expecting Nathan to have a secretary and so he was caught off balance, and was somewhat slow in responding to Judith John, who was forced to repeat her welcome message all over. By this time Anthony got going, asking: "May I speak with Nathan?"

Judith responded succinctly: "Nathan cannot come to the phone now, but may I give him a message?"

Anthony before continuing politely enquired: "To whom am I speaking?"

"Sir, you are speaking with Judith John. I am Nathan's sister." As she said sister she prolonged the sis – ta, almost as if she was getting bored with the conversation.

Anthony quickly caught on and replied: "I am really sorry to be a bane of bother, but I am calling in response to the conference that Nathan John is convening and I wish to speak with him."

Before Anthony could add to his sentence Judith said: "Please hold on, here come Nathan. It was nice speaking with you sir," and she handed the phone to Nathan.

He and Anthony spoke for another hour as he explained his dreams for the hosting of the conference. Throughout this lengthy conversation Nathan never once told Anthony about Miriam, and the role she was playing and was about to play in the hosting of the conference.

Halfway during a most lively conversation, Anthony knew that he would stand shoulder to shoulder in making the 'Conference of the Un-Godly' a success. As he conversed he made mental notes of things he needed to get done. He reasoned, notwithstanding the hurdles, he was about to become an acolyte all over again, only this time there would be no angry Irish priest wanting to reign down blows upon him and his brother.

Nearing the end of their conversation, both men agreed that they would meet within a few days as Nathan indicated he had to brief his committee. What he really meant was that he had to brief Miriam, and convince her that Anthony, who he met at a pan yard and had an hour long phone conversation with, was his proposed candidate to become a committee member.

In the weeks and month ahead, as the work of the conference was carried out by an ever increasing group of organisers, Anthony would prove to be not only a capable organiser but more importantly one of the stabilising thinkers within the conference team.

Nathan in choosing Anthony also demonstrated his native leadership skills, which as the conference took flight, so too did he in asserting his own leadership among a wide and varied group of conference elders and workers.

Anthony would spend all of his available waking hours reaching across religious lines, convincing anyone who would listen to attend the conference. And to the doubters, he encouraged: "Now you could have your say. Come and tell the world what the clergy has been doing and hiding all these years."

It was felt among the registration committee that Anthony may have single-handedly brought more Trinidadians to the conference than anyone else. He undertook to assist Nathan John and that is what he did, before, during and after the conference which opened the door to the closets of the Roman Catholics, Christians, Muslims, Hindus and other religions, where so much is not spoken of nor addressed, nor remedial action taken to correct wrongs committed against ordinary little people who represented the congregations of hundreds of religious groups of varying shapes and sizes.

It would be precisely three days following the long successful conversation between Nathan the charismatic conference leader and Anthony the convert and soon-to-be acolyte, that Nathan and Miriam met at the offices of Suielman and Sons Limited at Frederick Street, Port-of-Spain. Phillip, despite protest from his wife Sammoy, decided that during the initial stages of the planning he would host committee meetings, and assigned a space in which he stored special merchandise to the purpose.

To make this possible, as Miriam left their home that fateful day of reunion, he called the office and spoke to Josephine, giving her instructions to empty the "special goods" store room and set it up conference style with a small corner space for a desk. He also said to Josephine: "Josie, also call the IT man and have him install telephones for five persons and an equal number of computers."

Phillip then called out a detailed list of items needed for the space, inclusive of stationery, tea, coffee... and the list went on and on.

This kind of planning was Phillip Suielman's strength. He would sit silently and allow his mind to walk, fly and wonder over the things he wished into life. He was not a dreamer in any sense, but what he did well, very well, was grasping the possibility out of the impossible.

He knew that unless he brought his magic to bear on the moment, Miriam with all her good will would not succeed, and he had no desire to see his dear daughter fail in the hosting of her conference which gladly facilitated her return to the Suielman family.

When Miriam called his office the day following her visit, he told her that he had set up a temporary office for the conference at Suielman and Sons and she should visit to inspect and advise if anything further needed to be done at this time. When Miriam did visit, it was two days following Nathan and Anthony's very deep conversation, and it was exactly six months to the date of the opening of the conference.

19

MIRIAM ARRIVED AT SUIELMAN AND SONS THREE hours ahead of the agreed start of the meeting with Nathan. She wanted to ensure all was in place as she wanted for her conference committee, even if it was meant to be temporary. She got to Suielman and Sons but never got to her conference space for another two hours and forty minutes. Upon arrival she would not be allowed by the employees of the company to waltz in and not speak with each of them individually. Today she wore her most fashionable Muslim attire complete with hijab, but even though covered all over, every employee recognised her as soon as they laid eyes on her.

There were some new employees who did not meet her before this meeting day, but they all knew of her and would listen intently as their colleagues told stories of the boss's daughter who had gone rogue on the Suielman clan. At least, this is what was said of Miriam at the level of the store floor.

To those who knew Marian from childhood, they said nothing of the beautiful daughter of Phillip and Dr Sammoy. To these employees she was a princess and would always remain a princess, and whenever their paths crossed on the streets of Port-of-Spain, they would hurry across the street to greet her. They all wanted to hug and cuddle her, but resisted these natural tendencies less it conflicted with the beliefs of the girl they knew, who had quickly become a woman, as they all witnessed the never-ending evidence of pregnancies.

Miriam did not know what thoughts or conversations were uttered or conceived of her, but she knew she must have been the subject of too many lunchroom and bathroom discussions. She in her quiet moments at Rose Hill wondered how the gossip and hearsay affected her mother, who was never one for gossip and shunned anyone with tendencies to rumour and bad talk.

Dr Sammoy said to her, even in her infancy: "Those who bring news are sure to carry news."

She never knew what was said, but she knew each time her daughter left her home, as someone would see her and if orchestrated by all who would bring the news, would gently say to Dr Sammoy: "I saw her this morning," or this evening or yesterday.

They saw Miriam, and Miriam knew before she reached her Rose Hill home that her parents would be alerted of her whereabouts.

Flushed from all the welcome back greetings, she went straight to the newly placed centre of the 'Conference of the Un-Godly.' Miriam deliberately did not go to the main office of Suielman and Sons, which housed her mother and father's offices, as she did not wish to be further distracted from her mission and very first meeting outside the Central Market.

As she entered the temporary business centre Phillip Suielman had created, she felt tears explode from her innermost being. She gasped wide eyed at the placement of meeting tables, desks and the positioning of the stationery centre. The environment suggested bigness, and the impact of the layout and the furnishings matched her thoughts of things to come, for and with the conference.

She looked at the space she knew well, yet she could not recognise the space of which she was familiar.

There were no longer any aisles for special silks or other pricey fabrics, nor did she see the special closed glass storage, which carried gems of varying degrees in value.

Now she looked upon a huge conference table with eighteen executive chairs situated in the southern section of the centre. Her father had installed over the table special lighting, that both provided light to ease the reading process but not the kind of light which overpowered and negatively impacted the concentration of users of the space.

Using an open plan, Phillip spaced thirty chairs in a theatre seating format some twenty feet from the conference table, which allowed for two meetings to be held simultaneously. Between both areas he placed a coffee station, which allowed participants from both areas to access their needs of coffee or tea. Towards the extreme right of the theatre seating he placed a podium, and to the back of the podium which serviced the theatre seating he installed a row of four desks. To the front of each of the four desks were two chairs. One desk he slotted in the north western corner, upon which he placed a strip of masking tape: property of Miriam Suielman.

When she saw the note she smiled and promptly sat on the swivel chair placed at the desk.

Phillip's organisation of the centre imposed on Miriam an understanding of the undertaking, and forced her to flip her mental memory cards. As she did so it would seem as if she needed more space for her cards, which became full each time she contemplated a new thought.

During this mental attack Nathan loomed large in her memory, and she wondered whether he was having the same kinds of questioning thoughts or whether she was alone in beginning to question their joint abilities to pull off the conference, which would begin the rewriting and re-education process of religion not only in Trinidad and Tobago, but moreover across the world.

She looked at her phone and saw the time was nine minutes to the appointed start of the meeting.

Two minutes later there was a knocking at the main door. Josephine pushed her head through the door and shouted: "You are a fine one, you come to your office and you eh report to me," and having said this single sentence she broke out in laughter of a happy sound.

Miriam sprang to her feet and met Josephine almost midway between her desk and the door. Both women embraced each other as only an older relative clings to a younger relative. Josephine was one of the employees at Suielman who knew Miriam, as the people walking the streets of Port-of-Spain would say, "before she was born."

Miriam did not have to say anything to Josephine, nor indeed did Josephine need to say anything to her, as both knew that each was well informed of the other's journey over the past eighty months.

When Josephine did speak, she said to Miriam, "There is a young man for you at the front gate."

Nodding, Miriam said: "I am expecting a Nathan John, would you organise for him to come in? And is my dad in office?"

Josephine, never one to lose a beat, replied: "Both Dr Sammoy and Mr Suielman are in; will you be coming over to see them?"

Miriam caught onto Josephine's tone, which suggested she and her mother may not be seeing eye to eye, and immediately responded: "Let Mom and Dad know that as soon as our meeting is over I will bring Nathan over to meet them both."

As Josephine was departing, she turned and spoke directly to Miriam: "Miriam, I don't know what is going to come out of your conference, but I want you to know I fully support your ideas. Your dad explained to me what you hope to achieve, and I truly believe that if you succeed the outcomes from the conference can make the world a better place. I also want you to know that whatever assistance you need, you have only to ask and I am available to assist you."

With these words pointed and offered with sincerity she gave Miriam no space to reply, and she turned and retreated to usher Nathan into their conference headquarters.

Nathan was as happy as Miriam to meet with each other and to begin the long process of developing the plan for hosting the first of its kind conference in this century. Both tried to research when last, if at all, a conference was called to review religion and to critically examine just how clergy had used it to make war against the multitudes and to reduce little people to non-people.

What followed would serve as the backbone of plans for the conference. Miriam explained of her return to her family home, of her father's commitment and pledges of support, the creation of the conference administrative centre to which she introduced Nathan, and of her own to do list. She confided in Nathan that she had neither the blessings nor support of her husband, as she had not advised him of any of her plans.

Nathan was wide eyed about all he learnt from and of Miriam. He admitted being shocked to learn that his "partner in crime" Miriam was the daughter of the Suielman and Sons Limited Syrian Clan.

He admitted to Miriam: When I came to the address given to me, I did not connect that I was coming to this place. Coming upstairs I believed I was in the wrong place until I saw you," he added.

Miriam took it all in stride and exuded mannerisms of understanding. She never once chided Nathan for what she genuinely felt was unnecessary small talk, and sought to move their discussion to the reasons they agreed to meet.

Nathan, sensing some measure of care worn on Miriam's side, responded that she ought to be congratulated for establishing the conference centre, and requested of her that she thank her family for the considerations and accommodations.

Not one to miss a beat, Miriam replied to Nathan: "You will get a chance to do so yourself, as we will visit with them following our meeting."

Miriam shared with Nathan her long list of "things to do," and enquired of his list, to which he had no response. She indicated to him that a priority had to be the formation of the planning or organising committee, and asked of Nathan whether he had recommendations of persons who could be relied upon when the going gets tough. She added, not as an afterthought, but more to underscore her point, "And the going *will* get tough."

Nathan in response said: "I want to recommend Anthony Clarke." He proceeded to share with Miriam how he met Anthony, and the long conversations they'd had since that first meeting. He further shared with Miriam Anthony's desire to present at the conference, and confirmed he had already prepared his paper. Miriam listened, and Nathan having completed his nomination of Anthony Clarke, she nodded in agreement. The committee of two thus became the committee of three, then four, as Miriam saw a note to herself that her father and conference financier had expressed a desire to serve on the executive.

It was agreed that both Miriam and Nathan would co-chair the conference, and areas of responsibility would be assigned as the conference developed.

Key among the plans would be the issue of fundraising, of which Miriam proposed she would take charge and chair all fundraising activity for the 'Conference of the Un-Godly.' She informed Nathan that both co-chairmen, until staff members were recruited, would be required to keep the office as there were phones and computers to manage, as well as visitors who, whether out of genuine interest or curiosity, would soon be visiting.

Nathan sat through near ninety minutes as Miriam outlined and explained away the road map. He took notes when reminded – often, instructed.

Through it all, he soon recognised that there was a God above who, in his infinite wisdom, sent Miriam to assist him in doing what he felt driven to do. But the more he worked with Miriam the greater was his awareness of his needs versus his wants in hosting and staging of the conference.

20

HE HAD NOT PRAYED MUCH IF AT ALL IN RECENT years. However, from the first publication of the conference in the daily newspaper, Nathan began to see the importance of calling on his God for both guidance and assistance.

Whenever he and Miriam met he could not help feeling there was a living presence guiding their discussions and decision-making. Meeting for the first time in their own offices, he could not help but compare their first meeting on the wooden boxes of the swizzle sticks vendor at the Central Market in Port-of-Spain.

There was no heat, or dust or flies, not even the enquiring vendor who eavesdropped on their first meeting, as she sought to discern whether he and the white Muslim woman were up to mischief, having chosen to meet behind her stall for a discussion. Now they were meeting both with the comforts of privacy and physical comfort, and if needed, a good cup of tea or coffee.

He never said anything to Miriam about his biggest fear, that of her husband, whom all of East Port-of-Spain knew and feared, if not respected. He knew long before the week of the conference the matter of the Muslin of Rose Hill would emerge to be a challenge, if not just to Miriam then to both he and her, and he knew the concerns he harboured were real and had to be addressed sooner rather than later.

Nathan's fears were born out of a society where the culture suggested everyone's business is everybody's business. It therefore was not surprising when one afternoon, following a meeting between he and Miriam, he out of character walked with Miriam from the market to the corner of George Street and South Quay, where she turned North on George Street to get to Rose Hill, and he continued on South Quay heading west to City Gate, where the majority of public transportation arrived and departed the City of Port-of-Spain.

Nathan often when approaching City Gate thought of New York City's Grand Central Terminal, as only at Grand Central one could easily find comfortable and mostly efficient train service. At Port-of-Spain's City Gate, you find varying sizes of buses – some called by the travelling public maxi-taxis. On that fateful day Nathan boarded a maxi-taxi for Arima, and was sitting minding his 'own business,' when a passenger sitting next to him looked him in the eyes and said: "Fella, you playing with fire."

Nathan was taken by surprise, and so responded: "What do you mean? Where is the fire?"

The young man, no older than sixteen years, replied: "The woman I see you with by the corner of George Street, she is the boss' wife. Stay away from she; that is trouble."

That ended the conversation as he said nothing further, and Nathan kept his thoughts to himself, not knowing what the future held for him, Miriam or the conference. Both the young man, with no obvious signs of being a Muslim, nor Nathan, looked in each other's direction. When the maxi-taxi arrived at Curepe, which is almost midway between Arima and Port-of-Spain, the young man got up to leave. However, as he did so he said: "Fella, remember what ah tell you," and he walked off the maxi-taxi.

Nathan was concerned, and pondered whether to discuss the incident with Miriam, but decided against doing so as he reasoned that there was no need to. He and Miriam were colleagues planning a conference, and he hoped the young man's warnings were just curious concerns.

As the meeting concluded, Nathan agreed that he would take charge of the office over the next two weeks while Miriam did her overseas promotions and fundraising for the conference. She showed Nathan a range of conference promotional and advertising material, which buoyed his spirit and enthusiasm and gave him reasons to smile. His conference was finally taking flight.

This moment gave him an opportunity, and he took it. He gently said to Miriam, as if speaking to his younger sister: "Miriam, you are going to be gone for two weeks – have you discussed this with your husband?" Before Miriam could respond he added: "And who is going to look after your children?"

This statement was like a lightning rod to Miriam, who replied with an expression as one with the world on her shoulder. "Nathan, I must thank you for this wake-up call, as I really do not have answers for any of your questions. Until this very moment I have simply put aside the issue of Thomas and children. If you must know, he is no ordinary person – so the matter is not as easy as I lead myself to believe. But I am neither turning back, nor am I going to allow the father of my six children to make a prisoner of me," she ended defiantly.

Nathan wanted to share his experience of the young man aboard the maxi-taxi, but decided to "leave well alone."

Together they got up off their chairs, with Miriam leading the way to the other side of Suielman and Sons, where Phillip and Sammoy Suielman were waiting to meet the young man who they both felt would add a new meaning to their beloved daughter's life.

Coffee cups were set around the coffee table inside Phillip's office, as too was a steaming pot of Arab style brewed coffee. There was a bowl of sugar and small teaspoons. When they entered the office Miriam's mother was seated in the chair she would normally occupy, directly facing the entry door. Her father was at his table with the phone to his ear, and the moment he saw them at the door he said to his caller: "I will call you back, I have important visitors." With these comments he got up, made a beeline to his daughter and as he always did, hugged the love of his life.

He released Miriam and she moved quickly to her mother, and the ritual of the hug took a new deeper form and far greater meaning.

Phillip approached Nathan, who was so amazed at the showing of love between Miriam and her parents that for a brief moment he did not hear Phillip say: "You must be Nathan John. I am Phillip, Miriam's father," all the while with his hand outstretched hoping to exchange a cordial greeting.

When Nathan finally recovered from the scene of affection, he was too embarrassed to speak – he merely shook hands with Phillip, and became sufficiently aware of the "real world" to say to Dr Sammoy: "Good day Mrs Suielman, how are you?"

The moment was as Nathan would later describe: "Not warm but not cold. There was unparalleled heat between Miriam and her parents, which was expected, but there was pointed business professionalism towards me. I felt they saw me as an invader, who had come to capture their prized property," he underscored.

Nathan, never one to drink coffee, declined joining the Suielmans in sharing a pot of Arab coffee. However he accepted a cup of Lipton tea, and when Phillip returned from the office pantry with a box of assorted Arabian pastries and handed it to Nathan, he quickly picked an almond filled biscuit, coated with honey. Nathan from childhood could never resist sweets, and Phillip unknowingly broke the ice and dispatched any doubts Nathan may have harboured about Miriam's parents, who he was meeting for the first time.

Nathan, growing up within Los Bajos, was essentially a person of east Trinidad, as opposed to the hosts who were west Port-of-Spain and west Trinidad. Both the geography and stratification of the society defined the Suielmans to be of the moneyed class, while Nathan coming from deep east Trinidad would at best be of the land owning class of small property, but surely not gentry.

Yet it was landless, poor Nathan who conceived and encouraged the daughter of the gentry to become excited at the idea of hosting a most controversial conference, that even on paper promised to rock the pillars of religion within and far away from Trinidad.

This first meeting between the Suielmans and Nathan lacked the magic anyone may have anticipated, given who he was and more importantly how he was now impacting their daughter's life – if not the lives of all members of the Suielman clan.

Conversation at the first meeting focused on the preparedness of the conference centre and the day to day administration of the office, with Phillip suggesting he would assign two of his trusted team members to the centre to provide the support which he thought would very shortly be needed. Perhaps the biggest focus was given to Miriam's impending fundraising expedition to Boston. It was this matter which offered much hope and equal concerns, though the latter had nothing to do with the staging of the conference and more to do with Miriam's growing concerns of her husband's likely response to the 'Conference of the Un-Godly.'

Approximately ninety minutes later, with most pressing matters discussed and agreements reached, the meeting was adjourned. Nathan politely reminded Miriam to call and keep him apprised of her success as well as challenges.

"Miriam," he stressed, "we are in this together – sink or swim."

These were just nine words, but to Dr Sammoy and Phillip Suielman they were the best nine words they heard throughout the meeting, and perhaps the nicest words anyone could have expressed to their daughter. Unknowingly, Nathan had expressed the words that were in every way representative of how Phillip saw his relationship with his wife and, in like manner, how Sammoy Suielman saw her relationship with her husband. To both of Miriam's parents life was about living for the other, and the concept of being in it together – sink or swim as now articulated by a stranger – tapped a reservoir of years of commitment between them and opened for Nathan a relentless outpouring of support.

Nathan having taken his leave, the three Suielmans sat quietly with no one speaking. When the silence was finally broken it was Miriam, who requested of her father a quiet moment. This was not uncommon among the three, as it could have easily been a similar request made of Dr

Sammoy. This was how Miriam grew up, and each of the trio knew no insult was given and none taken.

As Sammoy stood to leave the office she said to her daughter: "Miriam, when are you travelling?" She swiftly added, "Who will be caring for the children when you are gone?"

This very maternal question initiated a plethora of concerns about Miriam's challenges at her Rose Hill home. Miriam looked at her mother and could find no response. Her silence and the silence of the room were perhaps equal to the silence which comes with death.

Eventually Phillip, with all his street wise, said to his wife: "Don't worry, we will work it out."

Sammoy grasped her daughter's fears and said nothing. She shook her head and exited the room, and as she did so she prayed alone and aloud: "There is only one presence with my daughter Miriam – it is the power of God. No harm can come to her." She would walk all over Suielman and Sons affirming the aforementioned, and did so until Miriam and Phillip completed their daughter and father pow-wow.

Miriam looked her father in the eyes and said: "Dad, I am scared. I am worried that Thomas may do something rash when he fully recognises my/our roles in the hosting of the conference."

Phillip did not respond, as he wished to learn what was really troubling his daughter.

Miriam needed no prompting, and quickly but calmly added: "I need no one to advise me that I made an error in choosing Thomas as a partner. If ever there was love it is difficult for me to discern. What I do know is that I am six years older, and, I want to believe, wiser. I have spent much, much time reading and seeking to understand not only the Quran, but the Bible, the Bhagavad Gita and God knows what other religious book I might have put my hands on. Dad, as we speak, I know in my heart there is no peaceful nor fulfilling future with Thomas, and it is this that troubles me Given what I know of him and his past, my leaving him could cause him to become erratic and possibly do something untoward. I have also the children to think of. I must protect them and ensure they have a future far from Rose Hill."

Miriam opened her mouth to speak, and across from her Phillip put his index finger over his lips beckoning her to silence. As he did so he said: "Miriam, you know I don't even know the names of my grandchildren."

This statement by her father opened a floodgate, and her tears came in a torrent as she pondered how could it be possible that her parents who she loved so much did not know the names of her six children. When she finally found her composure, she gave a history of her life over the past six years tagging each birth by date and gender.

Phillip learnt of his four grandsons and two granddaughters, and despite the extreme stress associated with the revelations he welcomed the new information and vowed to do what he must to bring his grandchildren home. During the exchange, half of Phillip Suielman was in the office with his daughter and the other half of his being he imagined was outside the office, holding his wife's Sammoy's hand, giving her support in understanding and accepting the road Miriam had travelled the past six years. But of greater importance, he concluded, was the road she had ahead of her.

When Miriam completed her story of the life of the lady at Rose Hill, uncharacteristically Phillip did not smile nor did he speak. He sat as if in a world of his own with a look of pain. His appearance troubled Miriam, as she had never known her father to be lost for words or not instinctively proffer a plan of action. Phillip neither smiled nor spoke as the things he contemplated he would not discuss with his daughter, nor could he speak what was both in his heart and head.

Miriam did not know this was the second time in the last six years her father had gone inside himself, overtaken with grief over her choices. She could not imagine how her actions of marriage to Thomas turned her parents inside out, and caused her father to withdraw from life, family and friends for the greater part of eighteen months. Nor could she grasp the sleepless nights Dr Sammoy endured as she kept what was left of her family together. Miriam did not know of the long hours her mother worked at Suielman and Sons to keep the family business alive and healthy as her father withdrew into himself.

Miriam would, in the months following the conference, learn of the trials and tribulations of her family and the negative impact her actions had created.

On this occasion six year later, Phillip pulled himself out of his safe zone and returned to the real world, where his daughter waited on him and his strength to see her through the challenges which were ahead of her.

"What are you going to do with the children? " Phillip asked, as if he had no answer. His daughter looked at him with a wide, opened eyed stare, but gave no response. When Phillip was certain his daughter had no answer, he said, "We will take care of the children. Do you want me to pack them up?"

Hearing her father speak of her children both gladdened and frightened her, as she was happy to finally learn that despite her children's father's background, her father and their grandfather had so easily and willingly taken possession of her brood of six. Yet she knew her husband would never relent and give up his children without a fight, and if there was one thing that came as second nature to Thomas it was his response to the call for a battle.

21

MIRIAM AWOKE VERY EARLY SEVEN DAYS BEFORE her departure to Boston. She carried out all her maternal responsibilities, and as she did so she observed closely the demeanour of her husband. She knew she could not raise the subject when Thomas would not be receptive, and so she waited.

Two days later, just as Thomas was leaving Rose Hill, she in her almost normal, best whisper of a voice, said: "Thomas could I have a word with you?"

He turned to her and enquired, "What's the matter wife?" He addressed her as wife whenever he felt good about her, but more so when he felt good about himself. Today in the early hours of the morning he waited on Miriam to begin the conversation – she having sought his attention, which he willingly gave.

Miriam, not missing a beat, seized the moment and responded: "Thomas, I need to let you know I have become involved in the work of a group which will be hosting the 'Conference of the Un-Godly,' in a couple months here in Port-of-Spain. It is a planned international conference, and I am one of the key members of the organising team. The committee's work is fairly advanced, and I am due to travel to Boston shortly to seek to raise funds from my former university colleagues to assist in funding the conference. You may have heard me speak of my campus group – most of the women have done exceptionally well and are inclined to assist."

Thomas did not interrupt Miriam and even long after the moment Miriam remained baffled over his actions during the more break-than-make discussion. Given his silence

Miriam pressed on speaking, as if the agenda she set for herself was never ending.

"I know I have not discussed any of this with you before this morning, but it had to be this way, and I ask your consideration as we go forward as a family."

Even this statement brought no response from Thomas, who as the one-sided conversation continued, grew more emotional if not angry.

Miriam continued: "Thomas, during my absence from home and given your own work schedule, I have asked my parents to look after the children."

Something within this last statement caused Thomas to rise to his feet. With his fist clenched, he pointed at Miriam and said, in the most frightening tone Miriam could remember: "You could do what you want with your life, as I believe we have long been divorced, but don't plan for my children." Thomas knew his next statement could either end or force a continuation of the discussion, and so he added: "I will get someone to take care of the children, but they are not going to Goodwood Park."

Unknowingly, Thomas had crossed the line that Miriam had drawn in the sand during the past six years as she bent and accommodated his ill-founded wishes of not returning to her parents' home, nor indeed accepting support from them.

When Miriam next spoke, she did so with a clarity of mission and purpose. "You speak of Goodwood Park as if it is unclean, as if it is bad. Yet it is the spoils of the Suielmans of Goodwood Park which I saved before I came to Rose Hill that have kept this household alive and fed. The food you eat each day, where do you think it comes from? The clothes, linen and food that ensure our six do not go unattended, where do you think it comes from? Thomas, you don't have a clue of how this home functions. And be assured, I am not leaving our children to be cared for by someone I don't know and I am pretty certain you really do not know."

She added defiantly: "You can do as you wish, but know during the time I will be away at Boston; I have made arrangements for our children to spend the time with my parents at Goodwood Park."

Miriam paused, seeking a rebuttal. But Thomas, who felt bruised and battered, would not normally engage anyone in a contest unless he had planned his strategies of offence and defence. In this battle, as he saw it he was caught off guard, unprepared and vulnerable.

He conceded defeat – he had lost the battle, but he consoled himself he would not lose the war.

As he looked at his wife he sought to conceal the disgust he felt, but he knew Miriam had declared war, whether she knew it or not, and he committed himself to do what he must to be victorious in the battles that lay ahead. He accepted that until a half an hour earlier he had underestimated Miriam – henceforth he would not make the same mistake.

Days later, with Thomas away at the mosque, Phillip Suielman, with directions given to him, arrived at Rose Hill for the first time in his life and at the door of his daughter's home.

Phillip Suielman, despite being what city folks described as a "town man," knew little of what existed "behind the bridge." He and his family, for all their lives, traded with and sold to the people from 'behind the bridge' all manner of goods, and in the case of the money lenders and pawn shop operators a range of services. So, too, Phillip Suielman employed residents from every nook and cranny within Port-of-Spain, yet he had never before set his feet on the soil of Rose Hill, where his daughter had lived for the previous six years.

He could not help being apprehensive as he knew not what he was about to encounter, but he would not have found himself at Rose Hill unless his daughter advised that he come to fetch his grandchildren. On reflection, Phillip smiled to himself two hours earlier as he listened to Miriam say to him, "Dad, you can pick up your grandchildren at eleven am." Until this moment the thought of grandchildren was something he and Sammoy had almost given up on, and now he was being asked by his beloved Miriam to collect her brood of six.

Neither he nor Sammoy knew what the grandchildren looked like. They knew the eldest was six years of age while the youngest was turning one year old. They knew that of the six, four were boys while two were girls. They also knew that the girls were sandwiched between the third and last boy.

Unknown to Phillip and Miriam, the news that 'the children' as she described her bunch would be spending time with she and Phillip awoke within Sammoy a spirit she often dreamed of, and which she had buried as she believed the idea of caring for grandchildren was something that her daughter and husband had ensured would not be possible.

When therefore Miriam called and asked: "Mother would you take care of the children while I am away?" she would not believe what she was hearing, and in the hours since this conversation she had cause to wonder whether she was dreaming a long dream, which she prayed would not become a nightmare.

She had Suzanna prepare two of the five rooms of the Suielmans' home. One she decided would be for the three older children, and the other for the two girls and the youngest, their baby brother.

Sammoy felt emotions about her home as she moved easily and with focus from room to room, ensuring linen, toothbrushes, toothpaste, bath soap and hand soap was in place. Above all she insisted good blankets were placed folded on all the beds the children were expected to occupy.

Sammoy was as excited about this moment, conscious it was the grandchildren's first visit to their grandparents' home. All these emotions pierced her spirit as nothing had before. She grasped the significance of the moment and embraced it all. She instinctively put away all her personal armour of defences and allowed the event to engulf her, as the events had already consumed Phillip, who was being carried by the tides, by the rush of the moment. And as she thought of this man who still called her Dr Sammoy, she truly understood unconditional love.

Together they would ensure Miriam's children were safe and well provided for, despite the reality that they as grandparents had the six children for just a few days. Sammoy had every intention that this visit would be as memorable for the children as it would be for her and her husband.

Phillip knocked at the door at Rose Hill, and he could hear his daughter respond: "Who is it?"

He knocked again and added: "Girl, it is your father, doing your bidding."

Miriam laughed one of her famous raucous laughs and hurried to open her front door.

Phillip stepped inside hugged his daughter and enquired, "Are the children ready?"

Phillip did not look around, nor did he show an interest in the space his daughter called home. He knew that any such action on his part would cause Miriam some measure of discomfort, and this he wished to avoid at all costs.

The six children came out of their bedroom all smiling, and together and in one voice said: "Good morning Grandpa." It was not rehearsed nor was it planned in any way, but each child approached Phillip and gave him a hug, to which he reciprocated with passion and tears in his eyes, though he did not allow them to break loose.

Each had a backpack and was ready to go. They said farewell to Miriam and each hugged her in a special way. All of this Phillip observed with admiration. He was about to pick up the youngest of the children, and suddenly realised grandfather did not know the names of his grandchildren.

He turned and looked at Miriam and moved his outstretched hands up and down, turning his palms inside out in a gesture to suggest 'what's going on?' and blurted out, "Miriam, I don't know the children's names." They both laughed, and Miriam took her time to introduce each child in the hope her father would remember each child's name, and would introduce each correctly to her mother and their grandmother.

Phillip seated each child inside the vehicle and ensured each was strapped in with seat belts. He placed the youngest in his car seat and strapped him in immediately behind the driver's seat. With bags loaded he hugged his daughter and parted with the words, "See you later Miriam."

22

PHILLIP DID NOT KNOW WHAT TO SAY OR WHAT TO do as he made his thirty-two minute drive from Rose Hill, East Dry River, to his driveway at Goodwood Park. His passengers were all six years and under, and could not relate to the thoughts which swirled in his very silent cerebral.

As he pulled up at the entrance to the kitchen, the greeting party of Suzanna and Sammoy was waiting to welcome the children to what was, in Sammoy's heart and mind, their home.

As each alighted from the Prado, beginning with the two eldest boys who occupied the rear seats, grandmother smiled and hugged each of the boys. They, not used to either their grandmother or hugging, did not reciprocate with matched intensity, and were quite happy as Sammoy moved her attention to their younger siblings. Each child was given a hug, the nature of which Sammoy reserved for Miriam.

She picked up Abraham, the youngest and not quite a year old, and as she did so she looked piercingly into his eyes and was convinced she was looking into her husband's. "Yes," she said to herself, "This is Phillip." Sammoy was never one to address what she felt and seemed to be small things, but she could not get over the look she saw in the eyes of a child not yet one year old. She could not grasp the similarity of her last grandchild's eyes and that of her husband.

When all the children had been settled into the rooms assigned, she quietly knocked on their doors and enquired if they would like to have something to eat. Miriam had earlier instructed not to serve them anything with pork, which included ham and bacon and roasted pork, which the Suielmans quite often enjoyed at meals.

Sammoy and Phillip's next task was getting to know each child by name. They soon came to recognise the eldest was Hamid, the second was Yufus, the third Kamal with the fourth being Nafessar, the fifth Zida and the baby Abraham.

Well into their fourth day of babysitting, Sammoy and Phillip were having an afternoon coffee when the subject of the children came up.

Phillip, as if wanting to raise the subject, said: "Sammoy, I don't see Thomas in these children." Sammoy smiled, she being the partner who understood the science, and replied: "If you don't see Thomas, tell me what you see."

Phillip grinned as if suggesting to Sammoy she was making fun of him, and added: "Then you are seeing Thomas in these children. Thomas is a brown-skinned boy, but all these children are as clear- skinned as I am and I spend a lot of time in the sun."

Sammoy could not resist the urge to join Phillip in what she would normally describe as small-minded talk, but on this rare occasion she chimed in: "Phillip I believe you are correct, it seems the children are more Suielman than any other."

The complexion and facial features in another time would have mattered, however in the world in which Miriam and her brood shared with the population of Trinidad and Tobago, colour and the shape and size of your nose mattered little.

In the culture of this society, driven by hydrocarbons, those who possessed wealth could be of any race, any culture, any religion and, above all, any colour. What mattered is that you had deep pockets from which you could order your life as you wished, and in the context of the Suielmans, the children of Miriam had made the giant step of establishing the right to sit within the main office at Suielman and Sons Limited.

Their mother Miriam, the prodigal daughter, had unintentionally built a bridge for all six children to claim their space by merely accepting her father's invitation to babysit her children while she looked after the affairs of her conference.

In this moment Sammoy and her husband enjoyed their coffee, as the moment had far greater meaning. The significance of the previous seventy two hours and the seventy or so hours which lay ahead, both agreed was very special. They got to know each child in a special way, and the children got to know them and accepted them as their grandparents.

The sweetness of the moment seemed too good to be true, and it would be Sammoy who would first suggest that the peacefulness of the moment was almost troubling, for as night follows day, after joy is sorrow. She prayed that the peace she enjoyed, and the Suielmans now enjoyed, would become the new normal. Her daughter had not only returned home, she now had a full house of beautiful, well-disciplined grandchildren.

In Sammoy's thoughts she felt proud – her daughter had home schooled her grandchildren and had done a commendable job.

Despite all these beautiful thoughts, she could not help herself; she could not free herself from believing that after the quiet would come the storm.

23

MIRIAM GOT TO LOGAN INTERNATIONAL AIRPORT, and was familiar with the Boston Airport Terminal. She moved with the same ease she knew in deplaning at Piarco in Trinidad. She looked like any ordinary passenger entering the city of Boston. Miriam had consciously changed from her Muslim clothing to the more fashionable clothing she took from her closets at her last visit with her parents.

When she left home early that morning and said a less than friendly spouse-like farewell to Thomas, she was dressed from head to toe in her now common long flowing gowns complete with hijab. She checked in with the local carrier. She quickly whisked her way through immigration, and en route to the security checkpoint she paused outside the female bathroom.

Following a minute's pause she entered. When she emerged fifteen minutes later, she could and would not be recognised as the Muslim woman who had earlier entered the bathroom.

A light brown, slim built and astonishingly beautiful woman, dressed in slacks which clung at the hips and finished just above the ankles, emerged. Miriam sported a pair of canvas shoes, which revealed her well-formed, strong ankles. No one seeing this casually dressed woman would accept that she was the mother of six children. Despite the birth of six children in six years, her body showed no signs of the challenges associated with pregnancies. Her nosey neighbours at Rose Hill often remarked: "she had worn good."

She closed the female bathroom door slowly and exited almost as if in another world, and if remembering she had just minutes ago morphed into another person in appearance she pulled out a pair of sunglasses and placed them gently upon her face, completing the transformation.

It would be this Miriam Suielman, who despite being married for six years and who never bothered to change her name, would waltz off the aircraft and through the immigration and customs at Logan International, and finally would wave a taxi and depart for the sleepy little town of Wellesley, where she had made reservation at the college commons.

She knew this space well, for as a student she on occasion worked as receptionist, much to the annoyance of Phillip Suielman, who insisted that if she needed additional money, she merely had to ask. She on the other hand worked, not because she needed money, but she convinced herself that it was important to do the things that those less fortunate than herself did, if she wished to understand the true meaning of life's ups and downs.

Phillip Suielman considered all of this to be 'baloney' but finally gave in, allowing his daughter to make her own choices.

The college commons would be her home, she mused to herself, for the three nights; the thought of being alone on a queen bed for "three whole nights" caused her to smile.

Miriam as she landed had gotten a U.S. SIM card and inserted it into a cheap phone her father had given her, with the advice to make it operational as soon as she settled in, and to let him have the number so there would be open communication while she was in Boston. Miriam anxiously telephoned her parents; spoke with both her mother and father and asked to speak with her children one after the other. She spoke with her eldest, Hamid, last, and it is with Hamid she had the longest conversation. Hamid assured his mother that his brothers and sisters were, as he said: "Good." He however was mindful to enquire, "Mom, how is Boston?" and quickly added, "When will you take me there?" Miriam felt this last question deep inside, and though she had never given it consideration, the question posed by Hamid raised inside her a desire to travel with her children, as she so many years ago travelled with her parents. She quickly brushed these thoughts aside and bid farewell to her son with the promise that she would call daily.

Her next call was to Viveanna. During her time at Boston, Viveanna, or Vive as she was affectionately called, was the third of the trinity of Suzie Steffano, now Dr Steffano, and Miriam. The three when they got to Boston were all in their late teens. Suzie would leave her two friends and move to Yale, where she pursued medicine, while Viveanna opted to attend Harvard in pursuit of higher studies in Politics and Economics. She was back at her Alma Mater as a professor in the Faculty of Political Sciences.

Miriam also moved to Harvard's Business Faculty, where she distinguished herself obtaining a Magna Cum Laude in Business, and where her growing circle of friends and professionals assumed she would go for her PhD. She surprised everyone when she announced she was returning home to Trinidad as the time had come for her to begin building her family's business.

As young women at campus with no knowledge of the world around them, they were admired by their female colleagues and adored by an ever lengthening list of men of all ages. Of the "Trinity," one young Harvard man remarked: "Each were handmade by God." Of the three Miriam was the most outstanding as she carried in her veins the blood of many rivers, with no one able to say whether the Ganges or Nile had more influence. She most certainly was a naturally brilliant person, yet learnt her lessons well from her mother Dr Sammoy, who encouraged her daughter to appreciate hard work. "Do not accept that you are brilliant; even the brightest bulb must forever be dusted for it to continue shining brightly." Her mother having said this to her would add: "Don't ever forget that."

Miriam never forgot her mother's counsel, and throughout her academic pursuits applied herself with passion to her studies and dedication in pursuit of excellence.

Today she was calling Vive, who had as requested complied with her wishes and convened a series of meetings of varying sizes to facilitate her fundraising initiatives.

Vive arrived approximately an hour later, giving her friend time to freshen up and settle in. As the women greeted each other no one could accept that both were crossing thirty years old. Each looked not a day older than their mid-twenties.

They embraced and kissed each other on the lips. To any observer this form of greeting could have been wrongly interpreted. Yet between the Trinity, they had long established that a peck on the lips, even though they were women, would be their greeting, and so it was on this humid Wellesley afternoon.

Once they were seated in the car Vive handed Miriam a schedule of thirteen planned meetings, inclusive of four breakfast meetings and four luncheons.

Before starting the car Vive smiled leaned back in her seat and scrutinised her friend as if she was on an inspection parade. Miriam, forever aware, smiled and said: "What?"

Vive replied: "Can I not look at my friend?" and with this both women laughed. As she engaged the gears of the one-year-old 500 series Mercedes Benz, she said in her most southern accent: "Girl, you sure you have six children? You sure don't look like you have even one." With that said she rolled around the college commons round-a-bout and headed for Route 16, to take them to the first luncheon meeting in downtown Boston.

Viveanna arranged meetings with former colleagues, both male and female. Some came from across the globe, but made Boston and environs their home. Other native Bostonians were all doing well, having certified at the most prestigious centres of North America, and were all eager to see what had become of the not only brilliant but beautiful Suielman woman from Trinidad and Tobago.

Each meeting brought back memories of not so long ago. Some of these memories were made of much of the run of the mill stuff, but some were memories that, on reflection, Miriam had always cherished.

As the first two days closed, Miriam and Vive had much to feel good over. With five more events ahead of them, they had raised, based on pledges and cash contributions, close to one hundred and thirty-eight thousand dollars. Miriam did not share with Vive, but she hoped to raise the equivalent of one million Trinidad and Tobago dollars.

Miriam and Vive sat within one of Boston's famous Dumpling Cafes for an early dinner, during which Miriam shared with Vive what she had received both in pledges and cash, with all indicators suggesting she was about to surpass her target.

Vive respected Miriam to the max, and would never ask her of her goals with her fundraising efforts. During the previous four days she had the distinct pleasure of sitting back and listening to her friend sell her plans for hosting her conference for "the un-godly". With each presentation she became more convinced of the likely success of the conference, which she with her inherent objectivity knew could, by its very name, spark tremendous pushback from those who felt under attack by a conference being hosted specifically to review the operations of religious administrators across all religious lines. Vive knew that she would communicate her concerns to Miriam on the aforementioned before they parted and Miriam returned to her home in Trinidad. This would wait, as she wished to learn from her friend a little more of her life and her challenges beyond the conference.

She, over a cup of green Chinese tea, learnt of Miriam's choice of Thomas with all its challenges, her six children and the dramatic changes in lifestyle. Vive was a good listener and neither prodded nor probed her friend, but allowed her to tell her story in tones that suited her and as she wished.

Later that evening as Vive reflected on the hours before now, she tried to reconcile the union between Miriam and the person she had married named Thomas. She never knew Miriam to be impulsive, nor did she in the many years she spent in her company see Miriam make a decision without due care and consideration. In the seven years they knew each other, many beautiful people sought to get close to her. But Miriam was always very careful of who she allowed into her space.

Vive remembered with a smile Miriam's preference to not be tied to any one partner. She liked dancing, and even as they visited clubs she enjoyed being able to dance with the group and not necessarily with any single partner. The group who partied with Miriam all knew she was cautious of those she did not know, and she always gave herself time to get to know new people.

How then did she fall for Thomas? And even more remarkable, what was the magic potion Thomas used to convince her to convert to Islam and to get married in record time?

Vive closed her thoughts on this matter, as she now believed having seen and listened to Miriam Suielman over the last days, that if there was a time she was not in charge of her actions, that period was now over. The life of the Trinity of friends was back in charge of their own destiny.

In the morning they would meet with the faculty of their old college, and where she was now a senior professor. It would be her show, and she knew she would have to persuade her colleagues to both accept and support Miriam's conference proposal. In the context of faculties competing for the available budget, she as host had done her background checks on who was likely to assist and who would be just difficult.

Vive welcomed her colleagues and acknowledged she was beginning, despite the absence of the group's boss, the president of the campus, who would be somewhat late. She outlined that Miriam Suielman was a former distinguished student, who was based in her native Trinidad and was leading a team in hosting an international conference seeking to engage a critical review of the integrity of religion.

Miriam was warmly welcomed. As she scanned the audience she knew a number of the professional body, as some were at the campus teaching during her stay at college.

Being as single minded as she had always been, Miriam walked her audience through her goal and emphasised her desired outcomes. She knew that with this group the focus would be in defining what she expected to come out of the data she was likely to gather. When the question was raised by an Indian female lecturer from the social sciences faculty, Miriam dispassionately replied: "If we knew what the results would be, there would be no need for the conference.

"However it is our hope to encourage an opening of the door, but not only to rooms and closets. We are hoping some will present files with factual information, which when evaluated and reviewed will offer all an opportunity to establish a way forward in addressing the many and varied wrongs that have taken place. Some of these we already have a grasp of, but much of it we anticipate we will learn of at our conference later this year," she added.

Miriam Suielman spent another ninety minutes fielding and responding to a steady flow of questions.

When the final question was articulated, Miriam was for the first time that morning without an immediate reply. Not getting a response, another in the room said: "Mrs Suielman, it appears you missed the last question, and so it falls to me to restate it. Could you tell us what you want us to do to assist you with this historic conference?"

This time Miriam responded: "Good people, for starters we need as much legal funding we can get. Further, we would be happy if we could be given such services that can assist us with the organising and administration of our conference. Finally, it would be great to see as many of you that can spare the time in attendance to lift the quality of the work of our conference."

As Miriam took her seat, someone almost to the rear of the auditorium shouted: "Pass the hat!" The three words were echoed over and over as two stationery boxes mysteriously appeared and were passed from one row of chairs to the other, with participants adding their personal contributions to a conference many knew would cause, as is said on the streets of Port-of-Spain, 'fireworks.'

No one saw the institution's president slip into the last row of chairs as Miriam began her presentation. At the end of her presentation she felt proud to be the leader of an institution that produced such a forceful woman, who she concluded would be a change agent.

She approached Miriam as the audience began departing the event. She found herself seventh in queue wishing to have a word with Miriam, and waited with patience and pride to speak to a girl she taught during her first year on campus.

When Miriam's eyes made contact with her former lecturer, now president of her school of learning, she could not contain her joy. She reached out and embraced her, and received an equally warm embrace. "Lady, you have become quite a leader. We are all proud of you," the principal added.

Miriam replied: "President, I am merely the product of a purpose driven, professional and progressive institution."

Their moment together confirmed that Miriam would be assisted, but such details had to be worked out. For Miriam this was a giant step, and she was just as excited to ensure the follow up action be carried out.

With the departure of the last participant, Vive came up to Miriam with the two stationery boxes and handed both to her with the words: "Girl, you did well this morning. Be assured you will hear from members of this group in the months ahead."

Miriam placed the boxes on the head table and looked inside, and could not believe on the surface that the professionals she faced for two hours were truly moved by what they saw and heard, and responded by dipping into their pockets in the way they did. She knew she would not do an immediate account of the contents of the boxes, and requested of Vive a bag or a couple large envelopes.

Later in the evening, Vive and Miriam counted the collections together and were both surprised at the generosity of the group. When the final tally was confirmed Miriam was wide-eyed, and Vive was proud of her colleagues.

Their contribution of sixty four thousand dollars was a good contribution to the 'Conference of the Un-Godly.' Miriam's fundraising now stood at a total of 162,000 dollars. Both friends agreed that with each event the numbers improved, and the morning's session was more than useful.

Miriam continued her schedule of events, with each providing her with both knowledge on the hosting of her conference and varying sums of much needed funding.

Two days before Miriam was due to depart for home, and with one more event scheduled, Vive received a request from a group of social workers based within the New Rochelle, New York community, headed by a Trinidadian with ties to Jamaica by marriage, requesting a meeting with Miriam.

Miriam thought for a moment and enquired of Vive her opinion. "Should we or should we not go to New Rochelle for this meeting?"

It was agreed that they would add the meeting and extend her stay by one day.

Miriam successfully concluded her Boston schedule having raised 219,000 US dollars.

24

SHE AND VIVE PLANNED TO LEAVE EARLY THE following morning, getting to New York by mid-morning, for a planned lunch meeting with the New Rochelle group, which was scheduled to be held at a Chinese restaurant within the tiny New Rochelle Centre.

Vive suggested that she pack a change of clothing, as when they got to New Rochelle she would visit with a friend who she had alerted of their planned stick-of-a-fire visit.

Vive was happy for the opportunity to visit with Jeffrey, an old friend with whom she enjoyed a healthy relationship for just over a year and following their breakup remained good friends. She liked this about Jeffrey, and was happy to introduce Miriam to a man with whom she enjoyed a good but short relationship. When he left Boston for New York they continued dating for a short period, but soon found the distance between Wellesley and New York was a little too much for a fledging relationship.

Mariam asked no questions of Vive, as she was always guided by her father's maxim, "ask no questions and you will be told no lies." What she learnt of Jeffrey was what her friend shared with her, and what she observed by the interaction between her bestie and her old flame.

She knew Vive well enough to sense she still carried a fire for Jeffrey, and despite his attentiveness to her, Miriam could not see in Jeffrey the same intensity from him to her. Miriam closed these thoughts in her mind, as she knew whatever transpired would only be for a night, and in the early hours of the next day Vive would be heading to Boston, leaving Jeffrey in New Rochelle, New York.

The luncheon, though hastily organised, was unsolicited, yet it attracted the largest audience of the fundraising tour. Neither Miriam nor Vive knew the member of the organising group, and were taken aback by the numbers and representation of those who attended. The group comprised largely of professional and business people.

What was the attraction to the conference to these people? Miriam pondered to herself, and she met and chatted with members of her audience during a fifteen minute cocktail before the meeting was seated for lunch.

During lunch the chatter within the room came from seventy-three persons, inclusive of Vive, Jeffrey and Miriam. As the group began lunch Miriam and Vive became a little concerned, as they were neither welcomed nor introduced to Mary Chan Sing, the lady who extended the invitation to meet at New Rochelle.

With lunch now served, an agile and high spirited woman, who looked very much like Miriam given the mixture of Chinese and other blood, hurriedly approached the table to which Miriam and Vive had been ushered and occupied the vacant setting. She apologised for her lateness and introduced herself as Mary Chan Sing, president of the group Friends for Betterment. They were based at New Rochelle, given that the majority of its donors and participants lived at New Rochelle, but worked in Manhattan. This said, Miriam now grasped the chemistry of her audience, and in response replied: "You have invited me to quite a ball Ms Chan Sing."

She replied: "Forget the formalities; kindly call me Mary."

Mary enquired of Miriam: "How much time do you need at the podium?"

"I would rather field questions, but maybe twenty to thirty minutes maximum," was the quick response.

Such details concluded, and having barely taken a nibble of her lunch, she got up and went directly to the podium. Mary knocked a water glass with a fork, and immediately the chatter within the room ceased.

"Friends," she began. "Good day. I want to thank you for coming at such short notice. I wonder if you are here because

I said to you the speaker is a smart, but more importantly, beautiful woman?"

As Mary uttered these words came responses of "Here, here, here."

Continuing, Mary added: "We are really here for a most serious matter. Our guest is a driven individual, who unlike many of us is not prepared to sit back and do nothing while 'Rome burns.' She, in months from now, will be hosting a conference entitled, 'Conference of the Un-Godly,' which she will tell us all about. It is hoped that after we learn of such details, we will see the need to do something to assist this woman and her team to open the doors that most of us are afraid to even grasp by the doorknob, far less turn the key."

Miriam walked slowly to the lectern, and once centre stage, she exploded.

She spoke uninterrupted for twenty-four minutes, and while in stride broke her presentation to invite questions.

The co-chair gave the very same presentation she gave at her old university college, yet on this occasion, as if driven by an unseen hand, she placed the success of the hosting of the conference in the hands of the audience.

Miriam's opening salvo was simply brutal, as she noted: "When honesty, integrity, justice, sincerity, nobleness and respect for each other – yes, when standards of goodness – are lost, the law of the jungle emerges and the law of the absurd prevails, and this is what we are witnessing as we meet today."

This was her opening statement, to which she was warmly welcomed.

In the twenty-four minutes which followed, she would be only interrupted with applause after applause, yet she found her centre and clung to it to tell her story of the boy from Los Bajos and her team in Port-of-Spain, Trinidad, working many long hours to establish a conference which she believed the world needed but truly feared.

The questions were quick and equally strong. As the questions came, she could not stop herself from smiling as she remembered Nathan's comment in a similar situation during a fundraising meeting at Chaguanas when he remarked, "The questions came like rapid gunfire."

She did not need to dodge the questions, as she was prepared to respond with answers that left her audience in no doubt that an investment in her would be well spent. Unlike other meetings, no one passed the box. As each of the participants left, they shook hands with Miriam and committed: "I will leave you my contribution with Mary."

An Afro-American couple approached Miriam and smiled at her. They stepped back and looked at her. They stepped back and looked her over from head to toes, and then the gentleman said softly: "Lady you have guts, but we suspect you have God within you – you must be special. We bless your conference. We may not be there physically, but we will send you appropriate conference material, and last but not least we will leave you a little gift at the door. We want you to know that, though we represent the house of the Lord, we frown on the un-godly." With these words they disappeared within the audience.

Miriam was fascinated by both the vibrations and words of blessings she got from the most delightful couple, and stared at them as they took their departure. Others who queued to speak with Miriam offered constructive suggestions on what should be done to facilitate the outcomes Miriam said she sought from the conference.

The after-lunch was for longer than the actual luncheon as participants mingled and chatted, yet as each departed they visited with Mary who had set up a table near the exit door.

When all departed, Mary invited Vive and Miriam to have a coffee with her. This greatly amused Miriam, who said to Mary: "My Grandfather would die, God rest his soul, if he knew I was having coffee in a Chinese restaurant in New York."

In response Mary said: "So would my father, and he is alive," and laughed a most unladylike laugh, which might have summoned the waitress to the table.

Mary told her new-found friend that the luncheon raised one hundred and twenty-five thousand dollars, with the highest donation coming from the pastor of one of the leading Pentecostal churches within New Rochelle. "He gave you a cheque for twenty-five thousand dollars," she added.

Over coffee, Vive and Miriam learned that Mary received a call from one of the group suggesting the meeting, having learned of the conference online.

"He called me and said: 'President, I see your home country is having an important conference. I think we should support it.' I enquired of him if he knew who was involved, and he said to me the key person is at the moment in Boston on a fundraising tour, and maybe we could get her to come to New Rochelle and we will do what we can to assist. That is when I contacted you and I am happy you agreed to come," she added.

Despite the background details provided, Miriam felt something was missing. So she asked: "Mary, you could answer as you wish, but who precisely are those other people who are so generous?"

Mary looked at her newfound friends and replied: "These are ordinary good people who have all done well with their lives, and who from time to time meet to discuss the state of the world, but more importantly to determine and agree on small actions to make the world a better space."

"Did you do that this afternoon?" Miriam boldly asked.

"You will determine the answer at the end of the 'Conference of the Un-Godly,'" Mary replied, with a facial expression of an angel.

Mary realised Miriam was still baffled by the goodness of the group, and said to Miriam: "Lady, for what it is worth, I assure you no one present is CIA or FBI. So be assured, we just felt we should help others who are seeking to define the meaning of the behaviour of others to whom the world placed so much trust and had the trust destroyed. Yes, we would like your conference to succeed. Yes, we would like *our* conference to succeed."

Miriam was forced to finally accept that neither she nor her co-chair Nathan John were casualties of the poverty of brilliance within their native Trinidad and Tobago.

Others saw and believed in the importance of knowing and understanding why something like religion – which was intended and ought to be so pure – has over centuries divided, caused plunder, rape, sodomy, incest, domestic violence and a destruction of the human spirit.

This last leg of the visit to New Rochelle was not only successful, it was liberating. Miriam left New York accompanied by Vive and Jeffrey, who for reasons unknown to Miriam would be part of the motor car passenger load on the way back to Boston.

Miriam left Boston the next morning, having deposited with Vive the nearly three hundred and forty-four thousand USD, which when converted amounted to two million, four hundred and eight thousand Trinidad and Tobago dollars.

The trip to Boston was a success, and as she left she handed Vive an envelope in which she shared with her friend her appreciation for her support and love. Her note read:

My dear Vive,
You may not be able to fully grasp how much of a friend and sister you are, to have done all you did for me this past week. Know that I will, as always, be forever grateful. In the past you have always supported my sometimes wild dreams. However, you must believe me when I say to you on this occasion our work of the past week had nothing to do with Miriam Suielman, but more to do with a fundamental challenge which has troubled little people across the world for centuries. You dear sister have laid the foundation for a more enlightened society, where things that matter most must stop being of little importance to things that matter least.

I thank you for all your support in the service of the voiceless.
See you in Port-of-Spain.
Always your sister,
Miriam

When Vive finally read the note near midnight that evening she cried troubled tears, as she who believed she knew Miriam Suielman began to appreciate that the woman she once knew had morphed into a warrior whose path she would not wish to cross.

25

"OUR MANY VOLUNTEERS AGREEING TO DO WEEKS of work, and in some instances months of work, without expecting any compensation is a first for Trinidad and Tobago," said Phillip Suielman to the Credential Committee.

The committee members quickly came to accept Phillip as being 'irie,' and sound or just darn good. These feelings had nothing to do with Phillip being Miriam's father.

Phillip offered his advice with openness and sincerity. He never minced words, and one committee member concluded: "He was a good one, and with Phillip what you saw was what you got."

The fact that just over three scores and ten persons fashioned the conference staff, with all persons doing so for 'free of charge' as he put it, is an indication of the commitment to the 'Conference of the Un-Godly.'

When Anthony reported to the Steering Committee he knew he had the full backing of his sixteen-member team.

The months leading to the conference had been a whirlwind of activity for a committee, which began with Anthony, Phillip Suielman, Nathan and Miriam, and had grown to be a dedicated team of seventy-two with each volunteering to do what they did at no charge for the organisers of the conference.

The group consisted of team leaders, co-ordinators, rapporteurs, welcome and reception personnel, stationery attendants, printing and copying crews, and public address technical teams. This huge group of ever willing volunteers came together, and were for the past three months putting in place documents, both published and unpublished, much of which some anticipated would be the backbone of discussions and would fashion the direction and outcomes of the conference.

This moment in the life of the conference will always be recorded as the period when the committee began to cast aside its doubts as the increase in persons registering grew with each day, with the Credential Committee in the presentation of its daily report highlighting increased international registration in a separate column.

With two weeks to the opening of the conference, registrations illustrated that locals were as keen to be part of the conference as were the ever growing column which documented international registered participants.

Initially Nathan and Miriam grappled with very slow registration, but as the weeks went by the international registration became a reality and much of it in response to an online campaign Miriam orchestrated during her now famous Boston sojourn.

As the numbers initially trickled in, there was an atmosphere of anxiety among the group. It would take the counsel of Phillip Suielman to steady the ship, encourage the patriots and convert the disbelievers. The registration would pick up and this country would see the biggest and most successful non-governmental conference, he would say in response to those members who were melancholy and were by their downtrodden spirits creating a heavy atmosphere, which encouraged others to be pensive.

The topsy-turvyness with registration caused Miriam, Anthony and Nathan to meet more often than warranted, as each kept their eyes on the application forms coming in to the Credential Committee.

With seven days to the conference opening, overseas registration began to spark. Each day saw upwards of fifty new requests for confirmations, and with it the five direct lines assigned were off the hook all seventeen hours the secretariat remained open.

Seven days before showed signs of things to come. Five days before illustrated the likely outcome, with international numbers matching local numbers in a single day for the first time since the 'Conference of the Un-Godly' began registration.

Each overseas application, Phillip and Anthony took turns at scrutinising these forms. Having done so, they would approve or disapprove. This was followed by a joint examination of the form to determine if either missed a clue, to stop any fanatic from entering the Republic and with it causing problems for the conference and its bona fide participants.

Anthony and Phillip, during an early meeting with the local law enforcement, were advised that the best assistance the conference could provide was to stop all radicals at registration. which meant the Credential Committee had a crucial role to play in keeping the hounds outside the doors of the Republic.

Both men gave a commitment to do as requested, but also knew that despite their best efforts, it is likely trouble would, if it wished, ease its way past their due diligence and onto the conference floor. They were therefore relentless in their pursuit of seeking out the likely un-godly, and so spent many extra hours examining mostly international applications as requested by local security and law enforcement.

The issue of locally registered versus internationals was not only of interest to the committee. It soon became apparent that local authorities had become very interested in the 'Conference of the Un-Godly,' with firstly indirect enquiries. Then as the days to the conference shortened Nathan received direct communication, enquiring whether the conference needed any assistance from the state. This was followed by yet another verbal enquiry, as to whether the conference would consider an opening address from a very senior member of the Republic's administration.

The conference committee met to review and respond to the letter. Nathan read out the letter to the group, as he knew among the committee were members who had strong affiliations to the government and did not wish to bring down the wrath of the government on the conference.

In making the contents of the letter public to the committee a far bigger group had the information, and would be in a position to share with their known or unknown audiences. He as chairman never indicated the matter was confidential as he had done on previous matters.

Members of the committee surprised Nathan and Miriam, and responded in a forthright manner. The consensus was that the government had only become interested as it recognised the conference would likely attract a sizeable local and international audience, and wished to piggy-back on any likely successes.

Nathan also shared with his committee that he had earlier direct communication from the government, asking whether the conference needed any direct assistance from the state. He added: "Friends, I want you to know no responses have been made to the government on any of its enquiries or overtures."

The latter information encouraged a moment of discord, as some members openly made known their displeasure with what one member described as, "The government is trying to muscle in on our conference."

Another member put the request in the context of time, and noted: "Why only now are they seeking to mix their waters with holy water?"

The questions and responses continued, and for reasons best known to Nathan he allowed all members to be heard.

Those who carried loyalties for the government remained silent, knowing the ship of state was in murky waters with the majority of members of the committee for the 'Conference of the Un-Godly.'

Nathan was requested by resolution to politely decline both invitations, as members reasoned: "If we accept any financial assistance, we cannot refuse the state its second request to speak at the opening of the conference."

When finally Nathan did put the matter to the vote, all present voted not to engage the state with any of its requests.

Following the meeting, Nathan, Miriam, Phillip, Anthony, Mildred and Rosie met informally, and the take away was the government would not be happy with the refusal.

Miriam was most decisive in her take on the matter, as she said: "Whether we accepted their very late invitation or not is not the question to be answered. The bigger question would be how would the government's presence impact our conference, and more importantly how do we know what the government is likely to say and what impact such statements would have on the outcomes?" she ended.

Nathan waited for his colleagues to speak, and when no one did he endorsed Miriam's position, reminding all that there would be equally more difficult challenges in the weeks ahead.

26

WITH THREE DAYS TO GO, ALL AREAS OF administration and operations seemed to be on track for a successful hosting of the first 'Conference of the Un-Godly.' Nathan and Miriam spent more time together, bouncing ideas off each other. Both were more than delighted when Suzie Stefano and Viveanna joined the team and took up office, with Suzie sharing space with Miriam while Vive elected to share with Nathan.

At the end of the first day, after sharing a meal at Dr Sammoy's kitchen table, she said to Miriam: "I wish he was a little older or I a little younger," in reference to Nathan, who she found adorable and near perfect.

Suzie, who overheard the conversation, chimed in: "Vive, girl I can tell you professionally in this day and in this place there is nothing like too old or too young." And she drew the laughter of the Trinity not heard in a long time.

Miriam could not let the subject slip, and she said to her: "If I were not married I might agree with Suzie, and you would have competition."

At this statement Suzie and Vive looked at each other with wide eyes and raised cheeks, illustrating surprise.

No new surprises visited the path of the committee, and on the penultimate day before the conference, they met to dot the i's and cross the t's.

On this occasion the inner committee was introduced to faces which belonged to names mentioned by Nathan and Miriam, but mostly by Miriam over the months of meetings. Suzie, Viveanna and Mary Chan Sing from New Rochelle finally met officially the group they supported from afar, and committee members finally put faces to names they were now very familiar with.

There were two other strange faces to the wider committee, but known to Nathan, Miriam, Anthony and Phillip. Both persons were introduced as officers of local law enforcement. Phillip was pleased to introduce the female of the two, who he underscored was a senior superintendent and the officer leading the co-ordinating of the conference's state security.

The senior superintendent thanked the committee for the invitation to the meeting, which she deemed to be a very important meeting, and further commended the committee for its professionalism.

She did not end here.

"Committee members, I believe the responsibility is mine to underscore that this conference has attracted people from all kinds of places – some such places we did not know existed before now. On the evidence before us, we are convinced persons with evil intent may well use your conference to visit our shores and seek to set in motion disasters of one kind or the other. We do not now have evidence to support any of the aforementioned, but we must guard against the likely evils of life," she added.

Nathan softly enquired: "My Lady, could you advise what you require of our team?"

In response she smiled and said: "Mr John you must enjoy the best security, as we have been working with Messieurs Suielman and Clarke, and both are well instructed."

She followed this statement with an enquiry of any further questions, and when convinced she had the attention and support of all she and her assistant asked to leave the meeting.

The committee met for another ninety minutes, reviewing the now extensive checklist. On reflection both chairman and co-chairperson agreed that theirs was a most comprehensive checklist, which carried items to be addressed from the very first meeting between them.

All items completed and actioned were so marked, but not removed from the list as Miriam insisted it remained in all members' mindshare. Convinced the committee was ready in all areas of operations, the chair adjourned the meeting and wished everyone a safe journey home.

27

"PEOPLE WHO CONDEMN THOSE WHO HAVE committed crimes within the Church are not necessarily criminals, but are truly sinners. It is not for us to investigate, try and convict these people – it is our responsibility to force these fallen to seek repentance and to be forgiven." In response there was a huge collective ovation of sighs.

The conference was as one voice on the collective of wrong doers. As one unnamed participant declared: "It is not a collective of wrong doers, it is not a battalion of wrong doers – it is an army, a huge army of wrong doers, made up of all genders, races and religions. All these wrong doers cannot be forgiven as if they stole a cookie from the cookie jar. No, people, we are not dealing with people who are in possession of the missing cookies, as sinful as that may be. We are addressing rape, abuse and violence against children. This is not something petty; this is not something for which we turn the other cheek. I have come from a far place, and have come here to seek a measure of justice which I cannot and will not find in the courts of my native country. Yet I am very present, and very much fully aware that this is a conference and not a court of law."

She paused, which gave an opening to a male voice to the rear of the conference floor to shout: "Tell us why you are here."

She looked around, as if hoping to determine who wished to learn why she travelled from far off Eastern Europe to attend a conference in the little known destination of Trinidad and Tobago. Many who attended were just as curious of each other's backgrounds, and the true reason for attendance of a wide and varied attendance register.

The inner circle of the Conference Executive had over the months prior to the conference reviewed with more than passing interest the persons not only enquiring of the conference, but more importantly, Phillip Suielman as one of the convenors stressed the importance to review each actual applicant closely. It was Miriam's father, and now Conference Executive member, who believed greater effort had to be made to discourage applications from applicants who could turn out to be trouble makers. It was Phillip Suielman who not only insisted but demanded that the list of applicants be reviewed as the last item on the agenda, on each Friday leading up to the conference.

Secretly he kept in touch with Anthony, who chaired the Credential Committee, and each recognised the importance of keeping a 'tight lid', on persons registering, whether they came from east, west, north or south. Both men understood the importance of keeping any possible trouble outside the conference doors.

As the tempers began to flare, Phillip, standing at the rear of the hall, called on his walkie-talkie and whispered: "Be ready to move on my signal." Phillip had, with the agreement of all, been asked to head up the Security Committee, he being the eldest, most experienced and gifted from birth with a deep appreciation for safety and security, which he underscored to the Executive Committee from the first day they met.

Neither Nathan nor Miriam, in all of the thousands of thoughts which flowed through their minds, ever gave serious consideration to security being an important agenda item for the hosting of their conference. Both would often look at each other in shock, concern and amazement each time Phillip Suielman gave a reason why an applicant ought not to be approved for conference participation.

His reasoning seemed to suggest that based on a number of factors assessed to be negative indicators, the applicant may have interests that may not be in keeping with the goals and objectives of the conference.

During these sessions each member of the committee was allowed enough time to be heard, and brought to the table their unique senses which either altered or encouraged a reinforcement of a planned course of action. Phillip Suielman, in speaking to the approvals of foreign applications reasoned not why, but why not?

On this morning, a clean-shaven, low-cropped head of hair, with the head sitting on a bull-like structure of a man, continued to rant and rave with the drawl of a mid-west Yankee.

"Tell us why you come here. Tell us why you feel it so important to come to a place like Trinidad to speak about matters un-Godly," he shouted. He continued shouting, and the audience became restless as participants murmured among themselves.

Some not happy with the interruptions by the man, who continued to spew anger, the conference began to respond with shouts of their own.

"Hush, please stop it," a spritely Caucasian woman uttered. Next she rose to her feet and pleaded with the disruptor: "Sir, would you be so kind to allow those of us who wish to participate to get on with our business? If you need a break you are free to have a coffee, which is on the house, kind sir."

As she concluded, the conference erupted with a resounding round of applause. This plea with its mixture of professionalism spiked with sarcasm finally encouraged the gent with the bull-like body to relent.

He sat motionless, no doubt recovering from the polite tongue lashing he received from the little spritely woman who remained on her feet to address the conference. He appeared restless and uneasy as he looked around and shifted in his chair. He crossed his legs left over right, then right over left, at no time focusing on the speaker or the head table.

Throughout the period of the apparent discomfort caused by the man with the bull-like body, Phillip Suielman kept his eyes on him. Within the blink of an eye the man sprang to his feet, looked around the conference floor, turned and made his way to the green room, which was set up to encourage participants to enjoy a cup of tea or coffee and exchange ideas and good will.

Phillip followed him, but not before he said on his walkie-talkie: "Let's keep an eye on him." Phillip saw him now, wearing a conference t-shirt over a long sleeved shirt which read, 'Be the Change, Speak to Your Clergy.'

Phillip smiled, as he was seeing the printed T-shirt for the first time. He knew Miriam had done a lot during her time away, but never imagined she had gone beyond her meetings and into the printing of t-shirts. What Phillip would subsequently learn was the t-shirts represented part of a sponsorship package from the 'eager beavers,' a name Miriam gave to her support group from the upstate New York community of New Rochelle.

The messages on the t-shirts were also the wording of the group, as Miriam, though given to details and admittedly a dotter of Is and crosser of Ts, when asked by Mary Chan Sing if she would supply the wording chuckled and replied: "I am leaving that up to you." Two weeks later, one thousand t-shirts in varying sizes, colours and messages arrived at conference headquarters. The only constant on each t-shirt was a tagline which read: "Changing from impure to pure." When the Executive Committee saw the t-shirts it was unanimously agreed that the conference would adopt those words as the conference's tagline, or, as some suggested, its slogan.

28

INSIDE THE MAIN CONFERENCE HALL THE discussions on the behaviour of the clergy raged, with each participant having their own story to tell. One speaker noted: "I have come from the wilds of Brazil, and I am here not to tell any of you what is right or indeed what is wrong. I have come to this beautiful country and, based on what I have seen, it has a far superior Carnival Festival than my country's. I am here to share with you my story, which is not a good story.

"In my community there are many churches and places of worship. Our churches in our wealthy neighbourhoods are adorned with the most exquisite illustrations of our saints. Our crucifixes are professionally and especially crafted. The walls of these churches are made of the finest stone. The public address systems are so good, and such effectiveness communicates the sound of the sinners of the clergy in clear, uncluttered voice. If you don't know better you could believe it is the voice of the one above." To underscore her point she lifted her hand and pointed her index finger to the sky.

There were no whispers or murmurs, nor were there any interruptions. The lady from Brazil had the floor and the undivided attention of her audience.

She came from a little known community on the fringes of Rio de Janeiro, and her appearance suggested she was in her early middle-aged years and who in her earlier years must have caused many a young man's heart to flutter.

The diction, and the powers of both presentation and more importantly persuasion, created an atmosphere of deep thinking and rapt seriousness experienced for the first time since the conference opened its doors for discussion and debate.

Speaking in a near whisper, she continued: "Make no bones about it, at these churches you could find the best organs, pianos and if you can afford it still have your name placed on a pew. That is, if you could pay for it. In my world, if you have money you could not only rent a seat in the house of God, but you could pay to keep everyone in the community silent if you are a member of the clergy and you rape or abuse a child in the church's sacristy. This power of the clergy over those of us who believe in the upper most high must be reversed. Truth must become more important than the reputation of the church." She ended as if alluding to a personal experience.

The lady from Brazil had used up the time allocated to contributors. She was about to continue, when Nathan, now chairing the conference, said: "We must interrupt you, as you have been on your feet for seven minutes, which is two minutes over the allotted time. We thank you for your contribution, but I do suggest you continue your presentation at the committee stage. I believe the Redeemed Sinners Committee would benefit from what you wish to further share."

Nathan's timing was impeccable. The 'Conference of the Un-Godly' was, as the swizzle stick lady at the Central Market where Miriam and Nathan had their initial meeting would have said, in 'full swing.'

Nathan called the conference to order, and immediately more than a dozen participants were on their feet. He quickly scanned the conference floor, and was about to give the floor to a lady mid-way in the hall, when Miriam touched his elbow and said quietly: "The first person on their feet is the guy to the front, in the green shirt." Nathan needed no persuasion, and he promptly announced. "The chair recognises the gentleman to the front wearing green."

Immediately one of Phillip's team took the mic to the man in green. The conference welcomed him with silence and he promptly began.

"Thank you Mr Chairman. Let me congratulate you and the conference organisers for having the foresight to host this must needed conference. Let me say that the conference addresses in a most creative way the lessons of need versus want. To the person without athlete's foot, athlete's foot is not a very serious illness. But to a person with athlete's foot, he or she is often in pain and often feels very sick. Looking at it another way, some people wake up wondering about a meal, others about making money – I wake up and if I have no pains, aches, I am a very happy man."

The conference did not know where the speaker who held the microphone was taking it, but applauded none the less.

"Friends," he continued, "I am not here to create controversy. It is my hope that my contribution, as small as it may be, will help to fashion a better church. I had hoped my son would have been here with me today, but he elected not to come, as he believes this conference would be only a 'talk shop;' that is how he described the conference.

"He grew up in a Christian family and served as an altar boy in the parish church. Try as I might to convince him otherwise, he will not even look at the same church today. His disinterest in the church began seven years ago, after he came home from a church celebration. He never spoke of any incident, but his disposition to our church had changed. He said to his mother, 'I am never going back to that place,' and when she pressed him what place he finally said to her – 'That church...'

"During the period to present I have watched my son grow from a boy into a man, but a boy who lost his smile and as a man still does not know what a smile is. Even as a man he has not found the winning smile he once had."

The man in the green shirt told the conference it was his hope to have allowed his son to feel and listen to the testimony of the many who have attended, and have spoken what can only be their truths. "Some," he said, "have shouted, others have whispered their innermost thoughts."

This speaker knew he had a story to share, he understood how much athlete's foot had impacted his family's life, but he, despite years of frustrations of not knowing the true nature, knew he had run out of the power of belief.

Before he handed back the microphone and took his seat, he said: "I have seen an unknown event negatively impact our son and change the lives of every member of our family. Despite counselling and counsellors, which cost us resources we did not have, we are yet to know what happened within the parish church that has radically altered the life of our son and family. If today you ask me about my son, I would say to you his absence of faith is as strong as my lack of it."

He took his seat with all eyes focused on him. There was no applause or clapping, nor comment from fellow participants. This last speaker was all illustration of what the 'Conference of the Un-Godly' was all about.

It was finding the facts, both negative and positive, and fixing an impure clergy.

He came to Trinidad for the first time, and he would return to his Canadian suburb a happier person, better equipped to work with his son, who, if he were to have a normal life would have to find the capacity to address the ghost of his youth. As he sat down he knew his takeaway from the conference would be to stop wondering about his son, and despite not returning to parish church he would find the faith he once had and which influenced his life in a strong and positive way.

"The silence which followed his contribution was both a check and balance, and initiated a new direction of contributions," said Viveanna to her friend Miriam, and her conference chairman Nathan. Despite Nathan being a younger man than she, she found him the kind of man who she would look at not once but several times. When she first shared her thoughts about Nathan to Miriam all she got was a smile in return, leaving her to wonder of the true nature of the relationship between her friend and her conference chairman.

Over the months Miriam spent in close proximity to Nathan she never gave consideration to any personal feelings, and she enjoyed the fact that he never made advances towards her. What was very clear and surely obvious to committee members was the spiritual connection between Miriam, who was the mover and shaker of all things, and the conference chairman – Nathan.

As the foursome of Miriam, Viveanna, Dr Stefano and Nathan huddled for a cup of coffee, each had an opinion of the last speaker just before the break.

Listening to Viveanna, both Miriam and Nathan wondered aloud, what was likely to follow? In response Dr Stefano added: "The conference now starts. I am very excited at what is likely to be produced over the next two days."

Suzie was always objective, and she knew her friend Miriam and her colleague Nathan and their respective teams had worked tirelessly to bring their ideas to life. Suzie Steffano had that rare and unique ability to step back and to objectively assess the value of an idea, the strength of a plan and the success of its implementation. Suzie liked what she was seeing, and choked with admiration for this woman, Miriam, her best friend who she felt she had lost.

She smiled to herself, knowing that her friend was not lost and had never been lost. She was very much the cutting edge personality that in the past pulled both she and Viveanna forward when they got stuck, and needed a pillar to lean on and a waiting cart to move them from being stuck in the mud.

She marvelled at the thought that none of the three women sitting enjoying their cups of Hong Wing Coffee – nor Nathan John, the only outsider in the middle – who would ever know what each meant to the other. Above all, they could never fully grasp the magic of Miriam Suielman.

29

"CONFERENCE MEMBERS, I WISH TO DRAW TO YOUR attention that we received ninety-six advanced papers and presentations of various lengths, sizes and details, which will find its way into the final conference report. These documents are available and can be located at the conference centre. We encourage you to bring along your flash drives, or conversely you will be charged a market fee for any storage device of your choice, or naturally you can request to have the same transferred to your cloud account," announced Nathan.

The session opened with the same electricity of the morning session. The man with the bull-shaped body returned to his exact seat he occupied earlier, only this time he wore a conference t-shirt which he no doubt bought. Those who recognised him pointed him out to each other. One of Phillip Suielman's spotters sent him a WhatsApp message, "The bull is back." Immediately Phillip entered the rear door of the hall, where he could see the man who his instincts suggested was a trouble maker and nothing else.

As the floor opened for contributions there were dozens of participants who simultaneously sought the attention of the conference chairman. Nathan, recognising the difficulty he now had in identifying an order to the standing participants, announced: "All participants wishing to be heard are requested to queue behind the twelve microphones, strategically located within the auditorium."

Those standing effortlessly moved to the microphones and queued, underscoring organisation and a sense of discipline at the conference.

With the movement of participants, Nathan observed that Miriam was not in her chair seated next to him as she had done the day before during the first day's sessions. He spontaneously raised his head and began searching the conference floor to locate her. He saw no image of Miriam, who came to the conference dressed as she had done for the past six years, in her modest attire and her now recognisable smiling face with her head covered with her hijab. Nathan's eyes searched the conference floor row by row, and he did same with the aisles, but he could not locate Miriam.

In the matter of time, Miriam had been his teacher.

She insisted: "Time is precious; it is like money, you don't waste it."

All who knew Miriam learned the hard way her importance with late arrivals. Both Viveanna and Suzie, as younger women, often joked with Miriam that time will one day get the better of her, but she won out in the end, enforcing a rigidity in time keeping which soon became the way the trio did business.

Miriam, as she spent more time with Viveanna, shared with her the discipline of keeping time that was drilled into her by her mother. This became a way of life for Viveanna who grasped with all her spirit the significance of time and its importance of time to the professionalism she chose to live.

If time mattered so much to Miriam, where was she at this moment, as the conference was about to resume following a reasonably strong first day? It was not only Nathan who could not find his co-chair – all who cared for Miriam Suielman were beginning to enquire, as if her absence from the head table was observed not only by Nathan but by all who cared even a little bit for her.

Nathan pressed on with the conference, knowing that Miriam might have insisted: "Regardless of what, we begin on time." Nathan scanned the floor, and invited the person who wore white cotton loosely fitted pants and an equally loose fitted white top with an orange turban. Thus the first speaker on day two was a person wearing a turban, which is common attire for Sikhs of Punjab of India. Did he come all the way from India? Nathan wondered, and hoped to learn the participant's origin during his contribution. As the speaker said good morning, Nathan interrupted with an apology to remind contributors that each was being given no more than seven minutes to make contributions, given the demands of the conference agenda.

With the floor given to him, the man from Punjab, India, said: "Good morning for the second time," for which he elicited chuckles from some members. "Friends, let me state from the onset that this conference is not a holiday for me, though it ought to be. As I walk across this beautiful city of Port-of-Spain, I can't help but wonder how so many of my ancestors would have risked crossing the great seas to come to Trinidad. Each moment I have spent here so far suggests to me that regardless of what you believe there must be God, as I have met so many kind people – not only Indians whose roots are in Trinidad but whose ancestors are from the homeland of India. I never knew, in my ignorance, the importance of religion nor the impact it has on the truly spiritual nor in being part of this spiritual event, and that I would be forced to confront myself with what a conference with a title, 'Conference of the Un-Godly', with a tagline 'Changing from Impure to Pure', would be.

Yes, the message which is carried on T-shirts I have seen all over, and which some of us are wearing. This message is worth sharing across the world. Think of the message: 'Be the change, speak to your clergy.'

"Chairman John, I commend you and the conference for these two simple messages, which if any reasonable man, woman or clergy were to assimilate, they would come to realise that abuse or wickedness has no place in spiritual work, nor in any holy place of worship. Chairman, fellow participants, I encourage you to study my own spirituality. I will not impose the teachings of the Sikh on this conference, but make no bones of it, my spiritual space also has its weaknesses which must be rooted out," he added.

"We live in a terrible world, we live in terrible spaces. We live in space now dominated with and by wealth. People today will do anything for money, and so we must teach to our flock, which include our spiritual leaders, that 'You cannot have what you want, if you don't want what you already possess.' We can only find peace in understanding what we possess, and the importance of these possessions as instruments for a better world," he expanded. "What we need to do as spiritual leaders is to choose to do good and right in all matters, and we must forever resist the temptations to encourage hurt and suffering at all times."

He paused and turned to look at the clock on the western wall of the conference hall, and recognising he was well over his allocated time he said: "Mr Chair, I apologise for going over the time given to me, but you ought to have stopped me. Chairman, I thank you for inviting me to Trinidad and Tobago and for hosting a much needed spiritual awakening. I am Amanpreet, the one from Punjab, India," and he quickly took his seat to lusty applause.

Participants came to the microphone and told their stories, some of hate and bitterness, while others sought clarity on infractions and criminal activity committed by clergy of various religious platforms.

"If I felt sad over the revelations of abuse within Christianity I have fashioned, after two days at conference I am more dejected and saddened that I was when I conceptualised the notion of a 'Conference of the Un-Godly,'" Nathan said to Anthony, as they met within the office of the conference administrators. Nathan was not elated at the end of day two. Apart from the steady volume of dirt, pain and suffering which came out of the hearts and lips of so many participants, the details and information, looking at it from any perspective, grew sadder and encouraged an atmosphere of grief, which weighed heavily on too many participants.

Nathan and Anthony looked tired, but while Anthony remained with a buoyed spirit, Nathan wore his experiences of the day and conveyed unhappiness and grief.

Sitting with Anthony and having sipped his coffee, he remembered Miriam. He got up without saying anything and bolted, looking for Phillip Suielman to enquire of his daughter's well-being.

Nathan saw Phillip surrounded by a number of Conference Committee members and his heart missed a beat as he feared the worst for Miriam, for whom he kept his feelings tightly covered like a boiling pressure cooker.

He approached the circle and gently parted Justin and Jennene to join the conversation, as he anticipated the discussion was about the absence of Miriam from the day's conference. He chose not to ask questions, and listened hoping he would learn what kept the conference's heart and spirit away from the second of three days.

Earlier in the day, as he allowed his mind the luxury to wonder from the hundred who sat and stood before him with each person demanding his attention, he wondered what could have kept Miriam away. At his moment he thought the worst, and then he dismissed these negatives out of fear that just thinking such thoughts could give life to hurts he never wished upon his co-chairman, organiser, counsel, and "Yes, my special friend."

Many hours later, he was about to learn what kept her away from the job she chose.

Phillip Suielman spoke in a measured voice, and in a tone different from the one all committee members had become used to hearing. There was no swagger in his delivery – it was almost corporate, if one could ever describe a contribution by Phillip Suielman as being officious. He was a Woodbrook person through and through, one who loved his steelpan, his calypso and his Carnival. The truth be exposed, so too did his daughter, who had buried all these urges for the sake of her marriage to Thomas.

Now he explained: "Early this morning, Miriam was about to leave home when she was alerted by a neighbour that another of her neighbours was asking for her, as she needed assistance." He continued: "It turned out the neighbour in question is a woman with whom Miriam respected and enjoyed a healthy relationship. Miriam, on her way to our conference, visited with her neighbour Avalon, who lives four houses above Miriam's home. She befriended her six years earlier, and throughout those years Avalon looked up to Miriam – a woman many years her junior. She measured Miriam not by the colour of her skin as others had done, but by the warmth and people-ness of the spirit she generated.

"On this morning she knew she needed urgent assistance, and she knew the one person who would render the required relief was Miriam. And so she waited as she so often did, sat tight and listened to hear the first footsteps coming down the hill. When she finally heard such footsteps, she called out: 'Neighbour, neighbour, you going downhill?' To which the passer-by replied: 'Yes ah going to market.'

"In response Avalon shouted with all the strength she could muster: 'Could you tell Miriam I need to see her urgently?' The passer-by enquired: 'Who is Miriam?' Avalon was about to faint, and responded, 'The lady four houses down. Dey does call she Whitey,' she stammered. The message arrived, and Miriam as anticipated knocked on Avalon's unlocked door.

As she knocked, Avalon said: "Miriam girl, ah goh dead ah real sick."

When she saw her neighbour she could not believe this was the same spritely woman who always called out to her each time she passed her home. Avalon, a Black woman, was now ashen, gaunt in facial expression, had lost weight and was having trouble breathing. In summary she gave a death like appearance, and it frightened Miriam.

Avalon was correct in her judgement in reaching out to Miriam, who quickly determined the seriousness of Avalon's condition and was on the phone calling a familiar number. The person who answered was capable of bringing relief to the sick and distressed. Miriam explained to her mother what she saw, and in response Dr Sammoy enquired: "Does she have fever?"

Miriam went silent as she felt Avalon's forehead, and immediately said: "Yes she is very hot, and her pulse is very slow." Dr Sammoy did not say another word and Miriam knew her mother was on the way.

With her mother on the way Miriam's thoughts drifted, and she remembered her mother did not know where she lived. Immediately she called her mother back, who as she answered said: "You have to give me the directions to get to you."

Dr Sammoy entered the small wooden structure, largely made of ply boards and storage platforms, but she did not see the environment. She came to see a sick woman and to render professional service.

Miriam marvelled at the thoroughness of the questions and the examination. She at this moment became her mother's assistant, and enjoyed the feeling that she could be of support to Dr Sammoy at a moment such as this.

Dr Sammoy, after what seemed like a lifetime of questions and examinations, said to Avalon that she needed to be at a hospital, where a number of tests could be conducted which she could not do without specialised equipment.

Dr Sammoy enquired of Miriam: "You will be late for the conference?"

To which query Miriam replied: "Mom, I could not leave Avalon, as she has no other support." And with that they were off to the Port-of-Spain General Hospital. There Dr Sammoy used not only her name, but also face recognition to facilitate a smooth passage for Avalon from Accident and Emergency, or Casualty as it is called in Port-of-Spain, and got her settled on the internal medicine ward, where she assisted with the series of tests required.

Miriam observed her mother's quiet but effective approach to getting things done and even as she assisted the medical doctor in charge, it was difficult for the uninitiated to determine who was resident in charge and who was visiting.

A process which began at 10:00am finally concluded at minutes after two pm, and when Dr Sammoy was assured that Miriam's neighbour Avalon would be in good hands, they looked at each other and knew it was time to go.

Dr Sammoy looked at her daughter, who appeared exhausted, and like daughter so too Dr Sammoy was equally exhausted.

"Do you want me to take you to the conference?" Dr Sammoy asked Miriam, who seemed to be in deep thoughts.

Her mother smiled, thinking her daughter was in her mind at her 'Conference of the Un-Godly.'

Both women looked at each other. The older and wiser knew what to expect, but said nothing to the younger, who had grown in wisdom and replied: "No, the day is almost over. I will hear soon enough of the day and its successes or failures."

"Could we go grab an ice cream? And at the same time I will get some for my six, who all love the homemade ice cream at Panka Street, St James."

Miriam knew her absence from the conference would be noted by all, and she entertained the thought that Nathan would be furious if he knew the reason she missed the all-important day two.

She hoped her dad would return home early, as she trusted him to give a sound account of the day's proceedings. She wanted to call Nathan to question him of each hour of each segment, but finally decided against such action. She did not wish to hear Nathan ask: "How could you miss the conference over something Dr Sammoy could have easily attended to?"

"No," she said aloud, speaking to herself. "She could not attend to Avalon, I had to be present."

Dr Sammoy looked at her and wondered who occupied her daughter's mind share. She heard the last sentence of her daughter's outburst and she knew her mind was back in her conference, but what she could not discern was precisely who haunted her daughter's thoughts which caused her to blurt out her innermost feelings as she did.

Knowingly Dr Sammoy smiled, as she appreciated her daughter felt comfortable to be herself in her presence even if she did not willingly share her story. She understood the need to exhale, and while she smiled and sought to convince herself all was well with Miriam, she knew she would with time seek to encourage her daughter to share some of her burdens.

Dr Sammoy went silent for a moment as she reflected on her visit to Avalon, and it dawned on her that despite her visit to Avalon's home she had never visited with her daughter. Such thoughts pulled her apart, as she wanted to understand everything about Miriam.

Over the past six years she agonised of the distance between her daughter, she and Phillip. Now with the conference, which she did not support openly, her family was finally becoming a family, and she would do nothing to disturb the growing harmony.

Miriam got herself a medium sized tub of peanut and a small tub of soursop ice cream, and for her mother and father she bought a medium tub of coconut ice cream.

Upon her arrival at home she greeted her brood of six, who demonstrated all the signs of having settled into Goodwood Park, without giving a sense of having missed their mother or father. Neither sisters nor brothers spoke of their father during the days shared with their grandparents, and this intrigued Miriam.

This was the second visit of the children to their grandparents within a three month period. As Grandmother Sammoy said to Grandfather Phillip: "If we keep praying, we will one day get to enjoy much more of our grandchildren." Despite her feelings on the 'Conference of the Un-Godly,' it had opened the door for reunification of daughter and grandchildren with she and their grandfather. She talked to herself quietly: "Thank you dear Father for these huge blessings. Thank you for bringing her back to us, and above all thank you for our lovely grandchildren," said Dr Sammoy.

30

PHILLIP SUIELMAN, DURING HIS WINDING DOWN OF the operations of day two of the conference, moved methodically from room to room to ensure all spaces were secure. As he had done during the last week, he would check the committee room last and would normally end up in a discussion with his daughter, Nathan, Anthony and others.

It was still early evening. The sun was bright outside, and the setting sun pierced through the glass walls of the committee room, lighting it an almost orange glow. Phillip liked the light of Port-of-Spain's sunsets, and would sit holding the hand of his Dr Sammoy on evenings, enjoying the sunset on the west coast of Trinidad.

Both mother and father had taught their daughter the beauty of the setting sun, and encouraged her to pause ever so often to allow reflection on the rays of the sun, which so slowly said goodbye each evening only to say hello with each new day.

He entered the committee room and all eyes were on him. Those present wanted to know, what was the final news on Avalon, Miriam's friend? And more importantly, what happened to Miriam?

Phillip advised that he did not have additional information, but assured his colleagues: "I am sure she is alive and well."

The team held its usual daily post-mortem, with some members concluding that the second day opened many wounds and set the stage for a fiery final and third day of the conference.

Anthony, who managed the Credential Committee, remained focused during the months and weeks leading to where they now found themselves, with one day to go to bring the curtain down on a job many outside the committee found was beyond it.

Anthony knew first-hand the contributions made by Phillip Suielman to all the areas of the organisation and administration of the conference, but he particularly acknowledged Phillip's focus on security and his insistence in taking steps to ensure there were no actions by any participant to ruin the proceedings of the 'Conference of the Un-Godly.'

Today he raised with Phillip his concerns over a cluster of participants, who arrived separately over the last three days and who registered separately but appeared to know each other well. They sat together, and kept a specific number of seats vacant as if expecting colleagues.

When Anthony raised his concerns Phillip did not fully grasp what was on his mind.

"I don't think you appreciate my concerns. These six men have all registered upon arrival. Each arrived separately, but upon registration specifically enquired of the five other registrants and further enquired where they could be found. All five have unusual names, and all originated from the same location in Europe," he added.

Anthony paused to encourage a response from Phillip, who seemed to be lost for words. This silence was just the energy Phillip needed to respond to Anthony's observations. Anthony was about to speak when Phillip put his finger to his lips, and enquired: "Do you have their registration forms?"

Anthony, forever ready, handed Phillip a stack of papers all containing the information Phillip needed.

In between reading, he enquired: "What do these people look like and where are they staying?"

Having read the information on the forms before him, Phillip could make no case for alarm. Yet he believed Anthony's concerns were valid. He reread each form looking for clues that would give him a reason to join Anthony in his belief that something was amiss.

Upon his third reading of the forms he observed that on the forms before him the registrant omitted to fill in his religion. This struck Phillip as being odd; participants did not leave this question blank, as some who did not practice a religion merely wrote none.

Phillip hurriedly looked through the remaining five forms, which showed similar responses. Phillip also noted that all six forms carried blanks to the question: 'Where will you be staying during the conference?'

"This means this group of six could at this time be anywhere within the city of Port-of-Spain, or roaming across Trinidad and Tobago doing God alone knows what," said Phillip to Anthony, with a worried look on his face.

Both discussed the data and finally agreed to contact the security co-ordinator of the Police Service, who was assigned to work with the conference's co-ordinating team. When Phillip telephoned the senior superintendent she answered her phone following three rings. Phillip responded immediately and said: "Senior, this is Phillip Suielman from the religious conference."

She replied, "Mr Suielman, good evening. How is the conference going?"

Phillip explained his concerns, and in response she said: "Other than your concerns, did they do anything to suggest they are trouble makers?"

Phillip paused, processed his thoughts, and responded: "My lady, it is not what they did, it is what they did not do that troubles us. Of the fourteen hundred and thirty-nine participants registered, of which they are six, they are the only participants who did not fill in two telling questions on our registration form, and that suggests something out of the ordinary. You will recall your instructions to our security team to report anything out of the ordinary. If two of the six did not fill in the address question I would not be calling you."

Before Phillip could speak further the senior superintendent interjected: "Mr Sueilman, I understand, and we will look into this matter."

Phillip responded without fluff: "Thank you Senior, good night." As he hung up on the senior police officer he looked at Anthony and hunched his shoulders, to exude both concern and uncertainty.

Both agreed to leave the matter to the authorities, but would keep focus on the six throughout the last day of the conference.

Like the others, Anthony was beginning to feel the wear of the week. As he faced Phillip they looked at each other and both men were a mirror of the other. Each had been on the go for near nine months, and each had a bigger stake in ensuring everything was done to make the conference a huge success.

Anthony never said it to anyone, but from the moment he met Nathan John, near a year earlier, he secretly adopted him as the son he wished for but never had. Nathan was, in his mind, regal. He spoke softly but by no means effeminately. His speech was that of someone trained and well educated, and more importantly his general demeanour suggested to those who met him that he, as the locals would say: "comes from good stock." Anthony signed on to assist this young man Nathan, having had a chance meeting and a lengthy phone conversation. Now he was in 'the thick of things,' knowing that though there was one day left, this 'Conference of the Un-Godly' would continue for a long time beyond tomorrow.

Phillip, the other part of the pair, had listened to his daughter's innermost thoughts on why she signed on to assist the boy Nathan John. Phillip in turn, on the explanations of his beloved Miriam, climbed aboard the boat knowing it was an uncertain journey, with likely ups, and yes, an even greater number of downs.

Phillip like Anthony had bought horses in the race, and each wanted the duo of Miriam and Nathan to do well. They in turn worked tirelessly over the months to dot Is and cross Ts, guaranteeing the successful hosting of a conference no one worldwide had yet to conceive. At the other end of the spectrum, no one in tiny Port-of-Spain, Trinidad, not the Inter Religious Organisation (or IRO), nor the government, could have contemplated the success of this conference.

With all its expenditure to woo tourists and visitors to the twin island nation, it had not been successful in encouraging upwards of three hundred visitors to visit for a single event outside its hosting of Carnival, which it was strongly felt was a most impious affair.

By the time Anthony and Phillip re-engaged having emerged from their personal thoughts, the other committee members were getting ready to depart. Anthony begged a ride to his junction from Everton, who lived at Arima and would pass the Trincity Mall, where Anthony was only too happy to be taken. From this location he would walk the remaining one and near half of a mile to his home. He often did this as he enjoyed the exercise, while the walking outdoors gave him time and space to think, and he had a lot to think over after day two ended.

As Anthony was nearing his home in East Trinidad, Phillip, who had coerced Nathan to travel home with him, was arriving at his Goodwood Park home in West Trinidad. In all of this it was Nathan who was troubled, as he just did not know how he would find transportation to get to his home in Los Bajos. He was equally excited as he hoped to see his soul mate Miriam, and to personally learn of her well-being, but above all to share with her the efforts of the day's activities at "their" conference.

Phillip opened the kitchen door of his family's home and stepped aside. As he did so with one motion with his right hand, which held the door keys, he beckoned Nathan with a shoulder to hip wave to enter.

Nathan thoughtfully felt it inappropriate that he should enter Phillip's home ahead of him, despite being invited to do so, and waved to Phillip an invitation to enter his home first.

Inside the Suielmans', Miriam and her besties, Dr Suzie Stefano and the constant Viveanna, stood in line to greet Phillip and looked forward to being updated on the day's events. When Miriam and the group realised that Phillip was not alone and had brought Nathan John home with him, the women in residence at the Suielmans' went into uproar, largely in response to Miriam's remark: "Look what the cat dragged in."

Miriam embraced her father, and as she did so she whispered to him: "Thanks Pops, thank you so much." She next thrust herself forward to greet Nathan, and to the surprise of everyone she was clinging to Nathan with a hug Muslim women reserve for their spouses, within the privacy of their homes out of the eyes of all others. To the onlooker what they saw was not what they got.

Miriam was just happy after a long unplanned day to be sharing the moment with one who she had begun to reason had, knowingly or unknowingly, begun her own liberation from a rigid religious lifestyle, which she determined was suffocating who she believed she was meant to be.

In this person Nathan John was something she embraced, and together their joint efforts had produced perhaps the most meaningful development the range of spiritual and religious organisations had witnessed in the history of Trinidad and Tobago.

Miriam knew all the indistinct chatter at and in and around Rose Hill and environs required urgent action, if the society which resided in East Port-of-Spain were to be brought on par with the wider, more entrenched element of society. She also knew that religion was insidious to the well-being of the greater society. Equally she knew that the number of destitute who roamed Port- of-Spain would continue to grow in number, as the evidence suggested it was in the interest of the Church's shepherds to be seen to be ever helpful to the downtrodden and destitute.

On the other side, Nathan, in his much younger mind, was more focused on the evils of religion. Melded, he and Miriam became a most potent force for change in a small society that got news from the outside world very quickly and viewed and read the news with passion.

The 'Conference of the Un-Godly' was twice featured on the major networks, they having local representatives, who all clamoured for up close and personal interviews with Nathan, the boy who began it all, and Miriam, the white-skinned Muslim woman who lived at Rose Hill, East Dry River.

The committee of the 'Conference of the Un-Godly' had taken the decision that all information about the conference and/or its organisers would be disseminated in an organised manner. The committee was particularly firm that neither Miriam nor Nathan were to give off the cuff interviews, as these were the communications that were more often than not taken out of context, badly interpreted and presented, with the result of challenges for the persons making the statement having to spend unnecessary time in rebutting. This, the committee agreed, was not necessary, and given the skeleton of the conference did not wish to be caught off guard.

Neither Miriam nor Nathan opposed the approach, though along the way it would be Nathan who would most often breach the established code.

Nathan, in a fit of anxiety one evening at the corner of Independence Square and Henry Street, Port-of-Spain, would hotly say to a daily newspaper reporter: "If you people were doing your work uncovering wrongdoing within places of worship, we would not have to be spending time organising the very conference of which you are being overzealously critical."

Nathan had been baited by the particular news reporter for weeks, and Nathan's obvious silence encouraged far more attention than he deserved.

What followed, neither Nathan nor the committee anticipated.

The newspaper's front page headline read: "Newspaper accused of cover up of wrongdoing in local churches." To respond meant the committee would be forced to use its limited resources to engage in a war it could not win. The committee issued a tersely worded statement neither denying nor confirming the statement of its chairman, but noted his comments were unfortunately misinterpreted.

The committee moved on, having reminded its co-chairman of the need to exercise more prudence with members of the media.

Since that headline the conference organisers were able to adroitly negotiate their way with the media.

Tonight the co-chairpersons sat together, each remembering their first meeting at the Central Market. So much good had come of the meeting – Miriam was no longer lost, she had found her way home, and the conference, which was at that time an idea in the heart and mind of Nathan John, was well on its way to becoming a landmark in the reviews of religion.

Phillip and Nathan briefed the group of all that transpired during the day's conference.

Miriam asked questions about the Credential Report. Viveanna had already said to her not once but thrice that she felt the numbers were greater than the first day, yet still she asked questions of Nathan.

Viveanna could not let this pass, and immediately responded: "Madam, since when do you not believe information given to you by me?"

And the question of how many were in attendance came to an abrupt end.

Strangely, the atmosphere on the night of the second day, despite the obvious accomplishments of day two, was neither celebratory nor lacklustre. It was one which mirrored seamen on board an uncertain vessel, sailing calm waters with their port on the horizon, with each sailor fully aware of his duty to himself and to every individual sailor aboard. Each knew the conference would officially come to an end at 6:00pm at the latest the following day, with some participants electing to attend a field trip on the sister island of Tobago, while other visitors would be leaving for their respective home destinations, and still others elected to remain in Port-of-Spain getting to know a little bit about the rich history of the capital city.

However, for many the day after tomorrow underscored the true reason for being in Port-of-Spain – to attend and participate in Anthony's Redeemed Sinners Forum.

Nathan began smiling as if tickled with a classic joke, of which he and Anthony always had one to break the ice when discussions got rough. This time when pressed by Miriam to "share," he revealed that a participant from New Orleans stopped him to enquire of the Lapeyrouse Cemetery, as he had read that a former mayor of the city once described it as a memory book of the Republic's better days. Miriam, with her persuasive look, enquired: "What did you say in response?"

Nathan once again smiled and said: "That the mayor was one of our progressive minds, and if I may add I agree with him, but don't expect the memories at Lapeyrouse to be kept as orderly as they ought to be kept. Our order keepers are not as diligent as the then mayor would have wished, but there are many good memories and these are not going anywhere soon."

Miriam appeared bowled over by the issue of Lapeyrouse Cemetery turning up as a topic at the 'Conference of the Un-Godly,' and in response she said: "To think the tourism minister didn't see a connection between our conference and visitors."

Miriam, despite her earlier challenges, was fired up by the news of the day. Having listened to her father and conference chairman she secretly had great expectations for the final day. Attendance had grown during the second day, over the first day, and she could not forget the words of her father: "If more people attend we will have no place to put them."

Following a light evening meal Nathan asked to be excused as he needed to get home to Los Bajos, it not being next door. Phillip Suielman as always began with the end in mind, and knew it would be inappropriate to offer Nathan a room at Goodwood Park. He handed Nathan a room key and advised him that he should stay at the hotel tonight, given the work ahead of him in the morning. In handing over the key he said: "This is courtesy of Phillip Suielman and Sons Limited."

Phillip knew both Nathan and Miriam had made it a law within the committee that the conference would not pay for rooms for members wishing to overnight at the conference hotel.

Rubbing salt in the wound, Phillip added: "And you getting the lovely Dr Stefano to take you back to the hotel."

In response Nathan laughed his first real laugh for the day. He thanked his host, bid farewell to his colleagues and left the luxury of Goodwood Park for his one night of luxury at the leading Port-of-Spain hotel.

31

MIRIAM'S ABSENCE FROM DAY TWO OF THE conference, though not significant to all conference attendees, was of great significance to a small group of locals headed by a very athletic young man who walked and talked with unparalleled authority.

His group of approximately fifteen was seated ten rows down from the head table, and though fifteen in number occupied two rows of chairs. The leader sat in the middle of the fourteen, and while they wore corporate clothing their demeanour suggested they were of a religious sect.

Prior to the beginning of the morning session of day three, one of Phillip's spotters said to him that he wanted Phillip to observe the group, as something about their conduct disturbed him. He could not put his finger on what caused his anxiety, but he needed another opinion.

Phillip did indeed respond, and upon reviewing each individual stopped at a young handsome brown skinned man, of slim build and sharp facial features. Phillip finally smiled, knowing that the person who he was staring at was indeed a person of interest, and one in another space would have been clothed in Muslim attire. Today, Thomas his son-in-law was attending his wife's and Philip's daughter's conference dressed as would any of the Pentecostal pastors. All signs suggested Thomas had come in disguise.

Phillip reasoned that for him to have forsaken his Muslim wear meant he did not wish to draw attention to himself, and in these circumstances he knew he had to share this with the executive team.

When Phillip broke the news to his daughter she became flushed. She was red all over. On reflection, it might have been the way her father shared the news.

With Nathan and Miriam at the conference head table, settling in to open the day's proceedings, Phillip stooped between both and whispered, "Your husband is here."

To which Miriam replied, "Whose husband is here?"

Phillip curtly responded: "Thomas."

Miriam quickly adjusted to the reality that today she would know what troubles were on the mind of her Muslim husband. In the context of the 'Conference of the Un-Godly,' the only connection she surmised would entertain his interests was what would be said of Muslims and Islam.

"Dad, just where can I find Thomas?" asked Miriam, and once told where he was seated, she asked Nathan to give them a few minutes as she wished to speak with her husband.

Thomas saw her coming to his row of chairs and immediately got up, not to only greet her, but also because he did not wish to have his colleagues hear his conversation with his wife. His judgement was sound, as Miriam never gave him an opportunity to speak.

She looked at him with disdain. She could not accept that Thomas, in all his Muslim-ness, would attend a conference based on religion and not dress as he did in his Muslim clothing. It is in this context she spoke to her husband.

"You are here. Welcome. It would have been nice if you had come by the committee centre to say hello and to explain your appearance. No Muslim clothing this morning, does that mean you left Islam? Thomas, is it not that you are spying on your wife? Maybe I ought to share this revelation with the conference."

During all her remarks, she never gave Thomas an opportunity to speak.

"And I see you have dragged in a bunch of your group – have they also lost faith with Islam? Really Thomas, you are too much," she ended, and left her dumbfounded husband standing in the aisle ten rows behind his colleagues.

As she turned and walked away, the soundness of her observations reached him deep within his stomach. What he saw as she strode ahead was the most beautiful Muslim woman dressed as a Muslim woman should dress, and yet he, blinded by the frustrations of unwarranted jealousy, changed his wardrobe from Muslim to conceal who he was, and registered under an assumed name, as he had hoped to find his wife in wrongdoing.

Thomas attended all of day two but did not hear a single speaker. His focus was on the empty chair next to the conference chairman. During the eight hours, he got up as many times to prowl through the conference hall meeting rooms in search of Miriam. He expected to find her all dressed up in some fancy American outfit. He also expected to find out who was the person responsible for "encouraging" her to stray, or so he wrongfully convinced himself.

Finally that evening, when he returned to Rose Hill, he learned of Miriam and Dr Sammoy's assistance to neighbour Avalon. For this good deed, all of Rose Hill was hailing his wife a "boss lady." As painful as it was Thomas slept through the night, even more anxious of what the final day of the conference would usher into his life.

Still not convinced that his wife's conference was forced by her good neighbourly actions, he donned his suit and tie with the expectation that he would be present and not seen. This did not work, nor did it amuse Miriam – he realised perhaps too late that he did not have a leg to stand on.

Miriam returned to her seat and said to Nathan: "The devil works in all kinds of ways." Each looked the other in the eyes and smiled, conscious that the most important of the three days of conference was ahead and immediate recent revelations had delayed the start of the third day's work.

Miriam would later learn the actions of her husband began the day before, and she surmised her absence from the conference, which had only to do with the need to give support to Avalon their neighbour, must have caused Thomas untold moments of worry.

As she settled into her seat Miriam was deep in thought. She weighed thoughts of yesterday, today and tomorrow.

Nathan on the other hand was anchored with the work before them, and without much fanfare he elbowed Miriam to suggest time to begin. With that they began a day that would be remembered by the fourteen hundred participants who crowded every available space.

In this regard one newspaper writer noted: "Port-of-Spain hosts its biggest ever international conference, which was characterised by a sharing of information and camaraderie never before seen at an international forum."

Prior to this conference, the naysayers cried doom and gloom. The 'Conference of the Un-Godly' reached into the hearts and spirits of all in attendance, and in the process buried defeatism and created an epiphany of the possibilities to force all wrongdoers to account for their individual and collective misdeeds.

To the onlooker, the events unfolding must have been viewed as a parley of all the opposing forces, meeting as it were to find answers to the cacophony of evil committed by religion and in the name of religious leaders.

Nathan stood and said: "Good morning good people," and the loud chatter almost disappeared.

Continuing, Nathan said: "Friends, we have much to do today and tomorrow before our first conference comes to an end." As he said 'first conference' he looked at Miriam, who returned his look with opened eyes of appreciation. They had never discussed another follow up or annual conference, but Nathan without discussion grasped the moment and placed the matter artfully on the agenda.

"Friends, we have covered much ground during our first two days, and beyond a very tough agenda today we have our own breakout committee session tomorrow, which I assure you will assist you to lift your burdens off your shoulders.

"Today then is about you, about your concerns, about your neighbours, friends and relatives. The agenda is about the children, your children, your neighbour's children, the children you don't know who have suffered at the hands of people who should know better and who were given the responsibility to take care of these children.

"The data – note well I state data, and not stories or reports – all point us in a single direction. As an international village we have been at the mercy of the church, temple, mosque and other umbrellas of worship. Our children have been victims. Our boys as well as girls have been abused, physically and psychologically. Those who believe we are evil for speaking to truths are living in a state of fear that our conference will shatter the glass of the conspiracy against the weak and unprotected.

"Further, I wish to underscore that our concerns for the victim goes beyond religion. This assault on our families, women and children happens each day, each night, by companions, spouses, aunts and uncles, siblings and the list goes on. Yes, there is a consistency of wickedness, which runs as deep as it runs wide – ultimately destroying all it touches, and in some places it has remained as deadly as any other plague or pandemic for generations. Friends, the wickedness of incest is not a disease as some would have us believe – it is a violent and most vicious crime, which must be both stopped and punished.

"I say to you this morning, while we give focus to the abuse of our children, be it by the clergy, the teacher, the caregiver or the brother, sister, aunt, uncle or mother or father, and this list is endless, we must never forget the seeds of all this evil begins in our hearts and minds. And if this conference achieves one thing, it must be to find the ways and means to begin the process to give meaning to the words, 'Closer to the Church.'

"I believe it was Mark Twain who wrote: 'The two most important days in your life are the day you are born and the day you find out why.' If this be true, let us all find out today that the near two thousand of us present here at the Conference of the Un-Godly, were born to bring the evil of religion, after thousands of years of injustices and crimes against the weak and innocent, to an end by our individual and collective efforts. We must commit that today we know our birth was not meaningless but meaningful, and given to ferreting out of dark places such information that will define this period in history as the moment when we the people took a stand against the un-godly.

"I note well all the kind comments made of our country, but I assure you we do have our own troubles, which have been documented and can be found in your package of papers. We have reserved conference time for our visitors, but I assure you when our final report is documented it will embrace all the contributions that are serious and uplifting in intent.

"I believe it is appropriate and relevant to remind you the way of the wicked is darkness – they know not at what they stumble.

"What do we know, good people, and what stumbles are we likely to make in reviewing and examining in an objective way the data we possess, both by first hand experiences and the reports made to law enforcement of the highest levels of clergy across the world? We know enough to call to order this objective review, which must set the stage for a truly international review, and when it is done our work carried out over the last two days will be at the top of the agenda."

Without another word Nathan said: "I thank you," and took his seat. Nathan received a sustained applause, during which Miriam elbowed him both in support and congratulations.

His opening address set the stage for a 'day of fire,' as Suzie had prophesised, and if ever the spilling of the blood of the innocent was on the agenda for discussion and debate and decisive action. This was the time and place, and Nathan had skilfully made the case for all to grasp.

32

NATHAN ROSE FROM HIS SEAT ONCE MORE, THIS time to begin receiving contributions from the floor of the conference. As he rose to his feet the conference became silent. Reverence for the chairman had improved over the days as the conference goers became familiar with Nathan's calming spirit.

"Colleagues, kindly note the standing order of the two previous days has been adjusted. You are entitled to five minutes on the floor, and we ask that if you cannot complete your contribution within the established time that you make your document available to us at the secretariat."

Nathan got up once again, this time to acknowledge the overflowing auditorium of attendees, conscious that what the 'Conference of the Un-Godly' needed on it final day was a combination of truth and sincerity mixed with integrity and purpose, stirred with the passions of every religion, race and nationality represented.

He as conductor of the orchestra had the responsibility to guide the beat rhythm and tempo of the movement. During his quiet lonely moment, surrounded by the luxury of his five star accommodation, he had time to confront the final day's events and he saw before him a body that was not fully alive. He was driven to accept his mission from the one above, which must be to create a living organism of the multitude to become agents for good and for God.

His actions he knew were not his, but of the one who sent him long ago to repair the filters and position them to strain the evil, filth, anger, hate and bitterness from the spirit of man. And further, to assist the conference with one voice to reject the un-godly acts and actions of men and women who had chosen to serve in the interest of the most high, but had over the centuries documented so much hurt and bitterness to his children as grievous as the lashes and thorns inflicted upon he who walked on earth.

Nathan knew that the one who sent him would guide and direct him. As he looked across the hundreds of occupied padded chairs and side aisles, all overflowing with enthusiastic wide eyed participants, he said: "As we open the floor to contributors this morning I ask you to say to me with one voice, why are we here this morning?" And in response with one voice, thousands of unprompted spirits responded: "For God."

Driven, Nathan said: "I have one more question for you – will the work of the 'Conference of the Un-Godly' end today?" The response again came as if being sung by a well-rehearsed choir. "Never, never, never," was the refrain. The questions and answers was the magic Nathan sought over the first two days, and he finally knew he had found it as he called his first participant to the floor.

The lady who stood at the mic was of mixed race, and by her accent was of Trinidad and Tobago. She stood five feet ten inches, and was of slim build. She wore a business suit, grey in colour with her skirt flowing to her calves. On the surface she carried herself as if she came from affluence, but Nathan had learned over the months to neither judge a person by their clothes nor their demeanour, as both could lead you to arrive at inaccuracies.

Nathan hoped that as the first speaker on the closing day, she would burn brightly all day.

The lady wearing the grey business suit also had her hair covered in a head tie, which was common among religious working class Africans within Port-of-Spain. She held a clipboard, which carried her papers and notes. She stood awaiting a queue to begin, and Nathan sensing her need for signal said to the conference: "Friends we must begin. I recognise the speaker at microphone one."

"Good morning, fellow participants. The privilege is mine to open the batting on the final day, and I am moved by this God-given opportunity.

"Chairman, 'the way of the wicked is as darkness. They know not at what they stumble', Proverbs 4:19. I lived in the Church, but not in the sense that I was a dweller, hugging for myself a cosy corner of one of the many Anglican, Roman Catholic, Methodist or other churches which adorn the beautiful streets of Port-of-Spain. No. I was born into Church, and I grew into the world with a profound awareness of the doctrine which fashioned me, as indeed so many, of the importance of the Church. The parish priest, in our infantile minds, was more powerful than our parents, teachers, aunts, uncles, and just more powerful than everyone we deemed to be figures of authority.

"Yes chairman, we lived in Church. No. We are born into and we grew into our worlds aware of the doctrine of the Catholic Religion, with a sound appreciation of the dos and don'ts, which were required of us if we were to become good Catholics and in the process, find a place in Heaven."

The lady who wore the business suit with the afro-Trinidadian head tie held the attention of all assembled as one could hear if a pin fell.

She continued: "All these things are true, and thankfully as I stand with you this morning I am in a good place, as I can objectively say, you Catholics pray all day, you pray as if God never hears and sees your most secret thoughts. I ask with all objectivity, is this the reason why the Church appears to be in shambles?" she asked, and paused as if waiting for an answer.

A response came from the body of the floor almost as she was about to continue. The person replying shouted: "Today we have the best Pope. Our Pope is a miracle worker, he is doing all kinds of great things. Where do you get this nonsense of shambles?" the unseen person's response echoed through the conference hall.

Clearly incensed by the interrupter, the grey suited lady replied: "My name is Laila," she smirked, as if she was waiting to enjoin others in an across the floor debate. "Your Pope has spent his papacy buying arms in the hope that these arms will slaughter and bury the long list of evil which has characterised the behaviour of the clergy over the centuries.

"My friend, face up to it, your Church is mired in the abuse of children from one end of the globe to the other. My friend, I know you are not alone here this morning, and many would wish to stand with you to defend our Pope, but this is not the place. Today in this place we have come to exorcise the evil from all religions, and each of these religious bodies have stories to be told in words worse or equal to stories of the Pope and his well-weaved network of priests with all their unfounded piety."

The support of Laila was overwhelming, and the applause and shouts of support grew as she continued her contribution.

"Colleagues," she continued. "I am not saying that there are not good, honest, decent professional priests, but at this moment the only thoughts that hold the world's focus of the Church are the daily revelations found in the news, of assaults on children and adults alike. Of rape, abuse and buggery on children, which are now too many to count and too many to continue saying we now have a good Pope.

"You need more than a good Pope. You need a whole new, blessed and baptised Church if you are to compensate the millions who have suffered in the name of the Pope and the Roman Catholic Religion over too long a period. It is this long and lengthy period, with no signs ever of reform, which places your Pope and his flock before the grand jury of the 'Conference of the Un-Godly.' Today your Pope, his papacy and his Church is on trial here in this auditorium at this conference."

"Chairman, I rest my case on behalf of those in search of justice for the injured, brutalised, violated and lost souls. May they rest in peace." And she sat to a standing ovation.

Throughout the presentation by the lady who introduced herself as Laila, neither Nathan nor Miriam spoke, but Nathan felt the pinches and slight cuffs Miriam shared each time there was applause. During moments of exhilaration, neither Miriam nor Nathan gave consideration to the presence of Thomas and his interpretation of the innocent thumps and pinches.

Nathan immediately welcomed to the microphone a clean-cut Chinese young man of just over five feet, chubby at the waist and wearing heavy set spectacles. The young man carried a metal briefcase which he set on the floor next to the microphone and waited for no prompts.

"Chairman, conference, I am just excited to be here," and as he said this he laughed, and the conference joined him in laughter. "Chairman, one cannot be certain on where something is and where it is going. Nothing is certain, I think Hiesenburg said this, I don't quite know. What I do know, and I am certain of, is that despite all the evil of the Church, be it Christian, Hindu, Muslim or all the others, the Church is not going anywhere fast. We must accept this, and recognise it is our duty to find ways to be the police, the investigator and the ones who will, with serious work, ensure the Church behaves itself and provides the services it was intended to provide.

"I come from Canada, and we are well aware of challenges within our religious institutions, but most people are afraid, some too embarrassed, to do something to protect those in need of protection. This will only stop when all who participate in Church get only God and good, and nothing else.

"So Chairman, you must tell me how to organise to combat the evils of which so many have spoken, you must help me to understand how to fight." As he said fight he raised his left hand and pounded his left fist into his opened right palm. This gesture, though a serious display of his "need to fight," encouraged much laughter, which forced Nathan to intervene. He demanded that participants appreciate the comments by the last speaker, and his non-verbal gesture was an illustration of his commitment to become an active combatant in the battle against the un-godly.

Said Nathan: "Mr Chen, be assured we will be in touch with you to assist you in organising your community against the un-godly. We will teach you to fight."

In response there was loud applause, the conference having come to recognise the significance of the request of the Canadian participant.

As Mr Chen took his seat, Nathan recognised a balding African middle-aged man wearing an African patterned silk skirt with as many colours as could be found within the African dye chart. He was of slim build and carried himself in a stately manner, and he spoke with eloquence. He neither addressed the chairman nor the conference, and he confined his contribution to a number of relevant quotations without crediting the source of the information he quoted.

He, who neither gave his name nor his country of origin, said: "The energy that should be directed against the enemy is dissipated in internal strife and jealousies." He moved quickly to his second quotation: "Turn your thoughts now to the considerations of your life, this life as a child, thy life as a youth, your manhood, your old age, for in these also every change was death. Is this anything to fear."

Conference participants began to become quite restless, but Nathan called for quiet and encouraged the speaker to continue.

Continuing, the speaker said: "Time is as a river of passing events and strong is the current, so sooner is a thing brought to sight that if it is swept by and another takes its place and this too will be swept away."

At this point, Nathan stopped the eloquent speaker, who offered no common thread except that his quotations were of some relevance to the conference's theme, but were clearly quotations for which no credit was being given to the work presented. In this regard Nathan advised that while the conference appreciated his unusual contribution it would appreciate a written document with credits given to the persons whose work had been quoted.

Nathan next recognised a woman dressed in full Muslim attire. She gave her name only as Zaida, and noted she was from Trinidad and Tobago.

"Chairman, Co-Chairlady, I am here today to speak to the issue of the belief of Muslim men, that women are less than equal to men and are therefore treated as less than equal in all things.

"I have listened over the last four days as well as participated in some of the committee sessions, and I get the feeling we are more concerned primarily of the ills which confront the Christian churches. Lest we miss the point, the challenges of the Christians are very similar to the challenges of other religions," she emphasised as she moved her right index finger from left to right, reminiscent of an elder counselling a child. "Make no mistake in believing that only in the Christian families there is incest, and only in Christian places of worship members of the clergy are wanting and not of sound behaviour," she added.

Zaida as she spoke showed signs of being careful not to offend anyone, as she chose her words carefully. Likewise she frequently looked to her right and to her left, and occasionally she looked behind her as if she was expecting someone within the conference to intervene as she spoke her own truth, or so the conference attendees assumed.

Zaida was of African descent and looked approximately in her forties. She was not overweight, but looked bulky even in her full length Muslim clothing. She stood just about five feet and could pass for any one of the thousands who daily traversed the streets of Port-of-Spain. Zaida was neither dramatic nor dull, but the clarity with which she spoke encouraged her audience to give her its undivided attention.

As a community of the world, each day we count the reports of the trials of clergy who have done wrong, and all those reports are from Christian Communities," she added. Continuing, Zaida said: "There is a reason why we are now told of all those criminal acts. The Christian Church has lost its hold on its flock, and members of the Church, encouraged by persons for their own reasons, no longer fear the wrath of the Church as they truly believe God is in charge. In the case of my religion, the power to discipline for disobedience flows from the imam to the person who is the 'man of the house.' There is no escape from some form of discipline if you do not behave in strict compliance with the teachings – yet our men folk behave according to their own interpretation of the good book."

Another woman of Indian descent sitting behind Zaida was so moved by Zaida's contribution she could be heard saying: "Yuh talking sister, don't stop talking."

On the other hand Zaida needed no approbation – she had come to speak her truth but now she was being pushed from behind. She stopped and said: "Chairman, as I take my seat, all I ask of you and everyone present, is that we always remember the blood of the martyrs."

The audience remained silent as if waiting for Zaida to continue her contribution, and when it accepted she had said her piece, it exploded in rapturous applause.

Miriam sitting next to Nathan, and who enjoyed a bird's eye view of all the activities taking place, was fascinated as any of the participants with what she witnessed and heard. She was particularly moved by the contribution by Zaida the last speaker, and had hoped to hear much more of her views from the perspective of Islam, yet she was satisfied that Zaida got to tell her story.

Miriam felt the energy of the conference, which was far from over, and anticipated that if the conference continued with the magic she sensed, their work would make an impact. They would encourage and increase debate and discussion of the issues of the ugliness of religion, followed by corrective action within the hierarchy of international religion.

33

NATHAN BROUGHT THE CONFERENCE BACK TO order, and invited a burly, heavy set African man sporting a Rasta hairstyle to address the conference.

"Jah Rastafari Chairman," said the speaker. "Sir, I am really happy I have come from Jamaica for these talks. I did not know that all dem church is the same thing all over the place. Masta I thought is only JA they have wicked people in church, with bad pastorman who does steal you gyal and wife. When I decide to come here I come looking to have some fun as I believed I would find a nice church gyal, but listening to all speakers I know now more than ever Jah lives.

"Masta when I hear about the Hindu priest and what, he does do and how they forcing ten year old pickney to marry old, old man. I say it have more wicked priest in the world. I say Jamaica eh so bad.

"However, what I want you to understand is that man have to find out for himself who God is and when he find out that God is a serious man he will mend he ways. Yes sir, I want you to know that all them things de people say about the Church men happening wherever you go. Yes Chairman, Jah Rastafari." And he took his seat.

Nathan looked at Miriam, soliciting a response to the last speaker, and was rewarded with a broad smile.

Some members of the audience took the contribution by the Jamaican speaker as a cue to stretch their legs and find a refreshment of some kind.

Nathan in the interim called his next contributor, an elderly gentleman who no doubt had roots in Latin America. Nathan, in his desire to encourage as a wide cross section of speakers, was keenly observing those who stood in line waiting, but gave way to the elderly who caught his eyes. The speaker, who held the floor, fell into the latter category.

Speaking in English with a Spanish accent, the gentleman introduced himself as one who once administered the sacraments and for personal reasons no longer did so. "Chairman, I am simply overwhelmed to be a participant in one of the most important meetings on religion for a long, long time. What is interesting is that you are not only speaking about Church you are speaking of all religions. It is interesting, many who are here today know of and indeed know only of their religion, and so the un-godly in other religions, though equally vicious, go away unscathed.

"I say our 'Conference of the Un-Godly,' and note Chairman I take ownership, as it represents for me an appreciation of a reckoning of the long decades, centuries if you may, of the darkness of dark deeds carried out in the name of the Church. From unnecessary wars to the cruelty of those who carried the keys on a huge ring strapped to their waist being a custodian for Peter. There is no mystery or magic, though some over the centuries were given to believe and were insane enough to suggest they possess magical powers.

"Yes there is indeed no mystery about the evil committed. They all seem to have forgotten the song of the village, which underscores: 'The evil men do live long after they die.' They may have forgotten that the truth is the only thing which truly sets anyone free, and though it has taken hundreds of years, those who have been imprisoned by the darkness of the clergy will continue to see and find light as more people, good people like this gathering of truth seekers, search and ferret out the numerous wrongs committed in the name of Peter.

"How can we ever reconcile the list of wrongdoings of my Church, without acknowledging that the list could not have become as long as it is without the blessings from the highest levels of the Church?" he said with a passion which touched Nathan, who over a long period said the same words to anyone who would listen to him.

Nathan also sensed from the unnamed clergyman that he had lived a life according to the good book, but may have been let down at a point in the river. All of the words of the speaker seemed to mingle with his own words spoken at varying times, which now seemed so long ago.

He continued: "When you lead and one of your subordinates commits a wrongdoing, or even worse an immoral act that is both a violation of the laws of the state and Church, and you are made aware of this indecent and often both violent and wicked act, you cannot read the file and then misplace it. This is not the way either the Church or the State can ever be allowed to do business in the future. For centuries we have had both blind and deaf Popes, and rascals as senior members of the Church. Equally it would appear we have both blind and deaf state officials, as they neither saw nor heard the cries of thousands of children buggered into their own deafness and blindness."

The unnamed former clergy had the conference in his spell, and kept his audience in a trance as he presented his well-ordered thoughts on his Church of the Un-Godly.

Nathan, despite his familiarity with the data presented, could not help but accept the man who held the floor was a gifted orator, and concluded he must have been a most outstanding clergyman while he stood at his pulpit.

However Nathan reminded himself of the time limit given to each speaker, and discretely checked the time on his wrist watch to measure the time the unnamed former clergyman had been speaking and noted he had been at it for near seven minutes. He touched Miriam's elbow and whispered, "He is out of time. Should we extend his?"

Without taking her eyes off the speaker she nodded and raised her right hand with all five fingers, giving support to the suggestion of an additional five minutes being allowed the speaker.

This man might have had many past moments when he weaved his spells over his audience as he was doing on the last day of the conference. Nathan questioned whether he planned his moment, or did he feel inspired to intervene at the moment he did.

Continuing, he questioned: "What is to be the destinies of all religion? Will we rise together or will we falter and be rent asunder, leaving all to believe in whatever force they deem to be God? Will we, with appropriate and necessary cleansing and sorrowful repentance, on a timely basis, make such interventions that are necessary to save the platforms of religions that rule the lives of vast swathes of people the world over?

"As I think of this issue, religion, with its hierarchy of controls, mandates and clergy, rules the hearts and minds of more of the world than do the nations of the world. Make no bones about the matter; the reach and influence, not to add the discipline, of religion is boundless. The multitudes who see and feel only virtue in their priest, Indian pandit or shaman, are perhaps more likely to be preyed upon, and still not accept that the God they worship frowns, condemns and is angered over wrongdoing, especially by those who have volunteered and have been chosen to lead the flock.

"As I speak to you this day, I cannot and will not ever accept that my church's leadership could not know when hundreds if not thousands of children born of unwanted pregnancies in Ireland could be consigned to a faith which ended in agony and often death. How can any Church elder reconcile the roles played by priests and nuns in the systematic herding of children often grabbed from the womb of their mothers? They were mostly young strong women, who would have gladly cared for their children and who were denied this right, as the Catholic cause demanded that the new born babies be quickly banished to unknown places of sadness, where they grew in environments of squalor. And, in more than eight hundred known cases, where they died in unknown circumstances."

"Mr Chairman, in the context of abuses in the most Catholic of all Catholic societies, we have learned over long years of the sadness and inhumanity imposed on women, young women, very young mothers and girls at the hand of the Catholic priest and nuns. As you learn of these most terrible, slave-like operations, owned, operated and managed by the state and Church, you recognise they both operate in a state of perpetual hell. In Ireland the church was at one with its flock in administering the sacraments, which defined Heaven and Hell. One might reason the Church was in control of delivering Heaven and Hell, and none were spoiled the beatings administered to children that left a lasting impressions all their lives.

"In reference to young women they learned very early the term fallen women, and were indoctrinated not to fall prey to lust. Young girls were forever reminded to keep their legs locked together if they wished to get to heaven. With all the lack of information and no desire to encourage or promote sex education, the Church exercised all authority with devastating consequences. There is no other way to review the deaths at the establishments of the infamous Magdalene Laundries, which confined thousands of females from the cradle to their coffins.

"Yes there is a God, and often we believe He is not there when we need Him to act, but I know friends, He has been there and He is here with us today.

"Mr Chairman, that was Ireland. In the context the Germans recently awarded compensation to victims for sexual abuse by priests and politicians.

"How can we ever explain or understand the roles played by nuns who pimped out the children they were required to care for? Further, how do you record for posterity that the courts recently awarded a sixty-four-year-old man twenty-five thousand Euros for his claim that he was raped 1,000 times? How do you report the facts of the French priest, shot outside his church by the jealous husband of his lover? Friends, what of the known apologies by German authorities for killing four hundred witches centuries ago? The reality is there were twenty-five thousand murders of primarily women between the fifteenth and eighteenth centuries, all under the label, 'witches'.

"Mr Chairman, how I wish I could go on, but I know you have been kind having allowed me to speak my thoughts, and I say in all sincerity I have much more to say, but I will submit my full contribution to the secretariat as you earlier requested," he ended.

The unnamed member of the clergy was given and graciously received a standing ovation. The one with the Latin accent, who looked like a priest, spoke like a priest but said he once administered the sacraments, was the keynote speaker, even if he came from a land unknown and gave no prior indication that he would set tongues a wagging with his well-reasoned presentation.

The sustained applause he received is quite often the kind deserved for feature speakers. That evening at the 'Conference of the Un-Godly' an unknown speaker came to the floor armed with facts, charisma and the ability to communicate, and advanced the case against centuries of wrongdoings within the Catholic Church.

Regardless of where the church building sat, the "Latin One" placed at its doorstep demands which had to be answered.

Would the conference satisfy his wishes? All that would unfold in the weeks and months ahead, as Nathan, Miriam, Anthony and Phillip collated and withdrew from the mountain of files and submissions the appropriate contributions for the conference's final report.

Information arrived from every continent. Some material arrived by couriers and international mail, but above all many attending would, upon registration, come sheepishly and hand over packages containing contributions, which others may have researched and written, and which were delivered to participants with the simple request: "Kindly hand in at the secretariat."

Nathan and Miriam, in opening the door for written submissions, received such contributions by every channel of communication available.

A high number of submissions were received online. Those were already being processed by a special team, which made itself available from among the ranks of the New Rochelle, New York group and Miriam's Boston Colleagues.

Anthony, forever on the lookout for 'good people,' found within his team a number of excited and highly driven spiritual volunteers. Above all they were also professional researchers by profession. Theses volunteers thrust themselves into the task of opening and sorting the vast data into distinct files, in preparation for receipt of additional information they knew would arrive during and after the conference.

The team concluded, during the final day of the conference, that the volume of documents was far greater than anticipated, and they communicated their conclusion to Phillip and Anthony.

Despite all of the unseen work, the work at the conference floor continued.

Nathan was on his feet restoring quiet to the conference floor, as individuals queued to commend the 'Latin One' and to request from him his full paper, of which he possessed a small stack and which he willingly distributed. Nathan, anxious to push the agenda, appealed to participants to take their seats. He observed the still long lines of participants wishing to make contributions and this worried him.

His co-chair had seized the interruption to visit with her husband, who upon seeing her coming his way quickly got to his feet to greet her. She in turn had forgotten and forgiven him his deceit and underhandedness.

Before he could utter a word, Miriam said: "Thomas, would you join me for a coffee?"

He nodded his head in agreement and followed his wife to the meet and greet lounge, set up to encourage participants to communicate with each other on conference matters, and, as Phillip said: "To encourage a network of supporters of similar thinking."

Miriam and Thomas got cups of coffee and a couple of currant rolls and retreated to the only available seating, two empty seats in the middle. It dawned on Thomas as they sat among so many that no one paid any attention to either of them, nor indeed both of them sitting together chatting, which was unusual for Miriam who was considered the darling of the leadership. In the moment however, no one seemed to recognise her, and she recognised no one other than Thomas. They sat looking at each other, until Miriam said in the warmest of spirits: "Thomas, how are you and how have you been?"

Thomas responded but she did not hear him, as the computer brain she carried reviewed the events of the immediate past and recognised she had really seen little of her husband over the last weeks. How many weeks she could not recall, as she had been busy, very busy, doing what she had to do to create a conference that had produced the kind of day she was now sharing with Thomas.

She remained in this state of 'inbetweenity,' totally oblivious of everything around her, until the realism of the conference triggered her back to the real world and she smiled warmly at Thomas. He had been looking at her and wondering if she was fatigued and had drifted off to sleep, and had removed the coffee from her hand lest it fell onto her lap. When he realised she was back in conversation with him, he handed back her coffee and said: "Miriam I took your coffee out of your hand as you drifted off to sleep."

She reached over and placed her right index finger on Thomas' lip, and said: "I was not sleeping, I was thinking. Thinking if we had forgotten anything, missed anything with our planning. Thomas, are you enjoying my work?" she enquired and looked at him, not waiting to hear his words but more so to measure the messages she now read so easily with the movement of the lines of his handsome face.

In response he said: "I do believe you and the team have something good going on. Today is better than yesterday, and there is much more energy among participants," he added.

Miriam smiled and said: "Thomas, you have not answered my question. I did not ask you to describe the conference, but never mind." She held his hand and said: "I must get back, will you walk me back?"

Miriam took her seat back at the head table, and elbowed Nathan to report her return.

During Miriam's absence approximately six speakers had made contributions of varying levels. None, Nathan reported, were stand out contributions. Much, he said, focused on the Catholic Church and its ills, be it the rape and abuse of children, or the role the Church played in slavery and the attendant violence and the dehumanising of Africans.

Miriam's return was met by a first time contributor. A woman in her forties of upright build, small around the waistline and well-endowed in more ways than one, now stood at the microphone holding it gingerly with the tips of her right thumb and index finger.

She did not wait on the chairman to recognise her, but immediately addressed him.

"Mr Chairman, I sense we are all conscious that we are here today because of the mean-spiritedness of so many who operate religious institutions of one kind or another. But be warned, we are here as we too operate our own private centres, and, I repeat, where cussedness is what we appear to live for above all else.

"Be it Prince or pauper, we live lives with an absence of goodness. Often we speak of kindness and goodness, but we really mix up doctrine with being human," she added. "It is my hope that we will all commit to becoming better people in every manifestation that we could contemplate, individually and collectively.

"I know some of you are asking yourselves, what is this woman speaking of? Well, it is my hope that when we leave today we will all write on a slip of paper how we propose to ensure we cause the world to move from being in a potential state of wickedness, to becoming a place where everyone makes a daily extra effort to improve not only how we live, but to do that one action that will assist others to be better. I wish to suggest that as long as there is one evil person, angry and wicked, the virus of evil, anger and wickedness will continue infecting the earth. For us to truly be rid of the virus of evil, anger and wickedness, we must first destroy it at its roots. Conference goers, with the greatest respect, who among us here today – this last day of the 'Conference of the Un-Godly' – does not entertain evil thoughts, is not given to bouts of anger nor harbour thoughts of wickedness? If you are innocent of any aforementioned, raise your hand." She paused and looked across the conference floor, but did not see a raised hand.

"Friends, I ask this question not for an answer, but to encourage an awakening that the tasks we have debated all of three days illustrate that the world is changing, not for the better but for the worse. Further, if I am to be guided by the narratives of the last seventy-two hours, the world as we know it is not an improvement on the world of centuries ago. If anything is palpable, it is that the world is changing for the worse, and the people, regardless of race, religion, class or sex, are not pushing the pendulum in the direction of good and Godliness.

"We must stop being vicious and spiteful, even if it means you will be considered insane. I encourage all to believe in this time, you can take counsel at the fact that it is far better to be considered insane than thought to be vicious and spiteful.

"As you read your local newspaper, you will appreciate why neither the party of red nor of yellow can effectively lead your country away from the darkness that covers it. I have no intention of getting into your local politics, but I can't help but express what I have felt wherever I have visited since coming to your country that has been named for the Blessed Trinity.

"Chairman I am tempted, but the purpose is not political, and so Chairman Nathan, all I ask of our conference is for each of us to teach one another to be kind, to be gentle as well as generous. To encourage good and to resist evil, to embrace honesty and integrity, and to be brave and bold in saying to those who lead that nobleness, sincerity, honesty, and a kind and gentle spirit could be transformational.

"Oh yes, we need to transform – from bad to good, from being selfish and covetous to being generous, with a strong willing desire to give to others. We have got to constantly seek assurances to firmly establish that there is no space for darkness, as only light allows the unseeing an opportunity to find the way to the place we all seek."

When the applause began, Nathan, who was partially listening, wondered whether the conference was seeking to get the speaker to end her contribution. But he quickly realised the speaker had touched a 'nerve cord' of the conference, and was being rewarded with much deserved applause that gave added 'tempo' to the conference now speeding to its final hours.

Overwhelmed by the rhythmic and sustained applause, the contributor, who began her presentation holding the microphone gingerly with the tips of her index finger and right thumb, finally released her gentle grip on the microphone. She said with a look of satisfaction: "Chairman, how I wish this conference could become a permanent school, for that is what it has been for me during the last three days. It has been nothing but an education, in recognising good, rejecting evil and coming to know in a precise way the acceptance of God – thank you Chairman Nathan." And she moved quickly to her seat, as the earlier applause of thanks resonated throughout the conference floor.

34

THOSE WHO COULD NOT BE INSIDE THE MAIN HALL had crowded around well-stationed television monitors to follow the program of activities, which now engaged a packed main auditorium. Participants on the outside, though separated by walls of concrete and bricks, were just as moved by the speakers and the energy they generated deep within the main artery of the conference.

Nathan once again got to his feet to bring the applause to a halt, and to give approval to the next speaker who excitedly took the microphone.

As he stood he looked at the wall clock, which told a story he dreaded all evening. The conference had already overstayed its welcome by one hour, and the hotel management had cautioned of the need for the conference to keep its schedule with the main auditorium, owing to another event the hotel was committed to early the following day.

Nathan knew he could not continue much longer. He turned to Miriam and said: "My lady of all ladies," which was met with such a compelling smile that even Nathan, who had grown to know his co-chair, was moved to enquire: "What have I done to deserve such a smile?"

Miriam did not stop smiling, and despite her quick mind and sharp wit could only muster a polite: "Nathan, I am just happy."

Continuing his earlier trend of thought, he looked Miriam in her eyes and said: "I believe we are in trouble – I must have been sleeping, we ran out of time one hour ago. We are now forced to wind down our programme that could have gone on for hours."

Before Miriam could react, he added: "My lady of all ladies, I hope you will agree to close the conference, given that the boy from Los Bajos opened the innings," Nathan added, as he gave her a smile equal to hers so genuinely shared moments ago.

Miriam, as if unhappy with the suggestion, shook her head and pouted.

Nathan could not grasp her non-verbal response, and said: "Let me introduce our final contributor, followed by introducing you as the final presenter of the main conference."

Nathan stood and warmly welcomed the last speaker, a young girl no older than seventeen years.

She wore a conference t-shirt and carried her hair in a ponytail. She was petite as she was pretty, and it was clear she was of the two dominant races of Trinidad and Tobago. She was of mixed Indian and African blood lines, and was a sound example of a growing group long before described by poet, songwriter and calypsonian David Rudder in speaking of Trinidad: "The Ganges done meet the Nile." She was a perfect illustration of the Indian and African mix more commonly known in the village as a 'dougla.'

Nathan recognised her, and though he had seldom during the conference requested speakers to identify themselves, he felt moved to ask the speaker to identify herself, which she quickly did.

Stacy Ramnarine took the floor, and immediately brought the conference to an unnerving, amazing silence.

Being at a microphone was not an everyday experience for Stacy, and following her contribution, many enquired of her whether she was used to speaking publicly.

"Conference participants, I have come to you this evening, as late as it is, to take centre stage, as I believe the responsibility falls on me to speak on behalf of the young people of whom so much has been said at this conference over the past three days.

"As I listened to speaker after speaker, I learned of the challenges young people have encountered over centuries. It is not as if hand cuffs are a today invention. From all

CLOSER TO THE CHURCH

indicators, the young of the world, wherever they are, have been abused, beaten, raped, buggered and made to engage in all kinds of prostitution, be they male or female. As I listened, I absorbed the pains of millions of my peers over centuries, and I am neither addressing slavery, serfdom nor indentureship.

"I am giving focus to the new reality, that while I have suffered pains, my pains have paled into insignificance when compared to the pains of each unnamed child, teenager and young adult, who was persecuted in ways no different to the most wicked criminality imposed on Jews and Gentiles alike by Hitler and his squads of murderous cowards. Yes crimes of equal station committed in the name of religion.

"Before today I never knew of the Magdalene Laundries, nor indeed of the brutality meted out to both the mother and child of unwanted pregnancies in Roman Catholic jurisdictions across the world. I read recently of young girls who became pregnant being made to walk the ramp with one of two options. You either abort the baby or you get married, and if you chose neither option you were forced to put the baby up for adoption," Stacy continued.

"Fellow participants, I wish to share with you that this also happened here in our beautiful Trinidad – such was the influence and control of religion, intimately tied to the clearly defined class structure of our then colony. I would have you know I grew up thinking of my eldest cousin as my cousin, who I would later find out was my eldest sister. I have sought to reconcile in my head the tremendous pressures placed on my parents to overnight turn my sister into my cousin, she being their first-born. "These are small matters when compared to the unwanted pregnancies of our space, and we must be grateful, as my sister who became my cousin, was allowed to live and she became a respectable and good citizen," she stressed.

"Yet my pains do not end here.

"How do you address situations where the children you play with during the day are often afraid to go home to a house twenty feet away because their father, who should be protecting and caring for his daughter and son, is like the hellhound and has viciously attacked them for years? And despite the reports my own parents made to the local police and other relevant agencies, nothing was implemented to save my next door friends for years from the sex crazy father who repeatedly raped his own children."

"When I say to you I have pains, know my pains are real, and memories of these two who were like my brother and sister cause me to still become angry, so many years after the fiend was finally locked behind bars," she ended.

"Friends, over the three days I have also acquired the skill of not being angry, and equally I have now put on the armour and I am prepared to make the un-godly know that there is a God, notwithstanding who you deem him to be."

Like the speaker before her Stacy touched a nerve cord of the conference, and the hundreds responded with resounding and sustained applause.

She showed no signs of being intimidated by the moment, and raised her hand to encourage her audience to become quiet so that she could continue her contribution.

Stacy continued: "It is my sincerest wish that many of the very healing and strong recommendations made over the conference would be implemented. Chairman, even with the best intentions, I have learned in Trinidad that no good deed goes unpunished. I caution you and your lovely co-host to be weary of the punishments that are likely to follow as a result of the power of the cleansing nature of the work you have performed, in staging a most successful conference. I want you to know from the eyes of the unintimidated, your team's work represents not a good deed, but a great deed – just be cautious as you go forward," she ended.

Nathan was already on his feet restoring focus to his conference's programme. Said Nathan: "Friends, I must share with you that we are now past our closing by one and a half hours. I wish to advise that I propose to bring the curtain down by the end of the next half hour. I must draw to your attention that the programme for the Committee for Redeemed Sinners will begin promptly tomorrow at 8:00am, at Conference Room B on the sixth floor. If you have not yet registered I suggest you do so before departing this evening, as space is now limited."

Nathan was moving at a pace as he hoped to give Miriam as much time as she wished, and so he hoped he had not done her a disservice by not discussing the additional responsibility before he did.

He pressed on, and then looked at Miriam as if to suggest: "Are you ready?" Nathan began by appealing to the conference to welcome a very special person. He neither gave a name nor did he notion to the audience to look left nor right, as he had done so often during the three days of the conference.

"Fellow participants, this brings us to the end of our official programme, though we have our session tomorrow for the Committee of Redeemed Sinners and our field trip to the sister island of Tobago. But however important these events may be, the next speaker is by far one of the most important events on our programme. Friends, if I sat at this head table, chaired and oversaw the activities of the last three days, I owe it to the next speaker.

"Almost eleven months ago I gave an interview to a local newspaper, in which I announced I would host a 'Conference of the Un-Godly,' and requested if anyone was interested to call, and I gave my mobile cell number. For weeks I got no response, and honestly I did not have a clue how to even organise a picnic, far less a conference such as the one we have experienced this past week.

"Ladies and gentlemen, friends, then from out of the blue I got a call from a total stranger enquiring of the conference, and we finally agreed to meet. We met at the Central Market, and we sat on two boxes at the stall of a beautiful vendor who sells swizzle sticks."

At Nathan's mention of swizzle sticks, participants could be heard asking: "What is a swizzle stick?" Nathan got a whiff of the question and promised he would bring to the session the following day a swizzle stick to allow the visitors to appreciate the term.

Nathan explained that the next speaker not only gave life to his idea, but she introduced her parents to the idea of the conference, and her father signed on to assist the boy from Los Bajos.

"Friends, the next speaker single-handedly raised the much needed financial and other resources to make this conference a real and meaningful moment. Along the way she taught the entire team to think outside the box, and equally to understand the meaning of a team. There is no way we can repay her and her father Phillip, and her husband Thomas, for the sacrifices they have made to make this conference possible.

"Friends, I ask you stand and welcome our conference co-chairman Ms Miriam…"

For the first time Nathan realised he did not know Miriam's surname, be it Suielman or another which Miriam had never shared with him.

Miriam stood, surveyed the floor and caught the eyes of her father standing at the first entrance door. She smiled as she surmised that her father was standing there with other members of his security team, forever conscious that it was his responsibility to protect his prodigal daughter.

She looked in the direction where Thomas was seated and also caught his eyes. He looked at her and smiled a smile she had forgotten he was capable of – such a warm smile. She moved to the lectern almost measuring her steps.

35

MIRIAM GRASPED THE LECTERN WITH BOTH HANDS as if needing a prop, all the while the conference remained standing and applauding.

Next, Miriam did what would make her known as 'the most powerful female speaker' in her home country. Her reputation as a forceful speaker went beyond the borders of the Caribbean and reached across the globe as the years passed, and she and Nathan took the message of burying the un-godly to every community who shared the view of good overpowering evil.

"Good people, I don't know where you would like me to begin, but I must at the onset thank my father, who is standing at the first entrance door on the right. Yes people, that handsome man is my ever protecting father, Phillip Suielman. And I thank my mother, who is not at the conference as she is caring for our six children of four boys and two girls."

"I thank the entire team, who have worked for months, taking the idea of the boy from Los Bajos – our conference chairman, Mr Nathan John – from a simple idea, and creating this conference of which we are all proud."

"I would like you to put your hands together for a man who began this journey worried and troubled about whether his idea would become a reality, and then worked his butt off to give the conference the life it found long before we opened our doors. Friends, I have nothing but admiration for our conference chairman, who recruited his committee wherever he could find good people. He found Anthony, our most outstanding, at a Pan Yard. Anthony has been to this conference what a bus driver is to a bus. Could we give it up for Anthony?

"Really, I could go into the late night singing the virtues of each team member, and that is not possible. So I ask you to give it up for our full team, who are all volunteers," she underscored.

"Participants, I decided some time ago that as I live in this world I must do as I must to ensure that the lives of those for who I have responsibility must have their needs met, at the expense of no one else but myself. Mine is a responsibility to ensure that each good citizen, regardless of religious persuasion, race, class or other man-made separations, accepts that he too has similar responsibility to not only look after his personal needs, but equally he has the more important assignment to father the needs of those who, owing to little or no means, cannot look after his personal needs."

Miriam paused and looked across the hall, measuring her audience. Given all the speaking she did over the last year she had become tuned to the need to establish early bridges with her audience. Now she recognised she needed to step up her tempo.

"Friends, we have heard over the last three days and we have seen written presentations which suggest to us that we are not good people, and we all know when something is not good it is thrown into the garbage. If we are to measure the testimonies of the many, we are and have always been rotten to the core.

"The question is, why are we still alive? And why is it we are alive if we are so wicked and rotten? Why is it that God, whoever you deem him to be, has not come to us to demand our accountability for the millions of wrongdoings committed in the name of religion, or committed by the clergy of various sects?"

Miriam knew she now had her audience, and began to steam roll her ideas for a wide cross section to hear, but to review and to slash and burn. How she managed with a full media contingent did not matter to her. She knew at the end of the conference she would be forced to assist Nathan in defending their work, and she began her defence as she stood at the lectern before the full conference.

She pressed home her points, one following the other, pushing the un-godly's backs to the ropes.

"Every song has a story; what is the story told to us with the songs sung during the last seventy-two hours?" she questioned.

Without stopping she accelerated as if she was in a hurry to get to her destination. She knew the time limit given to her by Nathan. She however knew the unwritten assignment for which she enlisted that memorable morning at the Port-of-Spain Market, not too far from where she stood on this closing evening of the 'Conference of the Un-Godly.'

What Nathan now wished could not be completed within the time allotted to her, and she knew she would speak until the assignment was completed. She also knew her new lasting friendship with Nathan John guaranteed he would not put God out of his thoughts to interrupt her. She was now speeding to her destiny.

"May I also say, some think only of the moon, but every moon has its sun, and it is in pairing the moon with the sun that we find a smooth and effective balance, that allows the continuity that has kept us as part of the living.

"If we are fortunate to be part of the greatest architect's master plan, why then do we choose to create cracks and crevices which facilitate so much un-godliness? The question must be asked whether those who live within places of worship, be it a mosque, temple or church, or for that matter those who live on its doorsteps, have more trash in their lives than the trash they often harbour with the spirits of their being.

"Some people in our very religious society would, in my opinion, do most anything to attract the light spirited, weak of heart, and – I am bold enough to say – the unthinking. The numbers are reduced within the pews of their huge edifices, built with rock and boulders, fashioned into blocks by the skilled and not so skilled free slaves, who in many instances gave their sweat as they toiled to fashion the unshakable presence of the Roman Catholic Church within our Republic.

"Within these often empty structures you can find the best carved ornaments, the highest quality brass and silver, and equally the best sculpture you can find in Christendom. The majesty of it all reflects the power of the Church, with its clergy at the top of the pole, the one percenters closely behind, and followed by the varying subclasses with the parishioners of poverty at the bottom of the pole of Christianity.

"It is with equal pomp and pageantry that this Christian fellowship, not too long ago, planned, produced and took to the street a Carnival band, and encouraged the followers to join in to participate in Carnival. My position then as now remains unchanged – what business does the Church have with Carnival?" she stressed.

Miriam never heard a member of the audience midway in the hall shout: "Yuh damn right. Church is Church and Carnival is devil business." No one responded, as most were in Miriam's spell.

"Good people," Miriam said, and then paused. "I wish to raise with you a matter that I believe is unforgivable. We live in a small country with a relatively small population, characterised by a reasonably high presence of clergy. We have a beautiful presence of Christians of all kinds, we have Muslims by the mile and equally we have as any Hindus as we have temples and prayer rooms.

"Indeed we have them all. If we are to measure religion by places of worship and clergy our Republic ought to be heaven on earth, but the evidence suggests otherwise. I share with you that in this place named for the Father, Son and the Holy Spirit, only the clergy know for how many deities sad, wicked and evil deeds are committed, each hour of each day, of each week of each month of each year, and the lack of response by the clergy is astounding.

"How can the custodians of good remain silent in the face of overwhelming evil? If they remain silent are they not as guilty as the wrongdoers? If history has taught us one thing, it is evil often catches up and makes prisoners of the good that choose to remain silent," she underscored.

Miriam at this point was ebullient, and systematically argued her case against the un-godly.

"How do you reconcile that an eleven year old is murdered at an upmarket birthday party, and decades later, despite the evidence, no one is tried nor convicted and a plethora of clergy says nothing. The bodies of our young women keep turning up mutilated, often raped and with all visible signs of torture, and our multitude of clergy remain silent. What troubles me are the daily murders and the lack of response by a clergy, which restricts its responses to its pulpits and lecterns."

"To these goodly ordained, I ask, why do you restrict your much needed messages to the converted? We need you to open the doors to your places of worship and let your voices be heard across every valley and river and stream. If ever there was a time our Republic needed a combined delivery of the messages of healing and redemption, it is in the now; it is in this period when we seem to be experiencing hell right here on earth."

Miriam gestured, pointing her right index finger in a downward fashion, in a way illustrating that she was speaking of and to Trinidad.

She would be later asked by a reporter if when she spoke of the un-godly she was referencing Trinidad. Her reply was pointed: "You live here – would you say you are in a country that can be described as Godly?"

Miriam, not done with her Republic, continued to marry the clergy's lack of words and actions to the evil all too common in the daily lives of the citizenry.

"What is the clergy's position on the ineptness of our courts at all levels? How are our courts responding to the cycle of viciousness, and to which the courts, police and state continue to dance macabre? Senior officials of the courts, police and prison are shot and killed, yet we hear nothing from the clergy."

She paused and pointed to her audience, and asked forcefully: "Would you like to hear the clergy speak with one voice on the evils of our society?" The response was instant and the "Yes!" could be heard on the plains of the Caroni, something of an hour's drive away from the conference.

"When a Senior Council is murdered and no one is held accountable, or politicians steal from our National Treasury and no one is ever convicted and forced to pay for their crimes, and the clergy remains silent, we know we are living in hell right here in Trinidad. And after hell in Trinidad, following our stay here, we will enjoy heaven."

There was sustained applause, whistles and stamping of feet.

Miriam, when she came to the microphone, met a conference which analysed, reviewed and unveiled a mountain of evil within religion, inside every crevice on lands near and far. Miriam, the keen listener she was, became absolutely certain the participants came to Trinidad armed to do battle with the clergy and all things evil.

Most saw the challenges with the clergy as being of religion, and therefore they argued on the basis of religion. So too did Miriam; she knew the significance of banging at the clergy's doors, breaking these doors down, and once inside the inner sanctum bringing the clergy to their reckoning for the evil committed, and for the lack of accountability for centuries of wicked deeds committed with no punishment administered to the wrongdoers.

Nonetheless she also recognised that the clergy could not have committed the vast levels of wrongdoing alone. In her mind there had always been others who knowingly assisted the clergy, and therefore were accomplices.

Miriam thought of what she saw from her Rose Hill window at East Dry River: illiteracy, poverty, box board housing, latrine pits, the availability of water only at public water distribution taps, rampant hunger, prostitution by both males and females, and though she did not see it she was advised of parents who prostituted their daughters to feed the family. In her mind she married all these social weaknesses with the work of the clergy, and felt strongly that the clergy was not only weak, but co-conspirators against the weaker of the society, and was determined to correct the obvious weakness. Today and at this moment she switched tracks from religion to politics.

"As we look beyond the weaknesses of our people all over the earth, we recognise their inactivity must be driven by fear of one kind or another. What we do know is that our God-fearing Church, temple and mosque goers are willing sufferers, as no one in recent times compels anyone to be a religious zealot. Hopefully, that was yesterday.

"There has been no diatribe by way of presentations, and in so many ways the arguments advanced have trumped the wrongs committed, as well as just who committed such vicious and fetid acts are now known."

"What perhaps we have failed to recognise are the roles played by clergy in not standing with their congregations and devotees in demanding what is justly due to them as citizens. What I do know is that the clergy is perhaps no better than the politician, who increases the burden on the citizen with a growing demand for new taxes, as indeed the clergy passes the basket with a quiet demand for collections, tithes and zakat. How then can we expect the clergy to speak out forcefully for the well-being of citizens who represent that group most in need?"

Miriam, in making a connection between politicians and clergy, had opened Pandora's Box, and it would remain unhinged for a long time. She moved from being just another member of a religious conference committee to a person now viewed in many quarters as a political mind.

Continuing, she said: "What are the roles of both clergy and politicians in the immiseration of so many congregation members, devotees and political party followers? By not doing or saying anything to defend the voiceless or mindless from criminal political people, we force an isolation on the dispossessed, which guarantees a continuation of the rancid class and caste structures which has kept the Republic from achieving together.

"On a personal note, as I look through my lone window at Rose Hill where I live, I see a situation where the young are trapped within the confines of their neighbourhoods. Upward mobility from a perpetual state of poverty for the residents of Rose Hill can only be imagined and truly never realised. Unlike the wealthy, who are blessed with their drains and infrastructure, the people of East Port-of-Spain are forever on bended knees begging for drains, to ensure that each time it rains the little possessions they own are not drenched and destroyed or, for that matter, their homes are not washed away.

"Everywhere you look across the horizon, from the plains of Caron to the hills of Goodwood Park, the wealthy enjoy such vast luxuries that they are unable to grasp or understand the challenges of the poor. Participants, it is precisely because the rich, wealthy and those of reasonable means do not know, that they often do not see the herculean burdens carried by the poor.

"However, the politicians and clergy know first-hand the full extent of the problems of the poor and they act in silence, as if their shackles of the constituents on the one hand and their congregations on the other hand is just a story of the few.

"Well friends, today we say to both pastor, imam, pandit and priest alike get up, and stand up for the poor wherever they inhabit a piece of this scorched earth."

Miriam, in linking clergy with politician and religion with politics, firmly established the long tradition of what clergy is to politician, what religion is to governments. "Each," she declared, "was an enabler of the other, with all its known iniquitous, never-ending silent attacks on little people."

She looked at Nathan, who guided her beats and tempo as she spoke, but at this moment she wished to gauge how much longer he would allow her to speak. Nathan, never disappointing, gave her the signal for five additional minutes.

Miriam did not delay; she immediately began her final pages of an unwritten but not an unrehearsed presentation.

Continuing, she added: "This is the sadness of our society – it is about class and cast; it is about religion; and worst of all, it is about race, which is firmly tied to our politics. Priests, pandits and imams, like politicians, understand the weaknesses of the races. They have over long, long decades tied each of the dominating races to their party, with the imam, pandit and pastor playing support roles with their never-ending silence."

"If the clergy was real, and genuinely leaders of men, they would not remain silent on what is good and noble, or for that matter what is best for their congregations or devotees. Each would counsel his flock and shepherd his away from what is not in the flock's best interest, but they do not do this," she exclaimed. "Those of African descent vote for one party and those of East Indian descent vote for the other party, and the clergy either directly encourages this measure of bondage or says nothing. They choose to remain silent, fully aware that indeed, silence is consent.

"This is a conspiracy that has kept the poor in poverty, while the rich grow richer. It is sinful, that the clergy has demonstrated this level of blindness to issues, which are rightfully theirs to address," she underscored. "More so, our Republic will never see its promised land until its political class accept that service to its people is the job for which they volunteered. The Republic must come to terms with its strengths as well as its weaknesses. It must accept that class, caste, and above all, race, have no place in religion."

Finally, Miriam added: "Friends, if there is one folly of our people, is that regardless of the performance of the clergy, we forget yesterday and return to our respective houses of worship. And in like manner, notwithstanding the unkept promises, poor delivery of goods and service, we continue to vote for "the party" – thus imposing on your communities another five years of bondage."

Almost in a pleading voice, she said: "All I ask off you is to accept that in religion as in politics you deserve the very best. No clergy or politician deserves that which is reserved for He who sent us. We all deserve far more than we have been served over centuries. The time has come to turn back both the underperforming clergy and state. I thank you for being such a kind conference."

Nathan was first to his feet. Whether Thomas saw or did not see mattered not to Nathan as he warmly embraced his co-chairman, and Miriam for her part welcomed the embrace and responded with equal panache.

Nathan spent another twenty minutes closing the conference and expressing his appreciation to a long list of people and organisations. He outlined plans for the following day, and highlighted the importance of an early start to the Redeemed Sinners Committee's work.

Nathan, as a final gesture of camaraderie and fellowship, asked his audience to hold hands and sing a popular hymn. Said he: "If you know the words I ask you sing lustily, and if you don't know the words hum to the melody." The hundreds did, creating a spirit of love and friendship matched only with the harmony, which came from all who opened their mouths in praise of the work done at Port-of-Spain to push back the un-godly and begin a rejuvenation of the little people, who have long made religion possible with their tithes and physical presence, and so many other sacrifices to ensure the brass was always shining on the altar of the church.

The Conference of the Un-Godly had taken a brick or two out of the wall, and as Suzie would later that evening add: "Who knows, the wall could come tumbling down."

Miriam and Nathan had dreamed big dreams about the 'Conference of the Un-Godly' and both had troubled themselves and so many others to make it all happen. Miriam's fifty-five minute closing address, which filled the cups of conference attendees to the point of over flowing, marshalled weeks of news coverage by curious media contingents from across the world. Media practitioners of all persuasions had arrived at Trinidad's Piarco International Airport, full of curiosity and anxious to hear from the people who hated the Church. When they left they did so richer and wiser, as they added to their basket of knowledge the realities that in Trinidad and Tobago clergy meant more than priest and deacon, but addressed a wide platform of religious organisations and administrators. Clergy was not cut and dried as in so many places, but its complexity is reflected in the standing Inter Religious Organisation, or I.R.O.

They also had the rare opportunity to witness the birth of a speaking celeb in the person of Miriam Suielman, who would in the months ahead become an in-demand speaker all over the world where the work of the clergy was being revived and scrutinised.

In like manner, Miriam established her committee's work as a key item of focus, and wherever she spoke she raised huge sums for her Trinidad-based committee.

36

THE COMMITTEE OF THE 'CONFERENCE OF THE UN-Godly' was winding down its scheduled Friday afternoon meetings at their Suielman and Sons offices, when Anthony raised his hand to get the attention of the chairman, Nathan John.

Nathan responded by asking: "Anthony, do you wish to add a point to the discussion?"

Anthony, over the months since he joined the committee, had become an influencer, as his contributions always seem to trend with Committee members. Anthony was a thinker, and often after a meeting he would turn over the details in his head, and if there were weaknesses in the thinking of the group he would likely find them and communicate them to Nathan. His interventions, the group came to accept, were either to fix or repair. Further, his suggestions gave added value to the group's planned programme for each area of the conference's work.

"Chairman, I wish that we give consideration to the establishment of a Redeemed Sinners Committee session for the programme."

No one grasped what he was proposing, which left the Committee speechless.

Finally Miriam said: "Anthony, would you elaborate on what you have in mind?"

Anthony, as if reading from a script, said: "I believe many who may come to the conference may be sinners. Sinners cannot be asked to speak of the un-godly without a feeling of guilt. If this is a sound assumption I believe sinners would be drawn to such a session, almost as addicted drinkers are drawn to Alcoholics Anonymous. We will be creating a forum for sinners to share with each other how they have sinned, and in the process openly confess and seek forgiveness," he elaborated. "We will assist in establishing an association of sinners known," he stressed.

Members of the committee were 'clean bowled,' with each recognising the importance of Anthony's suggestion. Anthony was asked to prepare a written detailed proposal, as it was agreed the Redeemed Sinners Forum would be one of the highlights of the conference, with all participants being given the option to attend.

Anthony, as chairman of the Credential Committee, saw up close the registration numbers of persons wanting to attend the Redeemed Sinners Forum, and with each positive response he smiled. His smile was one of satisfaction that good would finally prevail over evil and in his lifetime he would witness a day of reckoning for wrongdoing.

At the conception of the Redeemed Sinners Forum, Anthony did not see animosity towards sinners.

He had spent much of his life listening to scripture, and having served at so many high masses of the parish church in Latin, Anthony was always truly remorseful if he felt he had committed a wrong deed. That is how he believed it worked. If in his calculations he did a wrong deed it became not just a burden, it would genuinely cause him sleepless nights until he in his mind had resolved the wrong and brought about some form of healing to the person he believed he wronged.

There were no ifs or maybes with Anthony, in matters of good and evil. Anthony knew only right and wrong.

He was beneficent in all things, and his proposal for the Redeemed Sinners Forum carried his stamp, as all who knew him intimately accepted him with his overwhelming inflexibility on matters of good and evil.

Anthony fashioned a programme, which he planned would be driven by sinners themselves – whoever these growing numbers would be. Each application form which confirmed attendance at the Redeemed Sinners Forum also encouraged him to think outside the box, which so many were wont to say at planning sessions.

The Redeemed Sinners Forum would be the perfect addition to, and against the backdrop of, Nathan's 'Conference of the Un-Godly.'

He reasoned to himself it would be like public confession, without the clergy. With the vision of public confession etched firmly in his mind, he built his programme around this compelling idea. He convinced himself it would only become potent if truth emerged from the minds, hearts and voices of participants.

Anthony sought support from Nathan that he be allowed to be the chairman for the forum, as he hoped this forum, which he insisted be opened to the media, would encourage an intense media focus, bringing responses from all who knew the persons who sought to speak.

A week later, as the committee met and listened to his plan for the proposed Redeemed Sinners Forum, there was much anxiety amongst committee members, with each voicing varying levels of concerns regarding some aspect of Anthony's proposal.

Anthony listened intently and made notes of all contributions. He wondered silently whether those who voiced concerns had listened to his rationales for each segment of his proposal.

On one rare occasion during the planning of the conference when Mariam's comments were off target, she responded: "Anthony, are we going to stage our own Inquisition?" This alarmed but did not upset him, as he being through fires all his life felt the heat but ensured it did not burn.

Nathan, on the other hand, underscored his development as a leader when he spoke during the months of meetings. He, with his steady hand and ever growing grasp for possibilities, said quietly: "Good people, I like it. It is fresh, different and will have a lasting effect on all who attend. It will be like being in the confession box, but more importantly it will allow sinners in speaking of their sins to experience their own 'mourning ground.'

All looked at Nathan in amazement.

Anthony elaborated on his plans as he responded to his colleagues. He underscored his plan sought to give life and meaning to the very words used in the naming of the forum.

"It," he emphasised, "cannot just be about another day of the same issues and ideas. We have a responsibility, having assembled minds and bodies, to ensure each leave remembering the purpose of the 'Conference of the Un-Godly,' and to cleanse their spirits of all that have troubled each individual with his or her specific clergy. The energy we will generate during three days of conference will be very powerful, and will likely create the strength of thousands of whirlwinds," he emphasised.

What Anthony saw in his dreams he never shared, as he believed in his own powers of spirituality and the guidance he received from the ever present greatest of all architects. As he walked his colleagues down the path 'holding their hands,' he pointed to the colours of each flower or shrub. He in elaborating on his ideas would also explain to each member the fragrance and texture of the flower.

Anthony was the perfect teacher, having been involved in a milestone of community activities, some would say national service, which encouraged and enhanced his skill at persuasion. He never raised his voice, was polite to a fault and expertly encouraged others to see what they could not grasp.

His mission was to encourage everyone at the table, including Miriam, to agree to move forward on what would be a landmark feature on the conference's programme. He wasted no time on what he considered the small questions, yet he in the end answered the large, in between and small questions alike. When he paused he was greeted with eyes of the converted across the room, and yet he waited, as no one raised objection to his clarification on his plan for the Redeemed Sinners Forum.

On this occasion, no one but Phillip noticed his stop at Sinners. Phillip said: "Anthony, I am with you. We are dealing with sinners redeemed or otherwise."

Nathan did not carry the discussions further, and he quickly added: "All in favour?" Anthony received overwhelming support following his amplification of the road ahead, and the Redeemed Sinners Forum was baptised.

Officially, the main conference of three action-packed days had come to an end, with the sequel of the Redeemed Sinners Forum scheduled following the main agenda. This was also a call by Anthony, who did not wish to have this important forum serve as a distraction to the main conference's programme.

Two hours before the scheduled start of the forum, Phillip and Anthony were already very busy assisting the credential teams, ensuring all ushers were positioned to expedite timely seating of the participants. Anthony and Phillip continued to be a sound team, and on the morning of the Redeemed Sinners Forum were fully aware this session would provide the take aways to signal success or failure, and each wished to ensure success. In Phillip's mind he could not fail his daughter, and equally with Anthony he could not fail his 'adopted' son, Nathan. The queues for entry to the forum with ninety minutes to opening were far longer than Anthony and Phillip imagined it would be. Both knew there was more than enough accommodation, as seats were counted and allocated for each participant who at registration confirmed attendance and paid the additional twenty US dollars as fees for the special forum.

With half an hour to the scheduled start, Anthony excused himself and walked slowly to the head table to prepare himself for a day's work. He prayed this day would encourage all participating to find their centre of focus which he often thought was missing, not only within religion but in the very spirits of the people who pray often but remain unfulfilled in so many ways.

As he excused himself from Phillip and his team, he prayed that all would be well. Seated at the head table he noted that with less than thirty minutes to go near half the conference room was empty, and as troubling a thought it was he turned inside of himself, divorced himself from the world around him and connected with his God.

"Father," Anthony prayed, "grant me the wisdom and skill set to make crooked paths straight. May your light shine brightly on our work. These things I ask in your name."

He slowly returned to the conference space, now conscious of Nathan sitting to his left and Miriam to his right.

They all exchanged greetings, with Nathan adding: "I am counting on your prayers to guide us today."

In reply, Anthony said: "It is not the prayers to guide us, it is the most powerful, the unseen, to determine the outcome."

Miriam listened and added nothing to the exchange between her colleagues. She remained deep in thoughts of and about this part of the conference's work, which she believed Anthony would be forced to manage rigidly with his gavel.

37

ANTHONY, AT THE AGREED TIME, IMMEDIATELY GOT up and called his forum to order. "Fellow conference participants, we must begin," he said, with a measure of needed firmness. "If we are to conclude our agenda we cannot lose a minute. Therefore, could we all stand, and will you join each other in the universal prayer made famous by the Catholic, Francis?"

With these words, he said: "Lord, make me an instrument of thy peace..." Those who knew the prayer prayed in step with each other, and those who did not know the words listened as the full meaning of the words of the prayer reached their inner selves.

The prayer completed, an exuberant participant shouted: "Never heard it, but it is more than a prayer – it is an anthem for life." The positive comment elicited a welcome applause from the audience.

Anthony was already on his feet at the lectern. "Sinners," he said, "welcome." And this caused rapturous laughter among participants, with one participant shouting: "Chairman, I ain't no sinner," which was greeted with scattered applause. Continuing, Anthony added: "I ought to have said Redeemed Sinners."

The gentleman replied, "Chairman, that's more like it. I ain't sinning no more." On this occasion he was given rousing applause.

"Thank you friends. My name is Anthony, and I have the pleasure to lead this most important area of the conference, for which you have all paid a good rate to secure your seats. So we must work together, to ensure you do not waste the time we spend here," he emphasised.

Anthony took his audience through the dos and don'ts, and encouraged all to be disciplined about the use of time.

"I also appeal to you, if you wish to contribute and a contributor before you has made the points you wish to make, to advise the chair that the experiences of an earlier contributor mirror your experiences and be succinct with your comments.

"Finally," he added, "our format for this session will be an open forum, with all participants being free to get up and speak. We will not encourage participants to pose questions directly to speakers, as we will allow for questions and possibly answers during our final session. I trust you all understand the process, and I encourage you to observe the very short list of dos and don'ts. And now, I invite you to begin."

There were already approximately nine persons at each of the twelve microphones, which gave an indication of the work ahead.

The first speaker sought to speak, but for reasons unknown his microphone was muted. When this was corrected, he began: "Fellow conference participants I am a redeemed sinner." He paused, and the conference brought itself to a stillness not felt in the preceding three days.

Anthony looked right at Miriam and left at Nathan, hoping for a measure of feedback, but got none. His colleagues, like everyone in attendance, was locked onto the speaker who had the floor, and who with one sentence had weaved his spell.

"I am from Europe. I am now happily married and I am the father of two boys. Today marks nine years that I am married, but I am only happily married for the last two years," he underscored.

Continuing, he said: "For seven years I was married but not married, as during this period I continued to see and sleep with many other women and men. In so many ways I sinned against my wife and my family. Yet the worst of it was my wife began to complain, and I began to abuse her both mentally and physically. During these years of abuse of my wife, I was fully aware I was committing a dreadful wrong.

I knew that my actions constituted a most vile or – as the Catholics would say, mortal – sin, but I did nothing to correct the wrongs. I lived in two worlds: one in which I dressed each day in the best suits and went to my office, and often I would have lunch with someone who only brought me grief. In the evening, instead of going home to my darling wife, I would, like the rodent I had become, seek dark and dingy places to carry on with my drunkenness and illicit sexual activities.

"Am I or was I addicted to the immoral activity that threatened to destroy my life? I will say to you, no. I was not addicted; I was just a man with no morals, and, I believed at that time, with no purpose in life. Sometimes, when the Creator gives you too much too soon, you make mistakes. And even when you make mistakes, and even when you are made aware of your un-Godly behaviour, you refuse to get off the bus.

"Friends, the reality is very straight forward – if you fail to recognise the matter of good and evil you will be destroyed. You cannot hurt and continue to hurt good people without retribution. I saw the evil with which I was engaged, and I got off the bus and I spent a long time seeking redemption. I was very lucky I was guided by the Heavenly Father off the bus.

"Even as I bare witness before you today, I say publicly: "Father have mercy on me; I am a sinner. Father, I ask you to have mercy on my children's mother and my darling wife, who continues to hold my hand, and who has been and remains the light in all my darkness.

"Chairman, if you would permit me, I wish to introduce my wife, who I asked to join me at this special forum, if only to once again publicly atone for my most grievous sins."

Sitting two rows from where he stood, a woman of Caucasian ancestry rose and effortlessly joined her husband at the lectern. He put his hand over her shoulder and brought her closer to him. She placed her hand around his back and truly hugged him, with elegance and affection.

When the cameras focused on the couple there were many judgemental comments. The wife of the first sinner to speak was a strikingly beautiful woman who radiated an irresistible charm, not to be missed. Nathan, in his innocence not fully understanding, sought guidance from Anthony with a sentence that Miriam overheard. She looked at him with a smile and said: "I will answer you one day soon."

Nathan's question was on the lips of many at the conference: "How could a man who is married to such a beautiful person still be destructively unfaithful, and equally violent towards obvious godliness?"

Despite the sinner's transgressions his was a good start to the programme, and as Miriam said, the nature of his sins would be common today, and would reflect a reduced list of speakers as Anthony in his opening remarks sought to curtail repetition at the lecterns.

The newest speaker at the lectern also chose not to give his name, but elected to speak. When given the green light he said in a husky voice, as if suffering from an affliction of his throat: "You sit here and speak of being unfaithful," referencing the first speaker. Immediately Anthony interrupted him to remind him of the speaking guidelines, which demanded strict avoidance of the contributions of others. He in turn apologised, and enquired of the chairman if he could continue speaking.

"Chairman, as we sit here at conference speaking, I ask you, do you know a pandemic is approaching? Yes friends, a pandemic is well on its way, and it has everything to do with our sins. The nature of the pandemic will be felt across all continents, and citizens of each nation will be locked within their homes." All of that is to come as a direct result of sinners.

"If you are here today and you have not repented, do so today. Before I take my leave, I encourage all of you to get a branch of the olive tree, get your holy oil and paint a symbol of the crucifix on your entry door. Use all the oil you have, as it will ensure the pandemic passes your doors, leaving you safe.

As he ended he disappeared through one of the side doors of the hall. He answered no one who enquired of his source of information, but melted into the thick anxious crowd who were present and attended for all kinds of personal reasons.

Anthony and Nathan nudged each other whenever something unusual occurred on the floor of the forum. The last speaker left all participants wondering what brought him to the conference, and more importantly, what was the source of his information?

Anthony said to Nathan: "I have not read of any impending pandemic, but he may just be better informed than we are."

The comments by the speaker did not go away. They remained with Nathan as well as Miriam, who was noticeably quiet and withdrawn.

After the hubbub died away, the next speaker prepared to begin. She wore the clothing familiar to those who assisted at the Christian Centres across the United States. Her head was covered with a loosely fitted silk scarf. Her white top was buttoned up to the neck, and her short sleeves revealed arms that suggested they had been exposed to the sun for some time. Her skirt fell way below her knees, and she wore white cotton socks under her black strap sandals. Her horn rimmed glasses almost covered her face, and she had a distinct mole almost in the centre of her right cheek. When she finally spoke, she stuttered.

"Chairman, I have sinned, and I wish with all my heart to be forgiven for my sins. Yet the more I pray and seek atonement for my sins, the more burdened I become. Not a moment passes without my feeling my sins are so evil and bad that my Father has forsaken me. I believe my sins are so grave a nature that no amount of apologies and repentance will ever release me. I am a prisoner of my sins, and I ask all of you to pray that God will have mercy on me and set me free.

"You may wish to know the nature of my burdens, and rightfully so. As a good Christian, I was assigned by my Order to care for a sick elderly gentleman. From our first meeting, I knew the gentleman was on his last months by his actions. He confined himself to bed and refused to be assisted to do simple things like his daily hygiene. I used all my training and powers of persuasion, and eventually I encouraged my charge to choose life over death.

"In a matter of months the once bedridden was taking daily walks within his huge and beautiful garden, and I as his caregiver accompanied him. As the months went by, there were days when his illness got the better of him. And he being confined to bed, insisted that I remain in his chamber with him. At his insistence he asked me to join him on his bed.

"I told him my Order forbade such an action, and I could not accede to his request. In response he cried for three days, barely sleeping, and refusing to eat or bathe or even brush his teeth.

"His housekeeper, a good woman said to me, 'If he ask me I would join him, but it is you he has chosen to keep him warm.' To this day I hear his cries and his repeated request, 'Sister please join me, have mercy on a dying man.'

"I finally relented. I joined my charge in his bed, and he hugged me and he stopped crying. We remained in bed together all during the fourth day. Still he did not eat nor did his hygiene improve.

"I awoke during the early morning, feeling cold all over; my patient, my charge, had passed away.

"I crawled out of the bed, not convinced he was dead, and called the housekeeper. When she realised he was dead, she looked at me suspiciously and said: 'Sister, you killed the boss. You have real fire.'

"This was further compounded when I was summoned by the Mother Superior to advise me that I had to attend the reading of the Gentleman's will. She also asked if I could explain the rumours coming out of the deceased's household.

"At the reading I once again met his housekeeper, who was now dressed in high fashion and strutted about the mansion like a peacock. When I got to the mansion she greeted me at the door, and smiled a vicious smile while ushering me into the den.

"At the reading of the will, which was very short, the deceased's lawyer said: 'It would appear only one person has inherited my client's estate, so I will be quick about this task. My client has elected to leave all his worldly possessions to his caregiver of his last days, Sister ...' he ended.

As he completed his sentence, his housekeeper of many a year shouted: 'That terrible man! He leave everything to a nun who he slept with!'

I asked the lawyer: 'Are you making a mistake? Did he leave the estate to my Order?' But he replied: 'I am afraid not sister, everything is all yours.'

"I ran out of the mansion and returned to the Order, hoping to get the support of my Mother Superior. But this was not to be, and I was, without inquiry or investigation, deemed to be a sinner having slept in my patient's bed, and having been accused by a most foul-mouthed woman of killing him while having sexual intercourse.

"To date I have not used one cent of his inheritance, and I cannot give it away as I once tried to pass it to my Order. These burdens I have carried and continue to carry, and I have asked our Father for signs of forgiveness, but I never see any such signs. I say to you again, I am a sinner and I, Sister L... once again on bended knees, repent for my sins and my wrongdoings." As she said 'on bended knees' she dropped to them on the stage and bowed in supplication, begging for forgiveness for sins that she did not commit.

Anthony was numb by what he had heard. So too were Miriam, Nathan and the entire forum.

Simultaneously, the conference rose to its feet shouting: "You are forgiven, you have been redeemed." If ever God heard the conversations during the last three-plus days, it would have been at that moment as they all stood to say to the woman, "You are forgiven, you have been redeemed."

Nathan noted: "None of us can truly understand the work of the one most high, but if by chance the voice of the people is the voice of God, then there can be no doubt in Sister L's mind that she will not continue to be held accountable for any immoral acts that she did not carry out. She must be a free person from today."

Anthony heard his friend's comments, and knew that many would remember the Sister's testimony, and the response she received from twenty-five hundred believers of many religions and persuasions.

Sister L left the forum on its feet, as participants debated and continued to hug and touch her while shouting, "You are not a sinner."

Conscious of his time schedule, Anthony stood and said firmly: "There will be silence on the floor. Can we all take our seats?"

38

SPEAKERS OVER THE REMAINING HOURS TOLD OF their weaknesses, and shared information not normally shared publicly, but this was Redeemed Sinners Forum, which was designed to encourage sinners to confront their sins. And by sharing their real, imagined or perceived wrongs, they could find peace and forgiveness.

During the afternoon session, an odd presentation was made by a chubby-looking Chinese man. He sought to explain his and his family's role in a number of transactions, which involved some measure of kleptocracy from their country of origin.

Said he: "I am here to represent my two brothers and myself. We have sinned against many, but most of all against the memories of our parents, our wives and our children. Some people look at us and say we have stolen from them. I seek salvation in understanding if what others say is true.

"I am the eldest; you can call me Chubby. My second brother you can call Petty, and my third and youngest brother you can call Pretty. Many believe we are impious, but I assure you we are all men of sound scruples and we believe in God and the child."

'Chubby,' as he had given as his name, had clearly intended to protect his true identity. There were not hundreds of persons of Chinese origin at the conference, and so Chubby stood out and was remembered long after he walked away from the lectern.

He, without being prompted, spoke of the period during which he served as an official of government, and when as an official he facilitated the award of contracts and licences to himself, family and friends.

"Those who did not like us, and those who were envious of us, accused us of stealing from the accounts of children unborn. We have entered into arrangements with many over the years, and all these business arrangements have been strictly legitimate."

Continuing, Chubby said: "In many instances some of our businesses failed, and our friends and business associates lost their investments, but we did not do anything corrupt. There might have been companies where our reporting was weak and we failed to report to our shareholders, yet we never stole our partners' money.

"There is a lot of talk that we don't pay our bills, and we are bad payers. This is outright wrong. You see, many people believe and expect that once they send you a bill you must pay immediately. They don't know my cashflow; they don't know how many other bills I have to pay.

"I came to this conference for all you sinners, who know what it is to sin, to say to me whether or not you believe my brothers and I are sinners. Further, I wish to share with you that when I believe I may have committed a sin, I have retired to the sacristy of the holiest of nuns. There I pray for forgiveness for forty days, nonstop. The last time I did this was during a period when there was much uproar among the political class, as many sought to suggest I was favoured and given special rights in mysteriously securing a range of special approvals for several of our companies.

"I said to all, as I said to God – I can't give myself something. Someone has to give it to me. So I got down on my knees and prayed, asking God to forgive me if I had done something wrong," Chubby shouted.

As he spoke, another in the audience recognised the speaker. She, an aging woman with a full head of fluffed and curled silver hair, sat listening with focused interest on what Chubby was testifying.

As he said, "I go to the sacristy of the holiest of the nuns to repent," she said: "I know this man, he comes from my district. I remember him well, particularly during the heated days over the matter of special licences. Yes, he came for the thousandth time to pray. I remember him well. It was during my health challenges, and I too took to the sacristy to seek God's special blessings."

"He came, Bible in hand, looking solemn, wishing for salvation from the state, from the loud voices of the people and forgiveness from God. Yes, I remember him; he made his daily journey to the Blessed Sacrament in the beautiful popular church. To mine eyes, it seemed as if the ritual of prayer, fasting and seeking forgiveness was as much as a burden as a call for relief from what was likely to follow." What reasons caused this gentle spirit to recall the presence of Chubby, no one will ever know. But she continued to speak of a period past, but not one she had forgotten.

"Yes, I remember him. He once during his prayers, sitting in a pew two paces from me, said to the father that he was doing his penance on the counsel of his Catholic elders. He truly believed the forgiveness of his sins, and indeed repentance, could and would overturn the popular cries of the man-in-the-street. Yes, he genuinely believed enough prayers, direct from the holy book, could, if God wished, wash away his terrible sins and free him of a long jail sentence and his many other burdens.

"I remember him once during prayer say: 'There is nothing like money to focus the mind. Could you ever consume enough money while depriving shareholders of what is due to them?'

"Sometimes he was pleasant, and at other times he was mean in his appearance. The talk on the street was that he was like his second brother – mean, vicious, wicked and petty. Envious and jealous of relatives, of business associates and of people generally." As if to clarify the source of her information, she added, "Well, on this last point I can't verify, but this is what the people who know have said of those boys." She ended as abruptly as she had begun her recollection of Chubby.

Her memory of the threesome ended in sync with Chubby's final statement. Said he: "Who believes I and my family are sinners must say so to me, here and now. But be assured I, like so many, have come seeking total and final absolution for my sins. I say before all of you, with all who have ears to hear and to those who have eyes to see, 'Father, forgive me for my sins.'"

Satisfied he had made his peace with his God, he turned away from the lectern as if spooked by an unseen force, turned his back to face the stage, and quickly left the hall walking backward as if expecting a negative reaction – nothing followed.

In the aftermath of Chubby's presentation – or confession, for want of a better description – there was no applause, but participants began the debate that would go on for a long time.

Could he be considered a Redeemed Sinner?

Many a sinner present wanted to lean on the side that Chubby did confess his sins publicly, however they also questioned his genius or was it his ingeniousness, and pointed to Chubby having admitted that his focus was money.

A bold woman dressed in a faded white coloured sack dress, tied at the waist with a yellow chord and with eyes that shone brightly, said: "How do you reconcile that an obliviously greedy person, by admission, claims salvation by merely publicly repenting and hopes to satisfy the Father's criteria? Some people believe that by regurgitating the holy book you will find a place with the Father – this is not possible unless it represents a request from deep within. Yet we are not to judge, lest we ourselves be judged."

The chattering and debate was at fever pitch when Anthony intervened to call the forum to order.

"Participants, I know the last contributor has given us much food for thought, as evidenced by the intensity of the discussion across the house. It must be the Father's work that someone like Chubby, as he introduced himself, would come to us in the closing moments of our conference to pose before us his life, and to cause so many of us to so openly seek to judge him," noted Anthony. "I caution you, the very request he has made of you must be the work of negative forces. Any good spiritual being must know we have no power to judge anyone, least of all a being like ourselves, who has backed us into a corner demanding we judge him.

I ask you to postpone such judgement for a long time," he emphasised.

In response there were shouts of "yea, yea," and Anthony took this as his indicator to move forward.

He quickly recognised a bearded, middle-aged male wearing a black felt hat. He by appearance and demeanour suggested he was one of the international visitors. He walked with a bent back, and stood with it bent even as he held onto the lectern. His black felt hat was his headpiece, and dwarfed every bit of clothing he wore. No one remembered that he wore a pair of black trousers, with a black jacket above his dark blue shirt – he was referred to as the fellow with the black hat, so dominant was this garment.

His opening sentence, if intended to be an attention grabber, proved to be effective. No one uttered a word and the normal hum of chatter dissipated as 'Black Hat' said: "You come to a forum for and on Redeemed Sinners. But how do you know you have been cleansed your sins? Are we all playing God? Are we making jokes of serious people's business?" he said, as he aimed his guns at the heart of Anthony's special forum.

Miriam sat back in her chair for the first time throughout the day, slapped her right thigh and finally found the fear she sensed but could not put her finger on from day one of the planning of the Redeemed Sinners Forum.

She knew without being told that this was a conference breaker, and she had no intentions of having this gentleman, whoever he was, destroy the work which until this minute was achieving the objective of one big public confessional. She sat forward in her chair and simultaneously elbowed Anthony to alert him that she would wish to intervene if necessary.

Black Hat continued: "We know not who we are, nor do we know what we must do to repent. We have been taught from the cradle that we must seek forgiveness. But can we truly be redeemed for violating the Commandments? If we kill someone, and it is written, 'Thou shall not kill,' what are the consequences for killing? Can we simply stand up here today and say, 'You know, conference, I have killed a woman and I have never been caught by the law, and I seek absolution here and now?'" he emphasised. In a most sombre tone, he concluded: "Who amongst you have the power to offer the scope of redemption required for the salvation sought on the matter of murder by a remorseful spirit?"

Black Hat had not come to repent, nor did he question.

Anthony said in response to Nathan's question: "Is he seeking absolution?" This is written without Nathan's question deliberately.

Miriam joined in the discussion: "Judge and you shall not be judged."

Black Hat, like Chubby before him, walked away from the forum leaving in his wake much debate on his contribution. Anthony allowed the conference the liberty to discuss Black Hat's thread of discussion, as the point he raised bore relevance to the very title of the forum.

The debates among participants heightened, as the issues of redemption and absolution and the power to absolve now faced each participant in ways not experienced prior to the words spoken by the man wearing the black hat, and he like so many others had said what they came to say and simply vanished.

During the noisy pause Nathan passed a slip of paper to his co-chairman, which read:

"The conference is not about being comfortable. We planned, based on the material to surface, to take the world out of its comfort zone. When I met you and when I envisaged our conference, I never knew I would move from being a village boy to the place we find ourselves at this moment."

Miriam read Nathan's note and quickly scribbled: "I never knew you and I would leave our villages so quickly," and she signed 'M.'

39

ANTHONY MOVED WITH PURPOSE TO SPEED THE forum's agenda to conclusion. With time ebbing away he wondered whether he had underestimated the time needed to add substance to the full conference. He checked the clock on the wall and realised he had been sitting on the same place for near nine hours, having skipped lunch and all other scheduled breaks as he wished to allow as many possible to speak their truths in way only a true sinner could.

He knew that as much as he wished to go on he had obligations to the management, and unlike other items on the agenda of the conference, participants could not be asked to write their sins and leave them with the conference secretariat for review and inclusion with the final conference report.

This was a real and meaningful life changing experience for all who were participating, and he needed in the available time to hear as many a sinner as he could facilitate. There would be no tomorrow for those who sought salvation and could not do so because of time.

He put his foot on the pedal and pushed his forum for another ninety minutes, during which a record number of thirty-four speakers spoke of their trials and their tribulations.

Participants laconically gave vent to their innermost thoughts and deeds, for which they sought redemption. They lifted their hands to the sky for their sins, big and small, and collectively sought mass forgiveness.

When Anthony sought the chair for this special segment of the conference, no committee member could imagine this most invaluable experiment in human behaviour. None among the Committee, except Anthony, the author of the work, Miriam and to a lesser extent Nathan, could grasp the magic of sinners repenting in the full gaze of all who could physically witness the appeals for forgiveness within a public forum.

Anthony also remembered Nathan's observation that no one had volunteered to chair the Forum, and so he chose to chair a Forum he conceptualised. Some committee members, when presented with the plans, openly asked: "What could possibly come out of the Redeemed Sinners Forum?" This was a question which was repeatedly asked in the build-up to the conference's opening.

This question became a theme of members, who could not get it out of their minds that the plan would not work as individuals simply will not publicly share their sins. This view seemed a cancer among organisers, who had grown from a single table of four to a room full of believers and non-believers alike.

As he reflected, Anthony smiled. A simple idea with a focus on Christians had become a huge interwoven tapestry of religions not linked or limited to Christians, who he had initially hoped would be exposed for the centuries of corrupt practices by its clergy. So too he now anticipated persons of Islam, Hinduism and all other sects would be exposed, with all their known and unknown burdens of which the majority whispered, never wanting the truth to be known outside their circles of religion.

Listening all the day, he was forced to ponder that closer to the Church, temple, mosque or mourning ground are all cut from the same cloth.

Anthony, like Nathan and Miriam, listened from the head table as the "sinners" shouted their sad, sadistic, vile, vicious and conniving statements. They were tales that no one with an iota of self-respect would wish to share, out of fear of being rebuked and condemned as a blasphemer – if not as an outright liar – yet all told their stories.

Earlier in the morning, as Anthony watched the empty chairs before him, he silently pursued the thoughts of cause and effect, and though the registration was booked solid he had fears that his audience could get 'cold feet' and not bother to show up.

Still focused on the vacant chairs, he watched as the rows of seats became a sea of bodies, energetic, chattering bodies, which he found to be so similar in tempo and beat regardless of religion. These scenes of unoccupied chairs, followed by no empty seats with devotees all speaking at the same time as they waited on the clergy to begin the ritual, are a common feature to all places of worship, noted Anthony.

Moments such as the aforementioned also evoked in Anthony the questions he began asking of religion so long ago: how was it possible that, regardless of religion, under the vestments could reside so much evil?

How could a space named for the Trinity be weighed down by so much sadness and necromancy? At moments of reflection, these same questions and scenarios visited Anthony.

He grew up wanting always to serve both his God and his Church. Now, he quietly hoped he would find his God outside his Church.

Anthony had come to accept that in life you could not be certain where you will be at any given point until you get there, and in like manner, he simply did not know how his forum would end despite having under an hour to complete his agenda.

In his mind, sitting before hundreds in a most dramatic and dynamic environment, he knew where he was. He also knew where he wished to be, and he had it in his life's experiences the ability to get to where he wished so badly to arrive, on this final evening of a conference he assisted his young friend Nathan John in successfully planning and hosting the Republic's first international conference with a strong focus on religion."

One reflection gave rise to another as Anthony presided over the most important sociological experiment ever held within Trinidad and Tobago, given the importance of race and religion and its ominous ties to the Republic's politics.

His observation was on point as he muttered to Nathan: "Look at what is going on here. This is living sociology, and not one member from any of our universities is here to observe and study and learn. No wonder they produce so many politicians with nothing between their ears," he ended with a smile.

The hours passed quickly, and Anthony needed no signal to know his tour of duty had come to an end.

It was Anthony's turn to surprise Nathan the same way that Nathan did to Miriam the day before, in saying to him: "I am calling on you to close in fifteen minutes, and you can speak as long as you wish."

Nathan, with the ease of a seasoned speaker, moved to the lectern and basked for thirty seconds in the welcome applause. Then he said: "Thank you, you sinners," to which he was given just as rousing an applause as the welcome he received not a minute earlier.

Nathan had over the days of the conference become a good reader of his audience, and knew he could take the liberty of calling 'sinners' just that, 'sinners,' and be rewarded with electrifying applause.

Now he knew he had a job to do. Nathan stood silent, almost erect, not even blinking an eye, and during the moments of his stillness and silence he brought the packed hall to him in a way none had done during the conference. Jew and Gentile alike also came to stillness and silence, as a full forum looked up to the lectern and beyond it into the unblinking eyes of Nathan, their conference chairman, who was about to bring the curtain down on an event which drew only positive remarks from participants.

"You cannot blame the roots for all the rotten fruit, nor should you blame the tree for all of its rotten branches," said Nathan. "If we have learned anything these past four days, is that regardless of where we live or were born, or what religion we practice or of what race we belong, we are all God's children. And each of us has a personal responsibility to act, behave and consider ourselves in good, noble, decent, sincere and honest ways.

"We must also recognise that each of us, and that means each and every one of you who came from afar or very near, meaning Trinidad and Tobago, has a responsibility and role to play. You must police the spaces in which you live, and create not only a better space, but to make certain you police the clergy as it has never been done before," said an emboldened Nathan.

Continuing, Nathan added: "We cannot continue to speak of right and wrong and do nothing about guaranteeing that our words take life. The world as we know it today is covered with a thick, heavy blanket of evil and wrongs, which must be exorcised and reengineered to produce the quality of fruit we all seek.

"Good friends, I ask you to accept, as our world famous author V.S. Naipaul wrote so beautifully, 'The world is what it is.' And if we recognise this we will come to the realisation that despite our best efforts we will always be confronted by evil, and so we must forever be armed and ready to address such.

"Any society, be it big ones, the likes of which some of you originated, or our very small society, which has hosted you this past week, you cannot afford to remain deaf or silent on its corrupt members.

"How does the clergy treat the corrupt among its own? How does the clergy treat known paedophiles, both within its order and such miscreants from the outside? We can no longer stand silent and with duct tape on our mouths, as the dishonest and undesirable goes to the altar and is served Holy Communion. We must find ways and means to bring such wrongdoers to feel the burden of their sins – that is part of the task before us," he emphasised. As a group, each of us has individual and collective responsibilities to shine light in such areas of darkness that you might be aware of now or those you will encounter on your life's journey. If there is one such illustration that must be addressed, is that we must do all within our power to stop the acceptance of ill-gotten gains from corrupt persons being transferred to religious bodies. "The time is now; we must find ways to force out of all religions such corrupt persons from positions of influence. My fellow participants, we in this Republic live in a terrible society, one in which all our human and holistic values have vanished. The only thing that seems to encourage, empower and motivate so many is money.

"People would in this Republic do most anything for money," he said in a lowered voice. "I state this fact, conscious that Judas sold out Jesus for thirty pieces of silver. Silver, my cousins, was the currency of the period of the greatest betrayal. How then can we allow such un-godliness to remain a fixture within our respective religious institutions?" Nathan questioned.

"When we first contemplated this conference of answers – or was it a conference *for* answers? – I never envisaged that so many of you, from places I frankly did not know of, would show up and demand space. Some of you captured spaces. What is remarkable is all of you had one common demand: that you be given an opportunity to have your views heard. And you have each been given your own soap box, and your comments and remarks have been music to our ears. Each contribution is documented and will be included in perhaps the largest conference report ever to be written.

"With each speaker there were revelations of one kind or another, and each person who stood at the lectern evoked an individuality of thought with such light that even the sightless could interpret your writings.

"Yes, good people, what a joy it has been to sit silently and really listen to you who have so much to offer this near barren world of ours. What you have said is matched only by what you have not said, so fertile are the minds and bodies who have constituted the body politic of the 'Conference of the Un-Godly.'

"Like our Republic, religious bodies are over staffed both in front and behind the altars with phlegmatic people. These spirits of the aforementioned must be moved to action, to ensure that the efforts of the martyrs have not been for nothing."

Nathan paused, both to breathe and to enquire of Anthony how much more time. Anthony gave him the time was up sign.

"Friends, I know we have much still to communicate with each other. And I know we will be meeting again, and I hope not in the distant future but in the near future," and since he began speaking, this was the first applause which interrupted his speech.

He welcomed the intervention and allowed the conference to applaud.

"What has come to the forefront of the conversation these past days is that, whether our respective religions recognise it or not, we the parishioner, we the devotee, we the Christian, we the believers, want a better deal with our churches, temples and mosques. And equally, we underscore that this new deal requires transparency and accountability by all the clergy. We who keep the candles lit demand that our clergy be both responsible and accountable to the members of the flock.

"If there is to be a headline tomorrow, it must be: 'Time changes and so have we.'"

Before Nathan could move from the lectern, hundreds were on their feet giving him a deserved standing ovation as callers across the hall demanded: "more, more, more."

The conference was over, and Anthony grasped Miriam's hand. Miriam grasped Nathan's, and together they moved to the front of the stage to both acknowledge and be acknowledged by the hundreds who whistled, stamped their feet and applauded, as the public address played the gospel song, 'We Shall Overcome'.

The high energy generated within Port-of-Spain that evening would be long remembered by all who witnessed and participated in a simple yet spectacular closing to a week of dynamic contributors, from places known and some little known.

As the successful trio joined hands high above their heads, the rays of the evening's setting sun penetrated the glass windows of the conference hall with an intensity to be received. Orange rays lit up the hall and allowed reflections to dazzle one on top of each other, offering every conceivable image and shape possible.

For Miriam the sun was always her mojo. It represented so much upon which she built her operating principles. In the sun she saw light, and observed it was not always brilliantly clear, as at some moment it could offer a spirit of gloom though it offered pure crystal light.

She was most fascinated by the setting sun, and appreciated from a tender age that as the sun in all its brilliance set the moon would rise; both were a pair worthy of each other. She also held the view that both sun and moon were taken for granted, and in response she often articulated: "Too many never focus on the meaning of light which is provided by both the sun and the moon, but all too often give light to darkness."

Miriam, the woman of little visible emotions, consumed by the moment and the sun's rays, tugged at Nathan's hands and pointed him in the direction of the sun. He grasped immediately her desire to get out of the room to absorb the light that always lifted her spirits.

She released Anthony's hand, and still holding Nathan's they both ducked though a side exit door, which opened onto the board walk which adjoined the hotel. No sooner had they reached outside, the glory of a most beautiful setting sun said goodbye for yet another occasion.

They looked at each other, trying to understand their feelings for each other. Nathan could not say; nor could Miriam.

As the conference began to close shop, Phillip Suielman announced to as many of the committee members as he could locate that he was inviting all to the Suielmans' for an unplanned plate and beverage. Miriam found Thomas in the melee of activities, as participants lingered with no apparent desire to depart the conference hall which had become their home away from home during the past four days.

When she saw him, he was holding court with a group, which included his small team along with a number of persons she did not recognise. The topic being discussed had much to do with his defence of Islam in response to all that had been disclosed during the conference.

She touched him gently on his shoulder to get his attention. He was neither surprised nor unhappy to see his wife.

Miriam issued an invitation for him to join the group at her parents' home, and hoped he would agree. He looked at her as if she had insulted his every being with such a polite request. He shook his head and said to Miriam: "We will see."

On this occasion she didn't ask what he meant. Miriam smiled at her husband, with the fullest understanding of what tomorrow would bring, and walked away to search for her father who she knew would be waiting.

She stumbled into Nathan and Anthony still basking in the success of the day's work, and enquired of both men whether they would be joining the family.

In reply Nathan said: "I am honoured to be invited. Would you be so kind as to provide the boy from Los Bajos with a ride to Goodwood Park?"

Phillip and Sammoy Suielman laid out a buffet fit for kings, and committee members who had made friends with both local and foreign guests invited their newfound friends to the post conference get together. The Suielmans seemed to understand the moment, as each person who turned up at the house on the hill left well-nourished from a wide variety of sumptuous offerings.

Sometime during the evening, Miriam observed Thomas sitting away from the crowd and approached him. He did not get up to greet his wife; he merely looked up at her as if she were an invader in his space.

Not to encourage any argument, she said, "I believe I am disturbing you," and retreated to join her guests.

Sometime during the evening she felt a firm hand hold onto her wrist, and she turned to see Thomas staring at her. She smiled and said: "Thomas. How can I assist?"

His curt reply was: "We need to talk."

Without a response Miriam lead her husband back to the very spot she left him sitting earlier, and observed there were two chairs. She effortlessly sat and Thomas took the other chair.

Miriam said nothing and waited for Thomas to speak. When he finally spoke he asked Miriam: "When are you returning home with my children?"

Miriam was unprepared for the question, and so she said nothing.

"Miriam, you must know I won't let you take my children, and you must also know I won't let you leave me."

Miriam looked him in his eyes, and said: "You must think you are bad like crab to threaten me. I never gave consideration to leaving, but now that you have raised the matter, it is not such a bad idea.

"Thomas, until this moment I believed in my heart I had some feelings for you. But you just threatened my freedom, and that of our children. Note well that I said *our* children, although you have had little or nothing to do with their birth, growth or general well-being.

"Well, my dear husband, effective immediately I cease being a Muslim."

As Miriam said her piece she slowly removed her hijab, revealing her long hair that had been hidden for near seven years under her head clothing.

Thomas looked on fiercely, he too caught in a moment of his own creation, a moment which began near sixteen months earlier, long before the 'Conference of the Un-Godly' was conceptualised.

He turned and walked away, not knowing if he was still married to a woman he truly loved but did not know *how* to love.

EPILOGUE

THE STORY AFTER THE STORY BECAME THE RITUAL for weeks following the 'Conference of the Un-Godly.' Each day the trio of Nathan, Miriam and Anthony were pestered to answer questions; they answered as many times as the questions were asked of them individually.

This ongoing list of questions, despite a very comprehensive post-conference press release which gave more details than were required, continued even following the departure of the last international participant, who boarded a Caribbean Airlines 737 jet liner headed to New York and from there to disappear into the airline traffic to a small city in mid-eastern Europe.

Nathan, Miriam and Anthony took it all in good stride, and each would comment on the inaccuracies of the information contained in the news reporting. As Miriam said of the reporting: "It isn't that the reporters have a mean streak; they do their best, however, my father has always said: 'If you pay peanuts, you will get monkeys.' The reality is our media pays the lowest professional salaries."

Outside of managing the media, both local and international, each member of the team had specific roles to keep them busy. They were all so occupied looking after their areas of business that neither Nathan nor Anthony realised that Miriam had, in the days post-conference, stopped wearing her hijab.

Two evenings later, post-conference, Nathan was approaching his office positioned immediately next to Miriam's when he observed someone inside hers. He did not recognise the person, and wondered who was the person occupying his co-chairman's desk. Always cautious not to intrude, he moved to his desk having waved to the occupant next door.

As he settled in and began working in earnest he barely overheard the exchange of words next door, and dismissed it as the visitor may have been a relative of Miriam. Lost in his review of papers presented, which had been approved for inclusion in the final report by the Reports Group, Nathan was overwhelmed by the contents of submission and the level of research carried out by contributors.

Caught in his review, he never heard the three taps on his door. He responded as the door lock turned, and the door opened to admit a transformed Miriam Suielman.

Gone was the headwear, and in its place Miriam offered her jet black and slightly wavy hair. She now wore a relaxed fit pair of Levi's jeans and an airy pair of sandals. Miriam's top, also loosely fitted, could not hide the woman who only three days earlier wore clothing which covered her from the crown of her head to the soles of her feet.

Nathan looked at her in amazement with a half-smile on his face, and before he could say a word, Miriam asked: "What is wrong with you, has cat got your tongue?"

Nathan replied: "No, Lady Miriam, cat has not got my tongue. What has happened to you? What has caused this magical transformation?"

His reply neither amused nor caused her relief, as she knew all who saw her in the last forty-eight hours had the same questions. They just did not have the brass that Nathan possessed to ask the question as politely as he did.

It was apparent Miriam was, for the rare moment, stumped for words which normally came easily. At this moment Nathan was tempted to pick up the phone to enquire of Anthony if he had seen Miriam lately. He resisted the urge and wisely asked: "Miriam can, we sit and talk a bit?"

Nathan had read the moment correctly, as a troubled Miriam needed a trustworthy spirit to listen to her and to objectively give her the kind of responses that were neither partial nor supportive to her because they cared for her.

Nathan had seen Vive and Suzie earlier and enquired of Miriam. He knew Miriam wished to speak with him privately, but he believed her interest would be better served if she spoke with him in the presence of her besties. Nathan, throughout the build-up and during the conference, had come to respect the opinions of the older women, though they treated him as of their age group.

He proposed to Miriam: "Could I ask Suzie and Vive to join us for coffee?"

Miriam's reply was forthright: "No, I wish to speak with you without any referees."

She got up and made a beeline to the coffee station, got two coffees and returned instantly. She handed a coffee to Nathan and sat down in front of him, sipping her cup. Then she smiled and said: "Nathan, I am about to go through a very difficult period, which has already begun. Will you hold my hand through this unknown period?

"On Sunday, while at the after-conference 'lime' at our home, Thomas demanded that I advise him of my return to Rose Hill along with the fabulous six. He threatened me, indicating that I must know he would never allow me to leave him nor will he ever allow me to take his children. I literally said to him that he threatened me, and that is unforgivable. It was a most sagacious moment, as I immediately removed my hijab and advised him, with ebullience, that I would not be bullied by anyone."

Nathan, though some six years Miriam's junior, sat listening intently to what his newfound friend had to share as she poured her heart out to him.

During their conversation, it became clear to Nathan what a narrow and dangerous road he would be forced to traverse if he agreed to hold Miriam's hand during her withdrawal from her marriage and the separation from a most unpredictable husband.

He quickly came to his conclusion: Miriam sought him out and guided him in a way no other had ever done, and if she now needed his support it would be his to give and hers to enjoy, notwithstanding the consequences.

Miriam, having outlined her challenges, waited on a response from the wordsmith Nathan John.

Nathan, in turn, answered with a question: "What is your parents' position?"

Miriam responded cautiously: "My parents suspect I am about to make a quantum leap, but they will not ask me questions. They believe that when I am ready I will explain whatever challenges me to both of them, and I will do so in due course."

Before Nathan could ask another question, she said forcefully: "Are you with me in this most difficult matter?"

Nathan moved to sit closer to her, and said in a way only he could: "I will be with you to the end."

Miriam was buoyed by the fact that Nathan would be there when she needed to discuss her future. She deliberately chose not to involve her parents. Miriam had earlier shared with Suzie and Vive, and now she included Nathan, the third of her Trinity of friends, upon whom she hoped to receive advice if she needed counsel wiser than her own.

Miriam focused on Nathan, and said, "I am taking Vive and Ms Chang Sing to the airport this evening. Will you make the journey with me?"

Nathan did not verbally answer, but gave her the thumbs up sign to signal that he would join her.

She got up with her usual swift motions, and as she departed she said to Nathan: "We will be leaving at 5:00pm to beat the traffic; I will pick you up at 4:55pm sharp." She smiled for the first time her trademarked, beautiful, effervescent, wide-lipped smile, and Nathan knew she believed she was more troubled than her non-verbals communicated.

The hours passed all too quickly. As he opened another submission his desk phone rang, with the security at the main gate announcing: "Mr Nathan, Ms Suielman is here to meet you."

Nathan replied he would be at the gate in a minute and promptly left his office.

He greeted the women with a broad grin and a polite: "Good evening, que pasa?"

They all laughed as Miriam responded: "People be careful, the boy from Los Bajos has been having conversations with folks from Venezuela."

The farewells of both Vive and Ms Chan Sing were difficult on Miriam, who was saying goodbye to her bestie on one hand and on the other to a person who came to their support unsolicited and proved to be no fair-weathered friend.

Nathan had grown very fond of both women, but had developed a very special connection with Vive. Though he never said it aloud, he often wondered how a woman so beautiful in every way was still single, free and disengaged.

The tearful departures left the "Iron Lady" somewhat benumbed, and during the return journey to Port-of-Spain she said very little. Nor did Nathan, sitting next to her, feel he had any authority to break the silence which engulfed the SUV.

In the days which followed, each of the team leaders met with their team of volunteers, and with precision and professionalism closed the chapter which they willingly chose to write, and which they did while enjoying each other's presence.

The trio of Nathan, Miriam and Anthony established a winning corporate culture among all team members, and throughout its planning sessions encouraged all to, as Nathan so aptly put it: "Big up" each other. "Do not be embarrassed to say to each other, 'I like your idea,' or 'you have made a huge contribution.' We need to be each other's measuring tape of the progress we make. Conversely, if we are not doing well, we must man-up or woman-up and say, 'this is not working' or more importantly, 'you are not pulling your weight.'"

This call to an open level organisation produced a team which did the impossible and successfully produced the first conference of its kind, and not only in Trinidad and the Caribbean. In structure, participation and results it was not only a first, but its successes suggested a new standard for the world.

During the month post conference, mail both online as well as air and surface kept flowing into the secretariat. Much of it carried commentary of the conference. Some mail, a small percentage, carried complaints, but the majority of mail fell into the category of professional critiques of the conference's work with request for copies of the final report.

The conference posted a surplus of revenue over expenditure, largely due to the donations raised by Miriam during her Boston sojourn and the herculean efforts of Ms Chan Sing and the New Rochelle, New York Connection. When the final accounts were presented there was much banging of the table and fist bouncing, illustrating the relief committee members felt on having successfully hurdled its biggest challenge.

Yet the correspondence kept coming, and a new trend in the missives emerged. Invitations were being sent both individually and collectively to Miriam, Nathan and Anthony to attend religious based conferences across the globe. At some conferences invitations invited each to speak, but at others they were invited as feature speakers, with a common theme of topic: "The Story of the 'Conference of the Un-Godly.'"

The trio of Miriam, Nathan and Anthony had entered the work halls of the 'Conference of the Un-Godly' as locals, and left the conference door a month later marked as internationals

It would be Miriam who was first to agree to join a conference, at Cartagena, Columbia. Anthony would follow, being the second member of the team to accept an invitation to speak at a conference, in Budapest, Hungary.

With Nathan it was both invitations to speak and an enquiry whether he would give consideration to meeting with a team to discuss the hosting of the second 'Conference of the Un-Godly,' at Springfield, Philadelphia in the USA.

Nathan shared his invitation with the team, and did not surprise anyone when he admitted his interest had less to do with giving the feature address and more to do with the second 'Conference of the Un-Godly.'

THE END